PUFFIN BOOKS

THE ADVENTURES OF RUSTY:
COLLECTED STORIES

Born in Kasauli (Himachal Pradesh) in 1934, Ruskin Bond grew up in Jamnagar (Gujarat), Dehradun, New Delhi and Simla. His first novel *The Room on the Roof*, written when he was seventeen, received the John Llewellyn Rhys Memorial Prize in 1957. Since then he has written over five hundred short stories, essays and novellas (including *Vagrants in the Valley* and *A Flight of Pigeons*) and more than forty books for children. He received the Sahitya Akademi Award for English writing in India in 1993, the Padma Shri in 1999, and the Delhi government's Lifetime Achievement Award in 2012.

He lives in Landour, Mussoorie, with his extended family.

ALSO IN PUFFIN BY RUSKIN BOND

THE ADVENTURES OF RUSTY

COLLECTED STORIES

Ruskin Bond

PUFFIN BOOKS

An imprint of Penguin Random House

PUFFIN BOOKS

USA | Canada | UK | Ireland | Australia
New Zealand | India | South Africa | China

Puffin Books is part of the Penguin Random House group of companies
whose addresses can be found at global.penguinrandomhouse.com

Published by Penguin Random House India Pvt. Ltd
7th Floor, Infinity Tower C, DLF Cyber City,
Gurgaon 122 002, Haryana, India

Penguin
Random House
India

This edition first published in Puffin by Penguin Books India 2012

30 29 28

ISBN 9780143332220

Typeset in Sabon Roman by SÜRYA, New Delhi
Printed at Replika Press Pvt. Ltd, India

Contents

Contents

Introduction

Rusty and the Winning of Friends

Just the other day, when I was signing some of my books, I was surrounded by a group of bright youngsters from a school in Udaipur; and before I could scribble my name on a title-page, several of them chimed in with the request, 'Please sign as Rusty. Sign Rusty above your name!'

I was happy to oblige; at which, one bright spark asked, 'You *are* Rusty, aren't you?'

And I had to admit that Rusty the boy was the author as a boy. In part, anyway. Rusty's friends and adventures parallel my own experiences as a boy and as a young man. Fact becomes fiction; fiction becomes fact. As in great works like *David Copperfield* or *Robinson Crusoe* or *Huckleberry Finn*, they merge into one and create the story of a life.

Recently a smart critic wrote that Rusty was so-called because he had rusted like scrap iron, that he was old-fashioned, antiquated.

Wrong, my friend. My 'Rusty' comes from Rusty the Lion in the *Panchatantra*, that collection of wise and witty fables from ancient India and beyond. It consists of five parts, or five books, and one of these is called *The Winning of Friends*.

And that is what my Rusty is all about—the winning of friends.

For these are stories of friendship—discovering a different India with Somi and Ranbir; running away with Daljit; sharing a home with Kishen; looking for wild flowers with old Miss Mackenzie; finding love with Binya; getting into trouble with Sitaram; digging a tunnel with Omar. Their shared experiences bring them together. Their sincere, affectionate natures find a response in Rusty, a sensitive and often lonely boy. He puts his trust in friendship.

As Swift the Crow testifies to Spot the Deer:

'Tis hard to find in life
A friend, a bow, a wife,
Strong, supple to endure,
In stock and sinew pure,
In time of danger sure.

False friends are common. Yes, but where
True nature links a friendly pair,
The blessing is as rich as rare.

These verses come from Arthur W. Ryder's translation from the Sanskrit of *The Panchatantra*, first published in 1925 by the University of Chicago.

I am indebted to Sudeshna Shome Ghosh for her careful and sensitive editing of this new edition of the Rusty stories. I hope it finds many new readers, and that it pleases those who are already familiar with Rusty and friends.

RUSKIN BOND

All Creatures Great and Small

INSTEAD OF HAVING brothers and sisters to grow up with in India, I had as my companions an odd assortment of pets, which included a monkey, a tortoise, a python and a Great Indian Hornbill. The person responsible for all this wildlife in the home was my grandfather. As the house was his own, other members of the family could not prevent him from keeping a large variety of pets, though they could certainly voice their objections; and as most of the household consisted of women—my grandmother, visiting aunts and occasional in-laws (my parents were in Burma at the time)—Grandfather and I had to be alert and resourceful in dealing with them. We saw eye to eye on the subject of pets, and whenever Grandmother decided it was time to get rid of a tame white rat or a squirrel, I would conceal them in a hole in the jackfruit tree; but unlike my aunts, she was generally tolerant of Grandfather's hobby, and even took a liking to some of our pets.

Grandfather's house and ménagerie were in Dehra and I remember travelling there in a horse-drawn buggy. There were cars in those days—it was just over twenty years ago—but in the foothills a tonga was just as good, almost as fast, and certainly more dependable when it came to getting across the swift little Tons river.

During the rains, when the river flowed strong and deep, it was impossible to get across except on a hand-operated ropeway; but in the dry months, the horse went splashing through, the carriage wheels churning through clear mountain water. If the horse found the going difficult, we removed our shoes, rolled up our skirts or trousers, and waded across.

When Grandfather first went to stay in Dehra, early in the century, the only way of getting there was by the night mail coach. Mail ponies, he told me, were difficult animals, always attempting to turn around and get into the coach with the passengers. It was only when the coachman used his whip liberally, and reviled the ponies' ancestors as far back as their third and fourth generations, that the beasts could be persuaded to move. And once they started, there was no stopping them. It was a gallop all the way to the first stage, where the ponies were changed to the accompaniment of a bugle blown by the coachman.

At one stage of the journey, drums were beaten; and if it was night, torches were lit to keep away the wild elephants who, resenting the approach of this clumsy caravan, would sometimes trumpet a challenge and throw the ponies into confusion.

Grandfather disliked dressing up and going out, and was only too glad to send everyone shopping or to the pictures—Harold Lloyd and Eddie Cantor were the favourites at Dehra's small cinema—so that he could be left alone to feed his pets and potter about in the garden. There were a lot of animals to be fed, including, for a time, a pair of Great Danes who had such enormous appetites that we were forced to give them away to a more affluent family.

The Great Danes were gentle creatures, and I would sit astride one of them and go for rides round the garden. In spite of their size, they were very sure-footed and never knocked over people or chairs. A little monkey, like Toto, did much more damage.

Grandfather bought Toto from a tonga owner for the sum of five rupees. The tonga man used to keep the little red monkey tied to a feeding trough, and Toto looked so out of place there—almost conscious of his own incongruity—that Grandfather immediately decided to add him to our ménagerie.

Toto was really a pretty little monkey. His bright eyes sparkled with mischief beneath deep-set eyebrows, and his teeth, a pearly-white, were often on display in a smile that frightened the life out of elderly Anglo-Indian ladies. His hands were not those of a Tallulah Bankhead (Grandfather's only favourite actress), but were shrivelled and dried-up, as though they had been pickled in the sun for many years. But his fingers were quick and restless; and his tail, while adding to his good looks—Grandfather maintained that a tail would add to anyone's good looks—often performed the service of a third hand. He could use it to hang from a branch; and it was capable of scooping up any delicacy that might be out of reach of his hands.

Grandmother, anticipating an outcry from other relatives, always raised objections when Grandfather brought home some new bird or animal, and so for a while we managed to keep Toto's presence a secret by lodging him in a little closet opening into my bedroom wall. But in a few hours he managed to dispose of Grandmother's ornamental wallpaper and the better part of my school blazer. He was transferred to the stables for a day or two, and then Grandfather had to make a trip to neighbouring Saharanpur to collect his railway pension and, anxious to keep Toto out of trouble, he decided to take the monkey along with him.

Unfortunately I could not accompany Grandfather on this trip, but he told me about it afterwards.

A black kitbag was provided for Toto. When the strings of the bag were tied, there was no means of escape from within, and the canvas was too strong for Toto to bite his way through. His initial efforts to get out only had the effect of making the bag roll about on the floor, or occasionally jump in the air—an exhibition that attracted a curious crowd of onlookers on the Dehra railway platform.

Toto remained in the bag as far as Saharanpur, but while Grandfather was producing his ticket at the railway turnstile,

Toto managed to get his hands through the aperture where the bag was tied, loosened the strings, and suddenly thrust his head through the opening.

The poor ticket collector was visibly alarmed; but with great presence of mind, and much to the annoyance of Grandfather, he said, 'Sir, you have a dog with you. You'll have to pay for it accordingly.'

In vain did Grandfather take Toto out of the bag to prove that a monkey was not a dog or even a quadruped. The ticket collector, now thoroughly annoyed, insisted on classing Toto as a dog; and three rupees and four annas had to be handed over as his fare. Then Grandfather, out of sheer spite, took out from his pocket a live tortoise that he happened to have with him, and said, 'What must I pay for this, since you charge for all animals?'

The ticket collector retreated a pace or two; then advancing again with caution, he subjected the tortoise to a grave and knowledgeable stare.

'No ticket is necessary, sir,' he finally declared. 'There is no charge for insects.'

When we discovered that Toto's favourite pastime was catching mice, we were able to persuade Grandmother to let us keep him. The unsuspecting mice would emerge from their holes at night to pick up any corn left over by our pony; and to get at it they had to run the gauntlet of Toto's section of the stable. He knew this, and would pretend to be asleep, keeping, however, one eye open. A mouse would make a rush—in vain; Toto, as swift as a cat, would have his paws upon him. Grandmother decided to put his talents to constructive use by tying him up one night in the larder, where a guerrilla band of mice were playing havoc with our food supplies.

Toto was removed from his comfortable bed of straw in the stable, and chained up in the larder, beneath shelves of jam pots and other delicacies. The night was a long and miserable one for Toto, who must have wondered what he had done to deserve such treatment. The mice scampered about the place, while he, most uncat-like, lay curled up in a soup tureen, trying to snatch some sleep. At dawn, the mice returned to their holes; Toto awoke, scratched himself, emerged from the soup tureen, and looked about for something to eat. The jam pots attracted his notice, and it did not take him long to prise open the covers. Grandmother's treasured jams—she had made most of them herself—disappeared in an amazingly short time. I was present when she opened the door to see how many mice Toto had caught. Even the rain god Indra could not have looked more terrible when planning a thunderstorm; and the imprecations Grandmother hurled at Toto were surprising coming from someone who had been brought up in the genteel Victorian manner.

The monkey was later reinstated in Grandmother's favour. A great treat for him on cold winter evenings was the large bowl of warm water provided by Grandmother for his bath. He would bathe himself, first of all gingerly testing the temperature of the water with his fingers. Leisurely he would step into the bath, first one foot, then the other, as he had seen me doing, until he was completely sitting down in it. Once comfortable, he would take the soap in his hands or feet, and rub himself all over. When he found the water becoming cold, he would get out and run as quickly as he could to the fire, where his coat soon dried. If anyone laughed at him during this performance, he would look extremely hurt, and refuse to go on with his ablutions.

One day Toto nearly succeeded in boiling himself to death.

The large kitchen kettle had been left on the fire to boil for tea; and Toto, finding himself for a few minutes alone with it, decided to take the lid off. On discovering that the water inside was warm, he got into the kettle with the intention of having a bath, and sat down with his head protruding from the opening. This was very pleasant for some time, until the water began to simmer. Toto raised himself a little, but finding it cold outside, sat down again. He continued standing and sitting for some time, not having the courage to face the cold air. Had it not been for the timely arrival of Grandmother, he would have been cooked alive.

If there is a part of the brain especially devoted to mischief, that part must have been largely developed in Toto. He was always tearing things to bits, and whenever one of my aunts came near him, he made every effort to get hold of her dress and tear a hole in it. A variety of aunts frequently came to stay with my grandparents, but during Toto's stay they limited their visits to a day or two, much to Grandfather's relief and Grandmother's annoyance.

Toto, however, took a liking to Grandmother, in spite of the beatings he often received from her. Whenever she allowed him the liberty, he would lie quietly in her lap instead of scrambling all over her as he did on most people.

Toto lived with us over a year, but the following winter, after too much bathing, he caught pneumonia. Grandmother wrapped him in flannel, and Grandfather gave him a diet of chicken soup and Irish stew; but Toto did not recover. He was buried in the garden, under his favourite mango tree.

Perhaps it was just as well that Toto was no longer with us when Grandfather brought home the python, or his demise might have been less conventional. Small monkeys are a favourite delicacy with pythons.

Grandmother was tolerant of most birds and animals, but she drew the line at reptiles. She said they made her blood run cold. Even a handsome, sweet-tempered chameleon had to be given up. Grandfather should have known that there was little chance of his being allowed to keep the python. It was about four feet long, a young one, when Grandfather bought it from a snake charmer for six rupees, impressing the bazaar crowd by slinging it across his shoulders and walking home with it. Grandmother nearly fainted at the sight of the python curled round Grandfather's throat.

'You'll be strangled!' she cried. 'Get rid of it at once!'

'Nonsense,' said Grandfather. 'He's only a young fellow. He'll soon get used to us.'

'Will he, indeed?' said Grandmother. 'But I have no intention of getting used to him. You know quite well that your cousin Mabel is coming to stay with us tomorrow. She'll leave us the minute she knows there's a snake in the house.'

'Well, perhaps we ought to show it to her as soon as she arrives,' said Grandfather, who did not look forward to fussy Aunt Mabel's visits any more than I did.

'You'll do no such thing,' said Grandmother.

'Well, I can't let it loose in the garden,' said Grandfather with an innocent expression. 'It might find its way into the poultry house, and then where would we be?'

'How exasperating you are!' grumbled Grandmother. 'Lock the creature in the bathroom, go back to the bazaar and find the man you bought it from, and get him to come and take it back.'

In my awestruck presence, Grandfather had to take the python into the bathroom, where he placed it in a steep-sided tin tub. Then he hurried off to the bazaar to look for the snake charmer, while Grandmother paced anxiously up and down the veranda. When he returned looking crestfallen, we knew he hadn't been able to find the man.

'You had better take it away yourself,' said Grandmother, in a relentless mood. 'Leave it in the jungle across the riverbed.'

'All right, but let me give it a feed first,' said Grandfather; and producing a plucked chicken, he took it into the bathroom, followed, in single file, by me, Grandmother, and a curious cook and gardener.

Grandfather threw open the door and stepped into the bathroom. I peeped round his legs, while the others remained well behind. We couldn't see the python anywhere.

'He's gone,' announced Grandfather. 'He must have felt hungry.'

'I hope he isn't too hungry,' I said.

'We left the window open,' said Grandfather, looking embarrassed.

A careful search was made of the house, the kitchen, the garden, the stable and the poultry shed; but the python couldn't be found anywhere.

'He'll be well away by now,' said Grandfather reassuringly.

'I certainly hope so,' said Grandmother, who was half way between anxiety and relief.

Aunt Mabel arrived next day for a three-week visit, and for a couple of days Grandfather and I were a little apprehensive in case the python made a sudden reappearance; but on the third day, when he didn't show up, we felt confident that he had gone for good.

And then, towards evening, we were startled by a scream from the garden. Seconds later, Aunt Mabel came flying up the veranda steps, looking as though she had seen a ghost.

'In the guava tree!' she gasped. 'I was reaching for a guava, when I saw it staring at me. The look in its eyes! As though it would devour me—'

'Calm down, my dear,' urged Grandmother, sprinkling her with eau-de-cologne. 'Calm down and tell us what you saw.'

'A snake!' sobbed Aunt Mabel. 'A great boa constrictor. It must have been twenty feet long! In the guava tree. Its eyes were terrible. It looked at me in such a queer way . . .'

My grandparents looked significantly at each other, and Grandfather said, 'I'll go out and kill it,' and sheepishly taking hold of an umbrella, sallied out into the garden. But when he reached the guava tree, the python had disappeared.

'Aunt Mabel must have frightened it away,' I said.

'Hush,' said Grandfather. 'We mustn't speak of your aunt in that way.' But his eyes were alive with laughter.

After this incident, the python began to make a series of appearances, often in the most unexpected places. Aunt Mabel had another fit of hysterics when she saw him admiring her from under a cushion. She packed her bags, and Grandmother made us intensify the hunt.

Next morning I saw the python curled up on the dressing table, gazing at his reflection in the mirror. I went for Grandfather, but by the time we returned the python had moved elsewhere. A little later he was seen in the garden again. Then he was back on the dressing table, admiring himself in the mirror. Evidently he had become enamoured of his own reflection. Grandfather observed that perhaps the attention he was receiving from everyone had made him a little conceited.

'He's trying to look better for Aunt Mabel,' I said; a remark that I instantly regretted, because Grandmother overheard it, and brought the flat of her broad hand down on my head.

'Well, now we know his weakness,' said Grandfather.

'Are you trying to be funny too?' demanded Grandmother, looking her most threatening.

'I only meant he was becoming very vain,' said Grandfather hastily. 'It should be easier to catch him now.'

He set about preparing a large cage with a mirror at one end. In the cage he left a juicy chicken and various other delicacies, and fitted up the opening with a trapdoor. Aunt Mabel had already left by the time we had this trap ready, but we had to go on with the project because we couldn't have the python prowling about the house indefinitely.

For a few days nothing happened, and then, as I was leaving for school one morning, I saw the python curled up in the cage. He had eaten everything left out for him, and was relaxing in front of the mirror with something resembling a smile on his face—if you can imagine a python smiling . . . I lowered the trapdoor gently, but the python took no notice; he was in raptures over his handsome reflection. Grandfather and the gardener put the cage in the ponytrap, and made a journey to the other side of the riverbed. They left the cage in the jungle, with the trapdoor open.

'He made no attempt to get out,' said Grandfather later. 'And I didn't have the heart to take the mirror away. It's the first time I've seen a snake fall in love.'

'And the frogs have sung their old song in the mud . . .' This was Grandfather's favourite quotation from Virgil, and he used it whenever we visited the rainwater pond behind the house where there were quantities of mud and frogs and the occasional water buffalo. Grandfather had once brought a number of frogs into the house. He had put them in a glass jar, left them on a windowsill, and then forgotten all about them. At about four o'clock in the morning the entire household was awakened by a loud and fearful noise, and Grandmother and several nervous relatives gathered in their nightclothes on the veranda. Their timidity changed to fury when they discovered that the ghastly sounds had come from Grandfather's frogs. Seeing the dawn breaking, the frogs had with one accord begun their morning song.

Grandmother wanted to throw the frogs, bottle and all, out of the window; but Grandfather said that if he gave the bottle a good shaking, the frogs would remain quiet. He was obliged to keep awake, in order to shake the bottle whenever the frogs showed any inclination to break into song. Fortunately for all concerned, the next day a servant took the top off the bottle to see what was inside. The sight of several big frogs so startled him that he ran off without replacing the cover; the frogs jumped out and presumably found their way back to the pond.

It became a habit with me to visit the pond on my own, in order to explore its banks and shallows. Taking off my shoes, I would wade into the muddy water up to my knees, to pluck the water lilies that floated on the surface.

One day I found the pond already occupied by several buffaloes. Their keeper, a boy a little older than me, was swimming about in the middle. Instead of climbing out on to the bank, he would pull himself up on the back of one of his buffaloes, stretch his naked brown body out on the animal's glistening wet hide, and start singing to himself.

When he saw me staring at him from across the pond, he smiled, showing gleaming white teeth in a dark, sun-burnished face. He invited me to join him in a swim. I told him I couldn't swim, and he offered to teach me. I hesitated, knowing that Grandmother held strict and old-fashioned views about mixing with village children; but, deciding that Grandfather—who sometimes smoked a hookah on the sly—would get me out of any trouble that might occur, I took the bold step of accepting the boy's offer. Once taken, the step did not seem so bold.

He dived off the back of his buffalo, and swam across to me. And I, having removed my clothes, followed his instructions until I was floundering about among the water lilies. His name was Ramu, and he promised to give me swimming lessons every afternoon; and so it was during the afternoon—especially summer afternoons when everyone was asleep—that we usually met. Before long I was able to swim across the pond to sit with Ramu astride a contented buffalo, the great beast standing like an island in the middle of a muddy ocean.

Sometimes we would try racing the buffaloes, Ramu and I sitting on different mounts. But they were lazy creatures, and would leave one comfortable spot only to look for another; or, if they were in no mood for games, would roll over on their backs, taking us with them into the mud and green slime of the pond. Emerging in shades of green and khaki, I would slip into the house through the bathroom and bathe under the tap before getting into my clothes.

One afternoon Ramu and I found a small tortoise in the mud, sitting over a hole in which it had laid several eggs. Ramu kept the eggs for his dinner, and I presented the tortoise to Grandfather. He had a weakness for tortoises, and was pleased with this addition to his ménagerie, giving it a large tub of water all to itself, with an island of rocks in the middle. The tortoise, however, was always getting out of the tub and wandering about the house. As it seemed able to look after itself quite well, we did not interfere. If one of the dogs bothered it too much, it would draw its head and legs into its shell and defy all their attempts at rough play.

Ramu came from a family of bonded labourers, and had received no schooling. But he was well-versed in folklore, and knew a great deal about birds and animals.

'Many birds are sacred,' said Ramu, as we watched a blue jay swoop down from a peepul tree and carry off a grasshopper. He told me that both the blue jay and the God Shiva were called 'Nilkanth'. Shiva had a blue throat, like the bird, because out of compassion for the human race he had swallowed a deadly poison which was intended to destroy the world. Keeping the poison in his throat, he did not let it go any further.

'Are squirrels sacred?' I asked, seeing one sprint down the trunk of the peepul tree.

'Oh, yes, Lord Krishna loved squirrels,' said Ramu. 'He would take them in his arms and stroke them with his long fingers. That is why they have four dark lines down their backs from head to tail. Krishna was very dark, and the lines are the marks of his fingers.'

Both Ramu and Grandfather were of the opinion that we should be more gentle with birds and animals and should not kill so many of them.

'It is also important that we respect them,' said Grandfather. 'We must acknowledge their rights. Everywhere, birds and animals are finding it more difficult to survive, because we are trying to destroy both them and their forests. They have to keep moving as the trees disappear.'

This was especially true of the forests near Dehra, where the tiger and the pheasant and the spotted deer were beginning to disappear.

Ramu and I spent many long summer afternoons at the pond.

I still remember him with affection, though we never saw each other again after I left Dehra. He could not read or write, so we were unable to keep in touch. And neither his people, nor mine, knew of our friendship. The buffaloes and frogs had been our only confidants. They had accepted us as part of their own world, their muddy but comfortable pond. And when I left Dehra, both they and Ramu must have assumed that I would return again like the birds.

The Tree Lover

I WAS NEVER able to get over the feeling that plants and trees loved Grandfather with as much tenderness as he loved them. I was sitting beside him on the veranda steps one morning, when I noticed the tendril of a creeping vine that was trailing near my feet. As we sat there, in the soft sunshine of a north Indian winter, I saw that the tendril was moving very slowly away from me and towards Grandfather. Twenty minutes later it had crossed the veranda step and was touching Grandfather's feet.

There is probably a scientific explanation for the plant's behaviour—something to do with light and warmth—but I like to think that it moved that way simply because it was fond of Grandfather. One felt like drawing close to him. Sometimes when I sat alone beneath a tree I would feel a little lonely or lost; but as soon as Grandfather joined me, the garden would become a happy place, the tree itself more friendly.

Grandfather had served many years in the Indian Forest Service, and so it was natural that he should know and understand and like trees. On his retirement from the Service, he had built a bungalow on the outskirts of Dehra, planting trees all round it: limes, mangoes, oranges and guavas; also eucalyptus, jacaranda and the Persian lilac. In the fertile Doon valley, plants and trees grew tall and strong.

There were other trees in the compound before the house was built, including an old peepul which had forced its way through the walls of an abandoned outhouse, knocking the bricks down with its vigorous growth. Peepul trees are great show-offs. Even when there is no breeze, their broad-chested, slim-waisted leaves will spin like tops, determined to attract your attention and invite you into the shade.

Grandmother had wanted the peepul tree cut down, but Grandfather had said, 'Let it be. We can always build another outhouse.'

The gardener, Dhuki, who was a Hindu, was pleased that we had allowed the tree to live. Peepul trees are sacred to Hindus, and some people believe that ghosts live in the branches.

'If we cut the tree down, wouldn't the ghosts go away?' I asked.

'I don't know,' said Grandfather. 'Perhaps they'd come into the house.'

Dhuki wouldn't walk under the tree at night. He said that once, when he was a youth, he had wandered beneath a peepul tree late at night, and that something heavy had fallen with a thud on his shoulders. Since then he had always walked with a slight stoop, he explained.

'Nonsense,' said Grandmother, who didn't believe in ghosts. 'He got his stoop from squatting on his haunches year after year, weeding with that tiny spade of his!'

I never saw any ghosts in our peepul tree. There are peepul trees all over India, and people sometimes leave offerings of milk and flowers beneath them to keep the spirits happy. But since no one left any offerings under our tree, I expect the ghosts left in disgust, to look for peepul trees where there was both board and lodging.

Grandfather was about sixty, a lean active man who still rode his bicycle at great speed. He had stopped climbing trees a year previously, when he had got to the top of the jackfruit tree and had been unable to come down again. We had to fetch a ladder for him.

Grandfather bathed quite often but got back into his gardening clothes immediately after the bath. During meals, ladybirds or caterpillars would sometimes walk off his shirtsleeves and wander about on the tablecloth, and this always annoyed Grandmother.

She grumbled at Grandfather a lot, but he didn't mind, because he knew she loved him.

My favourite tree was the banyan which grew behind the house. Its spreading branches, which hung to the ground and took root again, formed a number of twisting passageways. The tree was older than the house, older than my grandparents; I could hide in its branches, behind a screen of thick green leaves, and spy on the world below.

The banyan tree was a world in itself, populated with small animals and large insects. While the leaves were still pink and tender, they would be visited by the delicate map butterfly, who left her eggs in their care. The 'honey' on the leaves—a sweet, sticky smear—also attracted the little striped squirrels, who soon grew used to having me in the tree and became quite bold, accepting gram from my hand.

At night the tree was visited by the hawk cuckoo. Its shrill nagging cry kept us awake on hot summer nights. Indians called the bird 'Paos-ala', which means 'Rain is coming!' But according to Grandfather, when the bird was in full cry, it seemed to be shouting, 'Oh dear, oh dear! How very hot it's getting! We feel it . . . we feel it . . . WE FEEL IT!'

Grandfather wasn't content with planting trees in our garden. During the rains we would walk into the jungle beyond the river bed, armed with cuttings and saplings, and these we would plant in the forest, beside the tall sal and shisham trees.

'But no one ever comes here,' I protested, the first time we did this. 'Who is going to see them?'

'We're not planting for people only,' said Grandfather. 'We're planting for the forest—and for the birds and animals who live here and need more food and shelter.'

He told me how men, and not only birds and animals, needed

trees—for keeping the desert away, for attracting rain, for preventing the banks of rivers from being washed away, and for wild plants and grasses to grow beneath.

'And for timber?' I asked, pointing to the sal and shisham trees.

'Yes, and for timber. But men are cutting down the trees without replacing them. For every tree that's felled, we must plant two. Otherwise, one day there'll be no forests at all, and the world will become one great desert.'

The thought of a world without trees became a sort of nighmare for me—it's one reason why I shall never want to live on the treeless Moon—and I helped Grandfather in his tree planting with even greater enthusiasm. He taught me a poem by George Morris, and we would recite it together:

Woodman, spare that tree!
Touch not a single bough!
In youth it sheltered me,
And I'll protect it now.

'One day the trees will move again,' said Grandfather. 'They've been standing still for thousands of years, but one day they'll move again. There was a time when trees could walk about like people, but along came the Devil and cast a spell over them, rooting them to one place. But they're always trying to move—see how they reach out with their arms!—and some of them, like the banyan tree with its travelling roots, manage to get quite far!'

In the autumn, Grandfather took me to the hills. The deodars (Indian cedars), oaks, chestnuts and maples were very different from the trees I had grown up with in Dehra. The broad leaves of the horse chestnut had turned yellow, and smooth brown chestnuts lay scattered on the roads. Grandfather and I filled our pockets with them, then climbed the slope of a bare hill and started planting the chestnuts in the ground.

I don't know if they ever came up, because I never went there again. Goats and cattle grazed freely on the hill, and, if the trees did come up in the spring, they may well have been eaten; but I like to think that somewhere in the foothills of the Himalayas there is a grove of chestnut trees, and that birds and flying foxes and cicadas have made their homes in them.

Back in Dehra, we found an island, a small rocky island in the middle of a dry river bed. It was one of those river beds, so common in the Doon valley, which are completely dry in summer but flooded during the monsoon rains. A small mango tree was growing in the middle of the island, and Grandfather said, 'If a mango can grow here, so can other trees.'

As soon as the rains set in—and while the river could still be crossed—we set out with a number of tamarind, laburnum and coral tree saplings and cuttings, and spent the day planting them on the island.

When the monsoon set in, the trees appeared to be flourishing.

The monsoon season was the time for rambling about. At every turn there was something new to see. Out of earth and rock and leafless bough, the magic touch of the monsoon rains had brought life and greenness. You could almost see the broad-leaved vines grow. Plants sprang up in the most unlikely places. A peepul would take root in the ceiling, a mango would sprout on the window sill. We did not like to remove them; but they had to go, if the house was to be kept from falling down.

'If you want to live in a tree, it's right by me,' said Grandmother. 'But I like having a roof over my head, and I'm not going to have it brought down by the jungle!'

The common monsoon sights along the Indian roads were always picturesque—the wide plains, with great herds of smoke-coloured, delicate-limbed cattle being driven slowly home for the night, accompanied by several ungainly buffaloes, and flocks of goats and black long-tailed sheep. Then you came to a pond, where some buffaloes were enjoying themselves, with no part of them visible but the tips of their noses, while on their backs were a number of merry children, perfectly and happily naked.

The banyan tree really came to life during the monsoon, when the branches were thick with scarlet figs. Humans couldn't eat the berries, but the many birds that gathered in the tree—gossipy rosy pastors, quarrelsome mynahs, cheerful bulbuls and coppersmiths, and sometimes a noisy, bullying crow—feasted on them. And when night fell and the birds were resting, the dark flying foxes flapped heavily about the tree, chewing and munching loudly as they clambered over the branches.

The tree crickets were a band of willing artists who started their singing at almost any time of the day but preferably in the evenings. Delicate pale green creatures with transparent wings, they were hard to find amongst the lush monsoon foliage; but once found, a tap on the bush or leaf on which one of them sat would put an immediate end to its performance.

At the height of the monsoon, the banyan tree was like an orchestra with the musicians constantly tuning up. Birds, insects and squirrels welcomed the end of the hot weather and the cool quenching relief of the monsoon.

A toy flute in my hands, I would try adding my shrill piping to theirs. But they must have thought poorly of my piping, for, whenever I played, the birds and the insects kept a pained and puzzled silence.

I wonder if they missed me when I went away—for when the War came, followed by the Independence of India, I was sent to a boarding school in the hills. Grandfather's house was put up for sale. During the holidays I went to live with my parents in Delhi, and it was from them I learnt that my grandparents had gone to England.

When I finished school, I too went to England with my parents, and was away from India for several years. But recently I was in Dehra again, and after first visiting the old house—where I found that the banyan tree had grown over the wall and along part of the pavement, almost as though it had tried to follow Grandfather—I walked out of town towards the river bed.

It was February, and as I looked across the dry watercourse, my eye was caught by the spectacular red plumes of the coral blossom. In contrast to the dry river bed, the island was a small green paradise. When I walked across to the trees, I noticed that a number of squirrels had come to live in them. And a koel (a sort of crow-pheasant) challenged me with a mellow 'who-are-you, who-are-you . . .'

But the trees seemed to know me. They whispered among themselves and beckoned me nearer. And looking around, I noticed that other small trees and wild plants and grasses had sprung up under the protection of the trees we had placed there.

The trees had multiplied! They were moving. In one small corner of the world, Grandfather's dream was coming true, and the trees were moving again.

A Tiger in the House

TIMOTHY, THE TIGER cub, was discovered by Grandfather on a hunting expedition in the Terai jungle near Dehra.

Grandfather was no shikari, but as he knew the forests of the Siwalik hills better than most people, he was persuaded to accompany the party—it consisted of several Very Important Persons from Delhi—to advise on the terrain and the direction the beaters should take once a tiger had been spotted.

The camp itself was sumptuous—seven large tents (one for each shikari), a dining tent and a number of servants' tents. The dinner was very good, as Grandfather admitted afterwards; it was not often that one saw hot-water plates, finger glasses and seven or eight courses in a tent in the jungle! But that was how things were done in the days of the Viceroys . . . There were also some fifteen elephants, four of them with howdahs for the shikaris, and the others specially trained for taking part in the beat.

The sportsmen never saw a tiger, nor did they shoot anything else, though they saw a number of deer, peacock and wild boar. They were giving up all hope of finding a tiger and were beginning to shoot at jackals, when Grandfather, strolling down the forest path at some distance from the rest of the party, discovered a little tiger about eighteen inches long, hiding among the intricate roots of a banyan tree. Grandfather picked him up and brought him home after the camp had broken up. He had the distinction of being the only member of the party to have bagged any game, dead or alive.

At first the tiger cub, who was named Timothy by Grandmother, was brought up entirely on milk given to him in a feeding bottle by our cook, Mahmoud. But the milk proved too rich for him, and he was put on a diet of raw mutton and cod liver oil, to be followed later by a more tempting diet of pigeons and rabbits.

Timothy was provided with two companions—Toto the monkey, who was bold enough to pull the young tiger by the tail, and then climb up the curtains if Timothy lost his temper; and a small mongrel puppy, found on the road by Grandfather.

At first Timothy appeared to be quite afraid of the puppy and darted back with a spring if it came too near. He would make absurd dashes at it with his large forepaws and then retreat to a ridiculously safe distance. Finally, he allowed the puppy to crawl on his back and rest there!

One of Timothy's favourite amusements was to stalk anyone who would play with him, and so, when I came to live with Grandfather, I became one of the tiger's favourites. With a crafty look in his glittering eyes, and his body crouching, he would creep closer and closer to me, suddenly making a dash for my feet, rolling over on his back and kicking with delight, and pretending to bite my ankles.

He was by this time the size of a full-grown retriever, and when I took him out for walks, people on the road would give us a wide berth. When he pulled hard on his chain, I had difficulty in keeping up with him. His favourite place in the house was the drawing room, and he would make himself comfortable on the long sofa, reclining there with great dignity and snarling at anybody who tried to get him off.

Timothy had clean habits, and would scrub his face with his paws exactly like a cat. He slept at night in the cook's quarters, and was always delighted at being let out by him in the morning.

'One of these days,' declared Grandmother in her prophetic manner, 'we are going to find Timothy sitting on Mahmoud's bed, and no sign of the cook except his clothes and shoes!'

Of course, it never came to that, but when Timothy was about six months old a change came over him; he grew steadily less friendly. When out for a walk with me, he would try to steal away to stalk a cat or someone's pet Pekinese. Sometimes at night we would hear frenzied cackling from the poultry house, and in the morning there would be feathers lying all over the veranda. Timothy had to be chained up more often. And, finally, when he began to stalk Mahmoud about the house with what looked like villainous intent, Grandfather decided it was time to transfer him to a zoo.

The nearest zoo was at Lucknow, 200 miles away. Reserving a first-class compartment for himself and Timothy—no one would share a compartment with them—Grandfather took him to Lucknow where the zoo authorities were only too glad to receive as a gift a well-fed and fairly civilized tiger.

About six months later, when my grandparents were visiting relatives in Lucknow, Grandfather took the opportunity of calling at the zoo to see how Timothy was getting on. I was not there to accompany him, but I heard all about it when he returned to Dehra.

Arriving at the zoo, Grandfather made straight for the particular cage in which Timothy had been interned. The tiger was there, crouched in a corner, full-grown and with a magnificent striped coat.

'Hello, Timothy!' said Grandfather and, climbing the railing with ease, he put his arm through the bars of the cage.

The tiger approached the bars and allowed Grandfather to put both hands around his head. Grandfather stroked the tiger's forehead and tickled his ear, and, whenever he growled, smacked him across the mouth, which was his old way of keeping him quiet.

He licked Grandfather's hands and only sprang away when a leopard in the next cage snarled at him. Grandfather 'shooed' the leopard away and the tiger returned to lick his hands; but every now and then the leopard would rush at the bars and the tiger would slink back to his corner.

A number of people had gathered to watch the reunion when a keeper pushed his way through the crowd and asked Grandfather what he was doing.

'I'm talking to Timothy,' said Grandfather. 'Weren't you here when I gave him to the zoo six months ago?'

'I haven't been here very long,' said the surprised keeper. 'Please continue your conversation. But I have never been able to touch him myself, he is always very bad tempered.'

'Why don't you put him somewhere else?' suggested Grandfather. 'That leopard keeps frightening him. I'll go and see the superintendent about it.'

Grandfather went in search of the superintendent of the zoo, but found that he had gone home early; and so, after wandering about the zoo for a little while, he returned to Timothy's cage to say goodbye. It was beginning to get dark.

He had been stroking and slapping Timothy for about five minutes when he found another keeper observing him with some alarm. Grandfather recognized him as the keeper who had been there when Timothy had first come to the zoo.

'You remember me,' said Grandfather. 'Now why don't you transfer Timothy to another cage, away from this stupid leopard?'

'But—sir—' stammered the keeper, 'it is not your tiger.'

'I know, I know,' said Grandfather testily. 'I realize he is no longer mine. But you might at least take a suggestion or two from me.'

'I remember your tiger very well,' said the keeper. 'He died two months ago.'

'Died!' exclaimed Grandfather.

'Yes, sir, of pneumonia. This tiger was trapped in the hills only last month, and he is very dangerous!'

Grandfather could think of nothing to say. The tiger was still licking his arm, with increasing relish. Grandfather took what seemed to him an age to withdraw his hand from the cage.

With his face near the tiger's he mumbled, 'Goodnight, Timothy,' and giving the keeper a scornful look, walked briskly out of the zoo.

Monkey Trouble

SOON AFTER TOTO passed away, Grandfather bought another monkey—Tutu—from a street entertainer for the sum of ten rupees. The man had three monkeys. Tutu was the smallest but the most mischievous. She was tied up most of the time. The little monkey looked so miserable with a collar and chain that Grandfather decided it would be much happier in our home. His weakness for keeping unusual pets was something that I, at the age of seven, used to heartily encourage.

Grandmother at first objected to having another monkey in the house since she had been especially fond of Toto and believed that Toto could never be replaced in her affections. 'You had enough pets as it is,' she said, referring to Grandfather's goat, several white mice, and a small tortoise.

'But I don't have any,' I said.

'You're wicked enough for two monkeys. One boy in the house is all I can take.'

'Ah, but Tutu isn't a boy,' said Grandfather triumphantly. 'This is a little girl monkey!'

Grandmother gave in. She had always wanted a little girl in the house. She believed girls were less troublesome than boys. Tutu was to prove her wrong.

She was a pretty little monkey. One of the first things I taught her was to shake hands, and this she insisted on doing with all who visited the house. Peppery Major Malik would have to stoop and shake hands with Tutu before he could enter the

26

drawing room, otherwise she would climb on his shoulder and stay there, roughing up his hair and playing with his moustache.

My Uncle Ken, Granny's nephew who came to stay with us now and then, couldn't stand any of our pets and took a particular dislike to Tutu, who was always making faces at him. But as Uncle Ken was never in a job for long and depended on Grandfather's good-natured generosity, he had to shake hands with Tutu like everyone else.

Aunt Ruby, who had been staying with us for a few days, had not been informed of Tutu's arrival. Loud shrieks from her bedroom brought us running to see what was wrong. It was only Tutu trying on Aunt Ruby's petticoats! They were much too large, of course, and when Aunt Ruby entered the room all she saw was a faceless white blob jumping up and down on the bed.

We disentangled Tutu and soothed Aunt Ruby. I gave Tutu a bunch of sweet peas to make her happy. Granny didn't like anyone plucking her sweet peas, so I took some from Major Malik's garden while he was having his afternoon siesta.

Then Uncle Ken complained that his hairbrush was missing. We found Tutu sunning herself on the back veranda, using the hairbrush to scratch her armpits. I took it from her and handed it back to Uncle Ken with an apology; but he flung the brush away with an oath.

'Such a fuss about nothing,' I said. 'Tutu doesn't have fleas!'

'No, and she bathes more often than Ken,' said Grandfather, who had borrowed Aunt Ruby's shampoo for giving Tutu a bath.

All the same, Grandmother objected to Tutu being given the run of the house. Tutu had to spend her nights in the outhouse, in the company of the goat. They got on quite well, and it was not long before Tutu was seen sitting comfortably on the back of the goat, while the goat roamed the back garden in search of its favourite grass.

Aunt Ruby was a frequent taker of baths. This met with

Tutu's approval—so much so, that one day, when Aunt Ruby had finished shampooing her hair she looked up through a lather of bubbles and soapsuds to see Tutu sitting opposite her in the bath, following her example.

One day Aunt Ruby took us all by surprise. She announced that she had become engaged. We had always thought Aunt Ruby would never marry—she had often said so herself—but it appeared that the right man had now come along in the person of Rocky Fernandes, a schoolteacher from Goa.

Rocky was a tall, firm-jawed, good-natured man, a couple of years younger than Aunt Ruby. He had a fine baritone voice and sang in the manner of the great Nelson Eddy. As Grandmother liked baritone singers, Rocky was soon in her good books.

'But what on earth does he see in her?' Uncle Ken wanted to know.

'More than any girl has seen in you!' snapped Grandmother. 'Ruby's a fine girl. And they're both teachers. Maybe they can start a school of their own.'

Rocky visited the house quite often and brought me chocolates and cashewnuts, of which he seemed to have an unlimited supply. He also taught me several marching songs. Naturally I approved of Rocky. Aunt Ruby won my grudging admiration for having made such a wise choice.

One day I overheard them talking of going to the bazaar to buy an engagement ring. I decided I would go along too. But as Aunt Ruby had made it clear that she did not want me around I decided that I had better follow at a discreet distance. Tutu, becoming aware that a mission of some importance was underway, decided to follow me. But as I had not invited her along, she too decided to keep out of sight.

Once in the crowded bazaar, I was able to get quite close to Aunt Ruby and Rocky without being spotted. I waited until they had settled down in a large jewellery shop before sauntering past and spotting them as though by accident. Aunt Ruby wasn't too pleased at seeing me, but Rocky waved and called out, 'Come and join us! Help your aunt choose a beautiful ring!'

The whole thing seemed to be a waste of good money, but I did not say so—Aunt Ruby was giving me one of her more unloving looks.

'Look, these are pretty!' I said, pointing to some cheap, bright agates set in white metal. But Aunt Ruby wasn't looking. She was immersed in a case of diamonds.

'Why not a ruby for Aunt Ruby?' I suggested, trying to please her.

'That's her lucky stone,' said Rocky. 'Diamonds are the thing for engagement.' And he started singing a song about diamonds being a girl's best friend.

While the jeweller and Aunt Ruby were sifting through the diamond rings, and Rocky was trying out another tune, Tutu had slipped into the shop without being noticed by anyone but me. A little squeal of delight was the first sign she gave of her presence. Everyone looked up to see her trying on a pretty necklace.

'And what are those stones?' I asked.

'They look like pearls,' said Rocky.

'They are pearls,' said the shopkeeper, making a grab for them.

'It's that dreadful monkey!' cried Aunt Ruby. 'I knew that boy would bring her here!'

The necklace was already adorning Tutu's neck. I thought she looked rather nice in pearls, but she gave us no time to admire the effect. Springing out of our reach Tutu dodged around Rocky, slipped between my legs, and made for the crowded road. I ran after her, shouting to her to stop, but she wasn't listening.

There were no branches to assist Tutu in her progress, but she used the heads and shoulders of people as springboards and so made rapid headway through the bazaar.

The jeweller left his shop and ran after us. So did Rocky. So did several bystanders who had seen the incident. And others, who had no idea what it was all about, joined in the chase. As Grandfather used to say, 'In a crowd, everyone plays follow-the-leader even when they don't know who's leading.'

She tried to make her escape speedier by leaping on to the back of a passing scooterist. The scooter swerved into a fruit stall and came to a standstill under a heap of bananas, while the scooterist found himself in the arms of an indignant fruitseller. Tutu peeled a banana and ate part of it before deciding to move on.

From an awning she made an emergency landing on a washerman's donkey. The donkey promptly panicked and rushed down the road, while bundles of washing fell by the wayside. The washerman joined in the chase. Children on their way to school decided that there was something better to do than attend classes. With shouts of glee, they soon overtook their panting elders.

Tutu finally left the bazaar and took a road leading in the direction of our house. But knowing that she would be caught and locked up once she got home, she decided to end the chase by ridding herself of the necklace. Deftly removing it from her neck, she flung it in the small canal that ran down that road.

The jeweller, with a cry of anguish, plunged into the canal. So did Rocky. So did I. So did several other people, both adults and children. It was to be a treasure hunt!

Some twenty minutes later, Rocky shouted, 'I've found it!' Covered in mud, water lilies, ferns and tadpoles, we emerged from the canal, and Rocky presented the necklace to the relieved shopkeeper.

Everyone trudged back to the bazaar to find Aunt Ruby waiting in the shop, still trying to make up her mind about a suitable engagement ring.

Finally the ring was bought, the engagement was announced, and a date was set for the wedding.

'I don't want that monkey anywhere near us on our wedding day,' declared Aunt Ruby.

'We'll lock her up in the outhouse,' promised Grandfather. 'And we'll let her out only after you've left for your honeymoon.'

A few days before the wedding I found Tutu in the kitchen helping Grandmother prepare the wedding cake. Tutu often helped with the cooking, and, when Grandmother wasn't looking, added herbs, spices, and other interesting items to the pots—so that occasionally we found a chilli in the custard or an onion in the jelly or a strawberry floating on the chicken soup.

Sometimes these additions improved a dish, sometimes they did not. Uncle Ken lost a tooth when he bit firmly into a sandwich which contained walnut shells.

I'm not sure exactly what went into that wedding cake when Grandfather wasn't looking—she insisted that Tutu was always very well-behaved in the kitchen—but I did spot Tutu stirring in some red chilli sauce, bittergourd seeds, and a generous helping of eggshells!

It's true that some of the guests were not seen for several days after the wedding but no one said anything against the cake. Most people thought it had an interesting flavour.

The great day dawned, and the wedding guests made their way to the little church that stood on the outskirts of Dehra—a town with a church, two mosques, and several temples.

I had offered to dress Tutu up as a bridesmaid and bring her along, but no one except Grandfather thought it was a good idea. So I decided to be an obedient boy and locked Tutu in the outhouse. I did, however, leave the skylight open a little. Grandmother had always said that fresh air was good for growing children, and I thought Tutu should have her share of it.

The wedding ceremony went without a hitch. Aunt Ruby looked a picture, and Rocky looked like a film star.

Grandfather played the organ, and did so with such gusto that the small choir could hardly be heard. Grandmother cried a little. I sat quietly in a corner, with the little tortoise on my lap.

When the service was over, we trooped out into the sunshine and made our way back to the house for the reception.

The feast had been laid out on tables in the garden. As the gardener had been left in charge, everything was in order. Tutu was on her best behaviour. She had, it appeared, used the skylight to avail of more fresh air outside, and now sat beside the three-tier wedding cake, guarding it against crows, squirrels and the goat. She greeted the guests with squeals of delight.

It was too much for Aunt Ruby. She flew at Tutu in a rage. And Tutu, sensing that she was not welcome, leapt away, taking with her the top tier of the wedding cake.

Led by Major Malik, we followed her into the orchard, only to find that she had climbed to the top of the jackfruit tree. From there she proceeded to pelt us with bits of wedding cake. She had also managed to get hold of bag of confetti, and when she ran out of cake she showered us with confetti.

'That's more like it!' said the good-humoured Rocky. 'Now let's return to the party, folks!'

Uncle Ken remained with Major Malik, determined to chase Tutu away. He kept throwing stones into the tree, until he received a large piece of cake bang on his nose. Muttering threats, he returned to the party, leaving the Major to battle it out.

When the festivities were finally over, Uncle Ken took the unnecessary old car out of the garage and drove up to the veranda steps. He was going to drive Aunt Ruby and Rocky to the nearby hill resort of Mussoorie, where they would have their honeymoon.

Watched by family and friends, Aunt Ruby and Rocky climbed into the back seat. Aunt Ruby waved regally to everyone. She leant out of the window and offered me her cheek and I had to kiss her farewell. Everyone wished them luck.

As Rocky burst into song Uncle Ken opened the throttle and stepped on the accelerator. The car shot forward in a cloud of dust.

Rocky and Aunt Ruby continued to wave to us. And so did Tutu from her perch on the rear bumper! She was clutching a bag in her hands and showering confetti on all who stood in the driveway.

'They don't know Tutu's with them!' I exclaimed. 'She'll go all the way to Mussoorie! Will Aunt Ruby let her stay with them?'

'Tutu might ruin the honeymoon,' said Grandfather. 'But don't worry—our Ken will bring her back!'

Animals on the Track

'ALL ABOARD!' SHRIEKED Popeye, Grandmother's pet parrot, as the family climbed aboard the Lucknow Express. We were moving from Dehra to Lucknow, in northern India, and as Grandmother had insisted on taking her parrot along, Grandfather and I had insisted on bringing our pets—a teenaged tiger (Grandfather's) and a small squirrel (mine). But we thought it prudent to leave the python behind.

In those days the trains in India were not so crowded and it was possible to travel with a variety of creatures. Grandfather had decided to do things in style by travelling first-class, so we had a four-berth compartment of our own, and Timothy, the tiger, had an entire berth to himself. Later, everyone agreed that Timothy behaved perfectly throughout the journey. Even the guard admitted that he could not have asked for a better passengr: no stealing from vendors, no shouting at coolies, no breaking of railway property, no spitting on the platform.

All the same, the journey was not without incident. Before we reached Lucknow, there was excitement enough for everyone.

To begin with, Popeye objected to vendors and other people poking their hands in at the windows. Before the train had moved out of the Dehra station, he had nipped two fingers and tweaked a ticket-inspector's ear.

No sooner had the train started moving than Chips, my squirrel, emerged from the pocket to examine his surroundings. Before I could stop him, he was out of the compartment door, scurrying along the corridor.

Chips discovered that the train was a squirrel's paradise, almost all the passengers having bought large quantities of roasted peanuts before the train pulled out. He had no difficulty in making friends with both children and grown-ups, and it was an hour before he returned to our compartment, his tummy almost bursting.

'I think I'll go to sleep,' said Grandmother, covering herself with a blanket and stretching out on the berth opposite Timothy's. 'It's been a tiring day.'

'Aren't you going to eat anything?' asked Grandfather.

'I'm not hungry—I had some soup before we left. You two help yourselves from the tiffin-basket.'

Grandmother dozed off, and even Popeye started nodding, lulled to sleep by the clackety-clack of the wheels and the steady puffing of the steam engine.

'Well, I'm hungry,' I said. 'What did Granny make for us?'

'Ham sandwiches, boiled eggs, a roast chicken, gooseberry pie. It's all in the tiffin-basket under your berth.'

I tugged at the large basket and dragged it into the centre of the compartment. The straps were loosely tied. No sooner had I undone them than the lid flew open, and I let out a gasp of surprise.

In the basket was Grandfather's pet python, curled up contentedly on the remains of our dinner. Grandmother had insisted that we leave the python behind, and Grandfather had let it loose in the garden. Somehow, it had managed to smuggle itself into the tiffin-basket.

'Well, what are you staring at?' asked Grandfather from his corner.

'It's the python,' I said. 'And its finished all our dinner.'

Grandfather joined me, and together we looked down at what remained of the food. Pythons don't chew, they swallow: outlined along the length of the large snake's sleek body were the distinctive shapes of a chicken, a pie and six boiled eggs. We couldn't make out the ham sandwiches, but presumably these had been eaten too because there was no sign of them in the basket. Only a few apples remained. Evidently, the python did not care for apples.

Grandfather snapped the basket shut and pushed it back beneath the berth.

'We mustn't let Grandmother see him,' he said. 'She might think we brought him along on purpose.'

'Well, I'm hungry,' I complained. Just then Chips returned from one of his forays and presented me with a peanut.

'Thanks,' I said. 'If you keep bringing me peanuts all night, I might last until morning.'

But it was not long before I felt sleepy. Grandfather had begun to nod and the only one who was wide awake was the squirrel, still intent on investigating distant compartments.

A little after midnight there was a great clamour at the end of the corridor. Grandfather and I woke up. Timothy growled in his sleep, and Popeye made complaining noises.

Suddenly there were cries of '*Saap, saap*! (Snake, snake!)

Grandfather was on his feet in a moment. He looked under the berth. The tiffin-basket was empty.

'The python's out,' he said, and dashed out of our compartment in his pyjamas. I was close behind.

About a dozen passengers were bunched together outside the washroom door.

'Anything wrong?' asked Grandfather casually.

'We can't get into the toilet,' said someone. 'There's a huge snake inside.'

'Let me take a look,' said Grandfather. 'I know all about snakes.'

The passengers made way for him, and he entered the washroom to find the python curled up in the washbasin. After its heavy meal it had become thirsty and, finding the lid of the tiffin-basket easy to pry up, had set out in search of water.

Grandfather gathered up the sleepy, overfed python and

stepped out of the washroom. The passengers hastily made way for them.

'Nothing to worry about,' said grandfather cheerfully. 'It's just a harmless young python. He's had his dinner already, so no one is in any danger!' And he marched back to our compartment with the python in his arms. As soon as I was inside, he bolted the door.

Grandmother was sitting up on her berth.

'I knew you'd do something foolish behind my back,' she scolded. 'You told me you'd got rid of that creature, and all the time you've been hiding it from me.'

Grandfather tried to explain that we had nothing to do with it, that the python had smuggled itself into the tiffin-basket, but Grandmother was unconvinced. She declared that Grandfather couldn't live without the creature and that he had deliberately brought it along.

'What will Mabel do when she sees it!' cried Grandmother despairingly.

My Aunt Mabel was a schoolteacher in Lucknow. She was going to share our new house, and she was terrified of all reptiles, particularly snakes.

'We won't let her see it,' said Grandfather. 'Back it goes into the tiffin-basket.'

Early next morning the rains streamed into Lucknow. Aunt Mabel was on the platform to receive us.

Grandfather let all the other passengers get off before he emerged from the compartment with Timothy on a chain. I had Chips in my pocket, a suitcase in both hands. Popeye stayed perched on Grandmother's shoulder, eyeing the busy platform with considerable distrust.

Aunt Mabel, a lover of good food, immediately spotted the tiffin-basket, picked it up and said, 'It's not very heavy. I'll carry it out to the taxi. I hope you've kept something for me.'

'A whole chicken,' I said.

'We hardly ate anything,' said Grandfather.

'It's all yours, Aunty!' I added.

'Oh, good!' exclaimed Aunt Mabel. 'Its been ages since I tasted something cooked by your grandmother.' And after that there was no getting the basket away from her.

Glancing at it, I thought I saw the lid bulging, but Grandfather had tied it down quite firmly this time and there was little likelihood of its suddenly bursting open.

An enormous 1950 Chevrolet taxi was waiting outside the station, and the family tumbled into it. Timothy got into the back seat, leaving enough room for Grandfather and me. Aunt Mabel sat up in front with Grandmother, the tiffin-basket on her lap.

'I'm dying to see what's inside,' she said. 'Can't I take just a little peek?'

'Not now,' said Grandfather. 'First let's enjoy the breakfast you've got waiting for us.'

'Yes, wait until we get home,' said Grandmother. 'Now tell the taxi driver where to take us, dear. He's looking rather nervous.'

Aunt Mabel gave instructions to the driver and the taxi shot off in a cloud of dust.

'Well, here we go!' said Grandfather. 'I'm looking forward to settling into the new house.'

Popeye, perched proudly on Grandmother's shoulder, kept one suspicious eye on the quivering tiffin-basket.

'All aboard!' he squawked. 'All aboard!'

When we got to our new house, we found a light breakfast waiting for us on the dining table.

'It isn't much,' said Aunt Mabel. 'But we'll supplement it with the contents of your hamper.' And placing the basket on the table, she removed the lid.

The python was half-asleep, with an apple in its mouth. Aunt Mabel was no Eve, to be tempted. She fainted away.

Grandfather promptly picked up the python, took it into the garden, and draped it over a branch of a guava tree.

When Aunt Mabel recovered, she insisted that there was a huge snake in the tiffin-basket. We showed her the empty basket.

'You're seeing things,' said Grandfather.

'It must be the heart,' I said.

Grandmother said nothing. But Popeye broke into shrieks of maniacal laughter, and soon everyone, including a slightly hysterical Aunt Mabel, was doubled up with laughter.

The Last Tonga Ride

IT WAS A warm spring day in Dehra Dun, and the walls of the bungalow were aflame with flowering bougainvillea. The papayas were ripening. The scent of sweetpeas drifted across the garden. Grandmother sat in an easy chair in a shady corner of the veranda, her knitting needles clicking away, her head nodding now and then. She was knitting a pullover for my father. 'Delhi has cold winters,' she had said, and although the winter was still eight months away, she had set to work on getting our woollens ready.

In the Kathiawar states touched by the warm waters of the Arabian Sea, it had never been cold. But Dehra lies at the foot of the first range of the Himalayas.

Grandmother's hair was white and her eyes were not very strong, but her fingers moved quickly with the needles and the needles kept clicking all morning.

When Grandmother wasn't looking, I picked geranium leaves, crushed them between my fingers and pressed them to my nose.

I had been in Dehra with my grandmother for almost a month and I had not seen my father during this time. We had never before been separated for so long. He wrote to me every week, and sent me books and picture postcards, and I would walk to the end of the road to meet the postman as early as possible to see if there was any mail for us.

We heard the jingle of tonga bells at the gate and a familiar horse buggy came rattling up the drive.

'I'll see who's come,' I said, and ran down the veranda steps and across the garden.

It was Bansi Lal in his tonga. There were many tongas and tonga drivers in Dehra but Bansi was my favourite driver. He was young and handsome and he always wore a clean, white shirt and pyjamas. His pony, too, was bigger and faster than the other tonga ponies.

Bansi didn't have a passenger, so I asked him, 'What have you come for, Bansi?'

'Your grandmother sent for me, dost.' He did not call me "Chota Sahib" or "baba", but "dost" and this made me feel much more important. Not every small boy could boast of a tonga driver for his friend!

'Where are you going, Granny?' I asked, after I had run back to the veranda.

'I'm going to the bank.'

'Can I come too?'

'Whatever for? What will you do in the bank?'

'Oh, I won't come inside, I'll sit in the tonga with Bansi.'

'Come along, then.'

We helped Grandmother into the back seat of the tonga, and then I joined Bansi in the driver's seat. He said something to his pony and the pony set off at a brisk trot, out of the gate and down the road.

'Now, not too fast, Bansi,' said Grandmother, who didn't like anything that went too fast—tonga, motor car, train or bullock cart.

'Fast?' said Bansi. 'Have no fear, memsahib. This pony has never gone fast in its life. Even if a bomb went off behind us, we could go no faster. I have another pony which I use for racing when customers are in a hurry. This pony is reserved for you, memsahib.'

There was no other pony, but Grandmother did not know this, and was mollified by the assurance that she was riding in the slowest tonga in Dehra.

A ten-minute ride brought us to the bazaar. Grandmother's
bank, the Allahabad Bank, stood near the clock tower. She was
gone for about half an hour and during this period Bansi and I
sauntered about in front of the shops. The pony had been left
with some green stuff to munch.

'Do you have any money on you?' asked Bansi.

'Four annas,' I said.

'Just enough for two cups of tea,' said Bansi, putting his arm
round my shoulders and guiding me towards a tea stall. The
money passed from my palm to his.

'You can have tea, if you like,' I said. 'I'll have a lemonade.'

'So be it, friend. A tea and a lemonade, and be quick about it,'
said Bansi to the boy in the tea shop and presently the drinks
were set before us and Bansi was making a sound rather like his
pony when it drank, while I burped my way through some
green, gaseous stuff that tasted more like soap than lemonade.

When Grandmother came out of the bank, she looked pensive
and did not talk much during the ride back to the house except
to tell me to behave myself when I leant over to pat the pony on
its rump. After paying off Bansi, she marched straight indoors.

'When will you come again?' I asked Bansi.

'When my services are required, dost. I have to make a living,
you know. But I tell you what, since we are friends, the next time
I am passing this way after leaving a fare, I will jingle my bells at
the gate and if you are free and would like a ride—a fast ride!—
you can join me. It won't cost you anything. Just bring some
money for a cup of tea.'

'All right—since we are friends,' I said.

'Since we are friends.'

And touching the pony very lightly with the handle of his
whip, he sent the tonga rattling up the drive and out of the gate.
I could hear Bansi singing as the pony cantered down the road.

Ayah was waiting for me in the bedroom, her hands resting on
her broad hips—sure sign of an approaching storm.

'So you went off to the bazaar without telling me,' she said. (It wasn't enough that I had Grandmother's permission!) 'And all this time I've been waiting to give you your bath.'

'It's too late now, isn't it?' I asked hopefully.

'No, it isn't. There's still an hour left for lunch. Off with your clothes!'

While I undressed, Ayah berated me for keeping the company of tonga drivers like Bansi. I think she was a little jealous.

'He is a rogue, that man. He drinks, gambles and smokes opium. He has TB and other terrible diseases. So don't you be too friendly with him, understand, baba?'

I nodded my head sagely but said nothing. I thought Ayah was exaggerating as she always did about people, and besides, I had no intention of giving up free tonga rides.

As my father had told me, Dehra was a good place for trees, and Grandmother's house was surrounded by several kinds— peepul, neem, mango, jackfruit, papaya and an ancient banyan tree. Some of the trees had been planted by my father and grandfather.

'How old is the jackfruit tree?' I asked Grandmother.

'Now let me see,' said Grandmother, looking very thoughtful. 'I should remember the jackfruit tree. Oh, yes, your grandfather put it down in 1927. It was during the rainy season. I remember because it was your father's birthday and we celebrated it by planting a tree—14 July 1927. Long before you were born!'

The banyan tree grew behind the house. Its spreading branches, which hung to the ground and took root again, formed a number of twisting passageways in which I liked to wander. The tree was older than the house, older than my grandparents, as old as Dehra. I could hide myself in its branches behind thick, green leaves and spy on the world below.

It was an enormous tree, about sixty feet high, and the first time I saw it I trembled with excitement because I had never seen such a marvellous tree before. I approached it slowly, even cautiously, as I wasn't sure the tree wanted my friendship. It looked as though it had many secrets. There were sounds and movements in the branches but I couldn't see who or what made the sounds.

The tree made the first move, the first overture of friendship. It allowed a leaf to fall.

The leaf brushed against my face as it floated down, but before it could reach the ground I caught and held it. I studied the leaf, running my fingers over its smooth, glossy texture. Then I put out my hand and touched the rough bark of the tree and this felt good to me. So I removed my shoes and socks as people do when they enter a holy place; and finding first a foothold and then a handhold on that broad trunk, I pulled myself up with the help of the tree's aerial roots.

As I climbed, it seemed as though someone was helping me. Invisible hands, the hands of the spirit in the tree, touched me and helped me climb.

But although the tree wanted me, there were others who were disturbed and alarmed by my arrival. A pair of parrots suddenly shot out of a hole in the trunk and with shrill cries, flew across the garden—flashes of green and red and gold. A squirrel looked out from behind a branch, saw me and went scurrying away to inform his friends and relatives.

I climbed higher, looked up and saw a red beak poised above my head. I shrank away, but the hornbill made no attempt to attack me. He was relaxing in his home, which was a great hole in the tree trunk. Only the bird's head and great beak were showing. He looked at me in rather a bored way, drowsily opening and shutting his eyes.

'So many creatures live here,' I said to myself. 'I hope none of them is dangerous!'

At that moment the hornbill lunged at a passing cricket. Bill and tree trunk met with a loud and resonant 'Tonk!'

I was so startled that I nearly fell out of the tree. But it was a difficult tree to fall out of! It was full of places where one could sit or even lie down. So I moved away from the hornbill, crawled along a branch which had sent out supports, and so moved quite a distance from the main body of the tree. I left its cold, dark depths for an area penetrated by shafts of sunlight.

No one could see me. I lay flat on the broad branch hidden by a screen of leaves. People passed by on the road below. A sahib in a sun helmet, his memsahib twirling a coloured silk sun umbrella. Obviously she did not want to get too brown and be mistaken for a country-born person. Behind them, a pram wheeled along by a nanny.

Then there were a number of Indians—some in white dhotis, some in Western clothes, some in loincloths. Some with baskets on their heads. Others with coolies to carry their baskets for them.

A cloud of dust, the blare of a horn, and down the road, like an out-of-condition dragon, came the latest Morris touring car. Then cyclists. Then a man with a basket of papayas balanced on his head. Following him, a man with a performing monkey. This man rattled a little hand drum, and children followed man and monkey along the road. They stopped in the shade of a mango tree on the other side of the road. The little red monkey wore a frilled dress and a baby's bonnet. It danced for the children, while the man sang and played his drum.

The clip-clop of a tonga pony, and Bansi's tonga came rattling down the road. I called down to him and he reined in with a shout of surprise, and looked up into the branches of the banyan tree.

'What are you doing up there?' he cried.

'Hiding from Grandmother,' I said.

'And when are you coming for that ride?'

'On Tuesday afternoon,' I said.

'Why not today?'

'Ayah won't let me. But she has Tuesdays off.'

Bansi spat red paan juice across the road. 'Your ayah is jealous,' he said.

'I know,' I said. 'Women are always jealous, aren't they? I suppose it's because she doesn't have a tonga.'

'It's because she doesn't have a tonga driver,' said Bansi, grinning up at me. 'Never mind. I'll come on Tuesday—that's the day after tomorrow, isn't it?'

I nodded down to him, and then started backing along my branch, because I could hear Ayah calling in the distance. Bansi leant forward and smacked his pony across the rump, and the tonga shot forward.

'What were you doing up there?' asked Ayah a little later.

'I was watching a snake cross the road,' I said. I knew she couldn't resist talking about snakes. There weren't as many in Dehra as there had been in Kathiawar and she was thrilled that I had seen one.

'Was it moving towards you or away from you?' she asked.

'It was going away.'

Ayah's face clouded over. 'That means poverty for the beholder,' she said gloomily.

Later, while scrubbing me down in the bathroom, she began to air all her prejudices, which included drunkards ('they die quickly, anyway'), misers ('they get murdered sooner or later') and tonga drivers ('they have all the vices').

'You are a very lucky boy,' she said suddenly, peering closely at my tummy.

'Why?' I asked. 'You just said I would be poor because I saw a snake going the wrong way.'

'Well, you won't be poor for long. You have a mole on your tummy and that's very lucky. And there is one under your armpit, which means you will be famous. Do you have one on the neck? No, thank God! A mole on the neck is the sign of a murderer!'

'Do you have any moles?' I asked.

Ayah nodded seriously, and pulling her sleeve up to her shoulder, showed me a large mole high on her arm.

'What does that mean?' I asked.

'It means a life of great sadness,' said Ayah gloomily.

'Can I touch it?' I asked.

'Yes, touch it,' she said, and taking my hand, she placed it against the mole.

'It's a nice mole,' I said, wanting to make Ayah happy. 'Can I kiss it?'

'You can kiss it,' said Ayah.

I kissed her on the mole.

'That's nice,' she said.

Tuesday afternoon came at last, and as soon as Grandmother was asleep and Ayah had gone to the bazaar, I was at the gate, looking up and down the road for Bansi and his tonga. He was not long in coming. Before the tonga turned into the road, I could hear his voice, singing to the accompaniment of the carriage bells.

He reached down, took my hand, and hoisted me on to the seat beside him. Then we went off down the road at a steady jogtrot. It was only when we reached the outskirts of the town that Bansi encouraged his pony to greater efforts. He rose in his seat, leaned forward and slapped the pony across the haunches. From a brisk trot we changed to a carefree canter. The tonga swayed from side to side. I clung to Bansi's free arm, while he grinned at me, his mouth red with paan juice.

'Where shall we go, dost?' he asked.

'Nowhere,' I said. 'Anywhere.'

'We'll go to the river,' said Bansi.

The 'river' was really a swift mountain stream that ran through the forests outside Dehra, joining the Ganga about fifteen miles away. It was almost dry during the winter and early summer; in flood during the monsoon.

The road out of Dehra was a gentle decline and soon we were

rushing headlong through the tea gardens and eucalyptus forests, the pony's hoofs striking sparks off the metalled road, the carriage wheels groaning and creaking so loudly that I feared one of them would come off and that we would all be thrown into a ditch or into the small canal that ran beside the road. We swept through mango groves, through guava and litchi orchards, past broad-leaved sal and shisham trees. Once in the sal forest, Bansi turned the tonga on to a rough cart track, and we continued along it for about a furlong, until the road dipped down to the streambed.

'Let us go straight into the water,' said Bansi. 'You and I and the pony!' And he drove the tonga straight into the middle of the stream, where the water came up to the pony's knees.

'I am not a great one for baths,' said Bansi, 'but the pony needs one, and why should a horse smell sweeter than its owner?' saying which, he flung off his clothes and jumped into the water.

'Better than bathing under a tap!' he cried, slapping himself on the chest and thighs. 'Come down, dost, and join me!'

After some hesitation I joined him, but had some difficulty in keeping on my feet in the fast current. I grabbed at the pony's tail and hung on to it, while Bansi began sloshing water over the patient animal's back.

After this, Bansi led both me and the pony out of the stream and together we gave the carriage a good washing down. I'd had a free ride and Bansi got the services of a free helper for the long overdue spring cleaning of his tonga. After we had finished the job, he presented me with a packet of aam papar—a sticky toffee made from mango pulp—and for some time I tore at it as a dog tears at a bit of old leather. Then I felt drowsy and lay down on the brown, sun-warmed grass. Crickets and grasshoppers were telephoning each other from tree and bush and a pair of bluejays rolled, dived, and swooped acrobatically overhead.

Bansi had no watch. He looked at the sun and said, 'It is past three. When will that ayah of yours be home? She is more frightening than your grandmother!'

'She comes at four.'

'Then we must hurry back. And don't tell her where we've been, or I'll never be able to come to your house again. Your grandmother's one of my best customers.'

'That means you'd be sorry if she died.'

'I would indeed, my friend.'

Bansi raced the tonga back to town. There was very little motor traffic in those days, and tongas and bullock carts were far more numerous than they are today.

We were back five minutes before Ayah returned. Before Bansi left, he promised to take me for another ride the following week.

The Photograph

I WAS TEN years old. My grandmother sat on the string bed under the mango tree. It was late summer and there were sunflowers in the garden and a warm wind in the trees. My grandmother was knitting a woollen scarf for the winter months. She was very old, dressed in a plain white sari. Her eyes were not very strong now but her fingers moved quickly with the needles and the needles kept clicking all afternoon. Grandmother had white hair but there were very few wrinkles on her skin.

I had come home after playing cricket on the maidan. I had taken my meal and now I was rummaging through a box of old books and family heirlooms that had just that day been brought out of the attic by my mother. Nothing in the box interested me very much except for a book with colourful pictures of birds and butterflies. I was going through the book, looking at the pictures, when I found a small photograph between the pages. It was a faded picture, a little yellow and foggy. It was the picture of a girl standing against a wall and behind the wall there was nothing but sky. But from the other side a pair of hands reached up, as though someone was going to climb the wall. There were flowers growing near the girl but I couldn't tell what they were. There was a creeper too but it was just a creeper.

I ran out into the garden. 'Granny!' I shouted. 'Look at this picture! I found it in the box of old things. Whose picture is it?'

I jumped on the bed beside my grandmother and she walloped me on the bottom and said, 'Now I've lost count of my stitches and the next time you do that I'll make you finish the scarf yourself.'

Granny was always threatening to teach me how to knit which I thought was a disgraceful thing for a boy to do. It was a good deterrent for keeping me out of mischief. Once I had torn the drawing-room curtains and Granny had put a needle and thread in my hand and made me stitch the curtain together, even though I made long, two-inch stitches, which had to be taken out by my mother and done again.

She took the photograph from my hand and we both stared at it for quite a long time. The girl had long, loose hair and she wore a long dress that nearly covered her ankles, and sleeves that reached her wrists, and there were a lot of bangles on her hands. But despite all this drapery, the girl appeared to be full of freedom and movement. She stood with her legs apart and her hands on her hips and had a wide, almost devilish smile on her face.

'Whose picture is it?' I asked.

'A little girl's, of course,' said Grandmother. 'Can't you tell?'

'Yes, but did you know the girl?'

'Yes, I knew her,' said Granny, 'but she was a very wicked girl and I shouldn't tell you about her. But I'll tell you about the photograph. It was taken in your grandfather's house about sixty years ago. And that's the garden wall and over the wall there was a road going to town.'

'Whose hands are they,' I asked, 'coming up from the other side?'

Grandmother squinted and looked closely at the picture, and shook her head. 'It's the first time I've noticed,' she said. 'They must have been the sweeper boy's. Or maybe they were your grandfather's.'

'They don't look like Grandfather's hands,' I said. 'His hands are all bony.'

'Yes, but this was sixty years ago.'

'Didn't he climb up the wall after the photo?'

'No, nobody climbed up. At least, I don't remember.'

'And you remember well, Granny.'

'Yes, I remember . . . I remember what is not in the photograph. It was a spring day and there was a cool breeze blowing, nothing like this. Those flowers at the girl's feet, they were marigolds, and the bougainvillea creeper, it was a mass of purple. You cannot see these colours in the photo and even if you could, as nowadays, you wouldn't be able to smell the flowers or feel the breeze.'

'And what about the girl?' I said. 'Tell me about the girl.'

'Well, she was a wicked girl,' said Granny. 'You don't know the trouble they had getting her into those fine clothes she's wearing.'

'I think they are terrible clothes,' I said.

'So did she. Most of the time, she hardly wore a thing. She used to go swimming in a muddy pool with a lot of ruffianly boys, and ride on the backs of buffaloes. No boy ever teased her, though, because she could kick and scratch and pull his hair out!'

'She looks like it too,' I said. 'You can tell by the way she's smiling. At any moment something's going to happen.'

'Something did happen,' said Granny. 'Her mother wouldn't let her take off the clothes afterwards, so she went swimming in them and lay for half an hour in the mud.'

I laughed heartily and Grandmother laughed too.

'Who was the girl?' I said. 'You must tell me who she was.'

'No, that wouldn't do,' said Grandmother, but I pretended I didn't know. I knew, because Grandmother still smiled in the same way, even though she didn't have as many teeth.

'Come on, Granny,' I said, 'tell me, tell me.'

But Grandmother shook her head and carried on with the knitting. And I held the photograph in my hand looking from it to my grandmother and back again, trying to find points in common between the old lady and the little pig-tailed girl. A lemon-coloured butterfly settled on the end of Grandmother's knitting needle and stayed there while the needles clicked away. I made a grab at the butterfly and it flew off in a dipping flight and settled on a sunflower.

'I wonder whose hands they were,' whispered Grandmother to herself, with her head bowed, and her needles clicking away in the soft, warm silence of that summer afternoon.

The Funeral

'I DON'T THINK he should go,' said Aunt M.

'He's too small,' concurred Aunt B. 'He'll get upset and probably throw a tantrum. And you know Padre Lal doesn't like having children at funerals.'

The boy said nothing. He sat in the darkest corner of the darkened room, his face revealing nothing of what he thought and felt. His father's coffin lay in the next room, the lid fastened forever over the tired, wistful countenance of the man who had meant so much to the boy. Nobody else had mattered—neither uncles nor aunts nor fond grandparents. Least of all the mother who was hundreds of miles away with another husband. He hadn't seen her since he was four—that was just over five years ago—and he did not remember her very well.

The house was full of people—friends, relatives, neighbours. Some had tried to fuss over him but had been discouraged by his silence, the absence of tears. The more understanding of them had kept their distance.

Scattered words of condolence passed back and forth like dragonflies on the wind. 'Such a tragedy!' . . . 'Only forty' . . . 'No one realized how serious it was' . . . 'Devoted to the child' . . .

It seemed to the boy that everyone who mattered in the hill station was present. And for the first time they had the run of the house for his father had not been a sociable man. Books, music, flowers and his stamp collection had been his main preoccupations, apart from the boy.

A small hearse, drawn by a hill pony, was led in at the gate and several able-bodied men lifted the coffin and manoeuvred it into the carriage. The crowd drifted away. The cemetery was about a mile down the road and those who did not have cars would have to walk the distance.

The boy stared through a window at the small procession passing through the gate. He'd been forgotten for the moment— left in care of the servants, who were the only ones to stay behind. Outside it was misty. The mist had crept up the valley and settled like a damp towel on the face of the mountain. Everyone was wet although it hadn't rained.

The boy waited until everyone had gone and then he left the room and went out on the veranda. The gardener, who had been sitting in a bed of nasturtiums, looked up and asked the boy if he needed anything. But the boy shook his head and retreated indoors. The gardener, looking aggrieved because of the damage done to the flower beds by the mourners, shambled off to his quarters. The sahib's death meant that he would be out of a job very soon. The house would pass into other hands. The boy would go to an orphanage. There weren't many people who kept gardeners these days. In the kitchen, the cook was busy preparing the only big meal ever served in the house. All those relatives, and the padre too, would come back famished, ready for a sombre but nevertheless substantial meal. He, too, would be out of a job soon; but cooks were always in demand.

The boy slipped out of the house by a back door and made his way into the lane through a gap in a thicket of dog roses. When he reached the main road, he could see the mourners wending their way round the hill to the cemetery. He followed at a distance.

It was the same road he had often taken with his father during their evening walks. The boy knew the name of almost every plant and wildflower that grew on the hillside. These, and various birds and insects, had been described and pointed out to him by his father.

Looking northwards, he could see the higher ranges of the Himalayas and the eternal snows. The graves in the cemetery were so laid out that if their incumbents did happen to rise one day, the first thing they would see would be the glint of the sun on those snow-covered peaks. Possibly the site had been chosen for the view. But to the boy it did not seem as if anyone would be able to thrust aside those massive tombstones and rise from their graves to enjoy the view. Their rest seemed as eternal as the snows. It would take an earthquake to burst those stones asunder and thrust the coffins up from the earth. The boy wondered why people hadn't made it easier for the dead to rise. They were so securely entombed that it appeared as though no one really wanted them to get out.

'God has need of your father . . .' With those words a well-meaning missionary had tried to console him.

And had God, in the same way, laid claim to the thousands of men, women and children who had been put to rest here in these neat and serried rows? What could he have wanted them for? Of what use are we to God when we are dead, wondered the boy.

The cemetery gate stood open but the boy leant against the old stone wall and stared down at the mourners as they shuffled about with the unease of a batsman about to face a very fast bowler. Only this bowler was invisible and would come up stealthily and from behind.

Padre Lal's voice droned on through the funeral service and then the coffin was lowered—down, deep down. The boy was surprised at how far down it seemed to go! Was that other, better world down in the depths of the earth? How could anyone, even a Samson, push his way back to the surface again? Superman did it in comics but his father was a gentle soul who wouldn't fight too hard against the earth and the grass and the roots of tiny trees. Or perhaps he'd grow into a tree and escape that way! 'If ever I'm put away like this,' thought the boy, 'I'll get into the root of a plant and then I'll become a flower and then maybe a bird will come and carry my seed away . . . I'll get out somehow!'

A few more words from the padre and then some of those present threw handfuls of earth over the coffin before moving away.

Slowly, in twos and threes, the mourners departed. The mist swallowed them up. They did not see the boy behind the wall. They were getting hungry.

He stood there until they had all gone. Then he noticed that the gardeners or caretakers were filling in the grave. He did not know whether to go forward or not. He was a little afraid. And it was too late now. The grave was almost covered.

He turned and walked away from the cemetery. The road stretched ahead of him, empty, swathed in mist. He was alone. What had his father said to him once? 'The strongest man in the world is he who stands alone.'

Well, he was alone, but at the moment he did not feel very strong.

For a moment he thought his father was beside him, that they were together on one of their long walks. Instinctively he put out his hand, expecting his father's warm, comforting touch. But there was nothing there, nothing, no one . . .

He clenched his fists and pushed them deep down into his pockets. He lowered his head so that no one would see his tears. There were people in the mist but he did not want to go near them for they had put his father away.

'He'll find a way out,' the boy said fiercely to himself. 'He'll get out somehow!'

Coming Home to Dehra

THE FAINT QUEASINESS I always feel towards the end of a journey probably has its origin in that first homecoming after my father's death.

It was the winter of 1944—yes, a long time ago—and the train was running through the thick sal forests near Dehra, bringing me at every click of the rails nearer to the mother I hadn't seen for four years and the stepfather I had seen just once or twice before my parents were divorced. I was eleven and I was coming home to Dehra.

Three years earlier, after the separation, I had gone to live with my father. We were very happy together. He was serving in the RAF, at New Delhi, and we lived in a large tent somewhere near Humayun's tomb. The area is now a very busy part of urban Delhi but in those days, it was still a wilderness of scrub jungle, where black buck and nilgai roamed freely. We took long walks together, exploring the ruins of old tombs and forts; went to the pictures (George Fornby comedies were special favourites of mine); collected stamps; bought books (my father had taught me to read and write before I started going to school); and made plans for going to England when the War was over.

Six months of bliss, even though it was summer and there weren't any fans, only a thick khus reed curtain which had to be splashed with water every hour by a bhisti (water-carrier) who did the rounds of similar tents with his goat-skin water bag. I remember the tender refreshing fragrance of the khus, and also the smell of damp earth outside, where the water had spilt.

A happy time. But it had to end. My father's periodic bouts of malarial fever resulted in his having to enter hospital for a week. The bhisti's small son came to stay with me at night, and during the day I took my meals with an Anglo-Indian family across the road.

I would have been quite happy to continue with this arrangement whenever my father was absent, but someone at Air Headquarters must have advised him to put me in a boarding school.

Reluctantly he came to the decision that this would be the best thing—'until the War is over'—and in the June of 1943 he took me to Shimla, where I was incarcerated in a preparatory school for boys.

This is not the story of my life at boarding school. It might easily have been a public school in England; it did in fact pride itself on being the 'Eton of the East'. The traditions—such as ragging and flogging, compulsory games and chapel attendance, prefects larger than life, and Honour Boards for everything from school captaincy to choir membership—had all apparently been borrowed from Tom Brown's Schooldays.

My father wrote to me regularly, and his letters were the things I looked forward to more than anything else. I went to him for the winter holidays, and the following summer he came to Shimla during my mid-term break and took me out for the duration of the holidays. We stayed in a hotel called Craig-Dhu, on a spur north of Jacko Hill. It was an idyllic week: long walks; stories about phantom rickshaws; ice-creams in the sun; browsings in bookshops; more plans. 'We will go to England next year.'

School seemed a stupid and heartless place after my father had gone away. He had been transferred to Calcutta and he wasn't keeping well there. Malaria again. And then jaundice. But his last letter sounded quite cheerful. He'd been selling part of his valuable stamp collection so as to have enough money for the fares to England.

One day my class-teacher sent for me.

'I want to talk to you, Bond,' he said. 'Let's go for a walk.'

I knew immediately that something was wrong.

We took the path that went through the deodar forest, past Council Rock where Scout meetings were held. As soon as my unfortunate teacher (no doubt cursing the Headmaster for having given him this unpleasant task) started on the theme of 'God wanting your father in a higher and better place', as though there could be any better place than Jacko Hill in mid-summer, I knew my father was dead, and burst into tears.

They let me stay in the school hospital for a few days until I felt better. The Headmaster visited me there and took away the pile of my father's letters that I'd kept beside me.

'Your father's letters. You might lose them. Why not leave them with me? Then at the end of the year, before you go home, you can come and collect them.'

Unwillingly I gave him the letters. He told me he'd heard from my mother that I would be going home to her at the end of the year. He seemed surprised that I evinced no interest in this prospect.

At the end of the year, the day before school closed, I went to the HM's office and asked for my letters.

'What letters?' he said. His desk was piled with papers and correspondence, and he was irritated by my interruption.

'My father's letters,' I explained. 'I gave them to you to keep for me, Sir—when he died . . .'

'Letters. Are you sure you gave them to me?'

He grew more irritated. 'You must be mistaken, Bond. Why should I want to keep your father's letters?'

'I don't know, sir. You said I could collect them before going home.'

'Look, I don't remember any letters and I'm very busy just now, so run along. I'm sure you're mistaken, but if I find your letters, I'll send them to you.'

I don't suppose he meant to be unkind, but he was the first man who aroused in me feelings of hate . . .

∾

As the train drew into Dehra, I looked out of the window to see if there was anyone on the platform waiting to receive me. The station was crowded enough, as most railway stations are in India, with overloaded travellers, shouting coolies, stray dogs, stray stationmasters . . . Pandemonium broke loose as the train came to a halt and people disembarked from the carriages. I was thrust on the platform with my tin trunk and small attache case. I sat on the trunk and waited for someone to find me.

Slowly the crowd melted away. I was left with one elderly coolie who was too feeble to carry heavy luggage and had decided that my trunk was just the right size and weight for his head and shoulders. I waited another ten minutes, but no representative of my mother or stepfather appeared. I permitted the coolie to lead me out of the station to the tonga stand.

Those were the days when everyone, including high-ranking officials, went about in tongas. Dehra had just one taxi. I was quite happy sitting beside a rather smelly, paan-spitting tonga-driver, while his weary, underfed pony clip-clopped along the quiet tree-lined roads.

Dehra was always a good place for trees. The valley soil is very fertile, the rainfall fairly heavy; almost everything grows there, if given the chance. The roads were lined with neem and mango trees, eucalyptus, Persian lilac, jacaranda, amaltas (laburnum) and many others. In the gardens of the bungalows were mangoes, lichi and guavas; sometimes jackfruit and papaya. I did not notice all these trees at once; I came to know them as time passed.

The tonga first took me to my grandmother's house. I was under the impression that my mother still lived there.

A lovely, comfortable bungalow that spread itself about the grounds in an easygoing, old-fashioned way. There was even smoke coming from the chimneys, reminding me of the smoke from my grandfather's pipe. When I was eight, I had spent several months there with my grandparents. In retrospect it had been an idyllic interlude. But Grandfather was dead. Grandmother lived alone.

White-haired, but still broad in the face and even broader behind, she was astonished to see me getting down from the tonga.

'Didn't anyone meet you at the station?' she asked.

I shook my head. Grandmother said: 'Your mother doesn't live here any more. You can come in and wait, but she may be worried about you, so I'd better take you to her place. Come on, help me up into the tonga. I might have known it would be a white horse. It always makes me nervous sitting in a tonga behind a white horse.'

'Why, Granny?'

'I don't know, I suppose white horses are nervous, too. Anyway, they are always trying to topple me out. Not so fast, driver!' she called out, as the tonga-man cracked his whip and the pony changed from a slow shuffle to a brisk trot.

It took us about twenty-five minutes to reach my stepfather's house which was in the Dalanwala area, not far from the dry bed of the seasonal Rispana river. My grandmother, seeing that I was in need of moral support, got down with me, while the tonga-driver carried my bedding roll and tin trunk on to the veranda. The front door was bolted from inside. We had to knock on it repeatedly and call out, before it was opened by a servant who did not look pleased at being disturbed. When he saw my grandmother he gave her a deferential salaam, then gazed at me with open curiosity.

'Where's the memsahib?' asked Grandmother.

'Out,' said the servant.

'I can see that, but where have they gone?'

'They went yesterday to Motichur, for shikar. They will be back this evening.'

Grandmother looked upset, but motioned to the servant to bring in my things. 'Weren't they expecting the boy?' she asked. 'Yes,' he said looking at me again. 'But they said he would be arriving tomorrow.'

'They'd forgotten the date,' said Grandmother in a huff. 'Anyway, you can unpack and have a wash and change your clothes.'

Turning to the servant, she asked, 'Is there any lunch?'

'I will make lunch,' he said. He was staring at me again, and I felt uneasy with his eyes on me. He was tall and swarthy, with oily, jet-black hair and a thick moustache. A heavy scar ran down his left cheek, giving him a rather sinister appearance. He wore a torn shirt and dirty pyjamas. His broad, heavy feet were wet. They left marks on the uncarpeted floor.

A baby was crying in the next room, and presently a woman (who turned out to be the cook's wife) appeared in the doorway, jogging the child in her arms.

'They've left the baby behind, too,' said Grandmother, becoming more and more irate. 'He is your younger brother. Only six months old.' I hadn't been told anything about a younger brother. The discovery that I had one came as something of a shock. I wasn't prepared for a baby brother, least of all a baby half-brother. I examined the child without much enthusiasm. He looked healthy enough and he cried with gusto.

'He's a beautiful baby,' said Grandmother. 'Well, I've got work to do. The servants will look after you. You can come and see me in a day or two. You've grown since I last saw you. And you're getting pimples.'

This reference to my appearance did not displease me as

Grandmother never indulged in praise. For her to have observed my pimples indicated that she was fond of me.

The tonga-driver was waiting for her. 'I suppose I'll have to use the same tonga,' she said. 'Whenever I need a tonga, they disappear, except for the ones with white ponies . . . When your mother gets back, tell her I want to see her. Shikar, indeed. An infant to look after, and they've gone shooting.'

Grandmother settled herself in the tonga, nodded in response to the cook's salaam, and took a tight grip of the armrests of her seat. The driver flourished his whip and the pony set off at the same listless, unhurried trot, while my grandmother, feeling quite certain that she was going to be hurtled to her doom by a wild white pony, set her teeth and clung tenaciously to the tonga seat. I was sorry to see her go.

∾

My mother and stepfather returned in the evening from their hunting trip with a pheasant which was duly handed over to the cook, whose name was Mangal Singh. My mother gave me a perfunctory kiss. I think she was pleased to see me, but I was accustomed to a more intimate caress from my father, and the strange reception I had received made me realize the extent of my loss. Boarding school life had been routine. Going home was something that I had always looked forward to. But going home had meant my father, and now he had vanished and I was left quite desolate.

I suppose if one is present when a loved one dies, or sees him dead and laid out and later buried, one is convinced of the finality of the thing and finds it easier to adapt to the changed circumstances. But when you hear of a death, a father's death, and have only the faintest idea of the manner of his dying, it is rather a lot for the imagination to cope with—especially when the imagination is a small boy's. There being no tangible evidence of my father's death, it was, for me, not a death but a vanishing. And although this enabled me to remember him as a living, smiling, breathing person, it meant that I was not wholly reconciled to his death, and subconsciously expected him to turn up (as he often did, when I most needed him) and deliver me from an unpleasant situation.

My stepfather barely noticed me. The first thing he did on coming into the house was to pour himself a whisky and soda. My mother, after inspecting the baby, did likewise. I was left to unpack and settle in my room.

I was fortunate in having my own room. I was as desirous of my own privacy as much as my mother and stepfather were desirous of theirs. My stepfather, a local businessman, was ready to put up with me provided I did not get in the way. And, in a different way, I was ready to put up with him, provided he left me alone. I was even willing that my mother should leave me alone.

There was a big window to my room, and I opened it to the evening breeze, and gazed out on to the garden, a rather unkempt place where marigolds and a sort of wild blue everlasting grew rampant among the lichi trees.

The Wish

LIFE SELDOM TURNS out the way we expect it to. The house in Dehra had to be sold. My father had not left any money; he had never realized that his health would deteriorate so rapidly from the malarial fevers which had grown in frequency. He was still planning for the future when he died. Now that my father was gone, Grandmother saw no point in staying on in India; there was nothing left in the bank and she needed money for our passages to England, so the house had to go. Dr Ghose, who had a thriving medical practice in Dehra, made her a reasonable offer, which she accepted.

Then things happened very quickly. Grandmother sold most of our belongings, because she said, we wouldn't be able to cope with a lot of luggage. The kabaris came in droves, buying up crockery, furniture, carpets and clocks at throwaway prices. Grandmother hated parting with some of her possessions such as the carved giltwood mirror, her walnut-wood armchair and her rosewood writing desk, but it was impossible to take them with us. They carried away in a bullock-cart.

Ayah was very unhappy at first but cheered up when Grandmother got her job with a tea planter's family in Assam. It was arranged that she could stay with us until we left Dehra.

We went at the end of September, just as the monsoon clouds broke up, scattered and were driven away by soft breezes from the Himalayas. There was no time to revisit the island where my grandfather and I had planted our trees. And in the urgency and

66

excitement of the preparations for our departure, I forgot to recover my small treasures from the hole in the banyan tree. It was only when we were in Bansi's tonga, on the way to the station, that I remembered my top, catapult, and Iron Cross. Too late! To go back from them would mean missing the train.

'Hurry!' urged Grandmother nervously. 'We mustn't be late for the train. Bansi.'

Bansi flicked the reins and shouted to his pony, and for once in her life Grandmother submitted to being carried along the road at a brisk trot.

'It's five to nine,' she said, 'and the train leaves at nine.'

'Do not worry, memsahib. I have been taking you to the station for fifteen years, and you have never missed a train!'

'No,' said Grandmother. 'And I don't suppose you'll ever take me to the station again, Bansi.'

'Times are changing, memsahib. Do you know that there is now a taxi—a motor car—competing with the tongas of Dehra? You are lucky to be leaving. If you stay, you will see me starve to death!'

'We will all starve to death if we don't catch that train,' said Grandmother.

'Do not worry about the train, it never leaves on time, and no one expects it to. If it left at nine o'clock, everyone would miss it.'

Bansi was right. We arrived at the station at five minutes past nine, and rushed on to the platform, only to find that the train had not yet arrived.

The platform was crowded with people waiting to catch the same train or to meet people arriving on it. Ayah was there already, standing guard over a pile of miscellaneous luggage. We sat down on our boxes and became part of the platform life at an Indian railway station.

Moving among piles of bedding and luggages were sweating, cursing coolies; vendors of magazines, sweetmeats, tea and betel-leaf preparations; also stray dogs, stray people and sometimes a stray station-master. The cries of the vendors mixed with the general clamour of the station and the shunting of a steam engine in the yards. 'Tea, hot tea!' Sweets, papads, hot stuff, cold drinks, toothpowder, pictures of film stars, bananas, balloons, wooden toys, clay images of the gods. The platform had become a bazaar.

Ayah was giving me all sorts of warnings.

'Remember, baba, don't lean out of the window when the train is moving. There was that American boy who lost his head last year! And don't eat rubbish at every station between here and Bombay. And see that no strangers enter the compartment. Mr Wilkins was robbed and murdered last year!'

The station bell clanged, and in the distance there appeared a big, puffing steam engine, painted green and gold and black. A stray dog with a lifetime's experience of trains, darted away across the railway lines. As the train came alongside the platform, doors opened, window shutters fell, faces appeared in the openings, and even before the train had come to a stop, people were trying to get in or out.

For a few moments there was chaos. The crowd surged backward and forward. No one could get out. No one could get in. A hundred people were leaving the train, two hundred were getting into it. No one wanted to give way.

The problem was solved by a man climbing out of a window. Others followed his example and the pressure at the doors eased and people started squeezing into their compartments.

Grandmother had taken the precaution of reserving berths in a first-class compartment, and assisted by Bansi and half-a-dozen coolies, we were soon inside with all our luggage. A whistle blasted and we were off! Bansi had to jump from the running train.

As the engine gathered speed, I ignored Ayah's advice and put my head out of the window to look back at the receding platform. Ayah and Bansi were standing on the platform waving to me, and I kept waving to them until the train rushed into the darkness and the bright lights of Dehra were swallowed up in the night. New lights, dim and flickering, came into existence as we passed small villages. The stars too were visible and I saw a shooting star streaking through the heavens.

. I remembered something that Ayah had once told me, that stars are the spirits of good men, and I wondered if that shooting star was a sign from my father that he was aware of our departure and would be with us on our journey. And I remembered something else that Ayah had said—that if one wished on a shooting star, one's wish would be granted, provided, of course, that one thrust all five fingers into the mouth at the same time!

'What on earth are you doing?' asked Grandmother staring at me as I thrust my fist into my mouth.

'Making a wish,' I said.

'Oh,' said Grandmother.

She was preoccupied, and didn't ask me what I was wishing for; nor did I tell her.

∾

We never made it to England. Grandmother passed away after a brief illness in Lucknow. Aunt Emily—in whose house we were staying before going on to Bombay to board our ship to England—made arrangements for her funeral and for me to be sent back to Dehra. My father's cousin Mr John Harrison who lived in Dehra agreed to let me stay with him and attend the day school in the town.

By a strange twist of fate therefore, my wish to return to Dehra was coming true after all. I did not know if it was something to now look forward to, or dread.

The Window

I CAME IN the spring, and took the room on the roof. It was a long, low building which housed several families; the roof was flat, except for my room and a chimney. I don't know whose room owned the chimney, but my room owned the roof. And from the window of my room I owned the world.

But only from the window.

The banyan tree, just opposite, was mine, and its inhabitants my subjects. They were two squirrels, a few mina, a crow and, at night, a pair of flying foxes. The squirrels were busy in the afternoons, the birds in the mornings and evenings, the foxes at night. I wasn't very busy that year; not as busy as the inhabitants of the banyan tree.

There was also a mango tree but that came later, in the summer, when I met Koki and the mangoes were ripe.

At first, I was lonely in my room. But then I discovered the power of my window. I looked out on the banyan tree, on the garden, on the broad path that ran beside the building, and out over the roofs of other houses, over roads and fields, as far as the horizon. The path was not a very busy one but it held variety: an ayah, with a baby in a pram; the postman, an event in himself; the fruit seller, the toy seller, calling their wares in high-pitched familiar cries; the rent collector; a posse of cyclists; a long chain of schoolgirls; a lame beggar . . . all passed my way, the way of my window . . .

In the early summer, a tonga came rattling and jingling down the path and stopped in front of the house. A girl and an elderly lady climbed down, and a servant unloaded their baggage. They went into the house and the tonga moved off, the horse snorting a little.

The next morning the girl looked up from the garden and saw me at my window.

She had long black hair that fell to her waist, tied with a single red ribbon. Her eyes were black like her hair and just as shiny. She must have been about ten or eleven years old.

'Hello,' I said with a friendly smile.

She looked suspiciously at me. 'Who are you?' she asked.

'I'm a ghost.'

She laughed, and her laugh had a gay, mocking quality. 'You look like one!'

I didn't think her remark particularly flattering, but I had asked for it. I stopped smiling anyway. Most children don't like adults smiling at them all the time.

'What have you got up there?' she asked.

'Magic,' I said.

She laughed again but this time without mockery. 'I don't believe you,' she said.

'Why don't you come up and see for yourself?'

She hesitated a little but came round to the steps and began climbing them, slowly, cautiously. And when she entered the room, she brought a magic of her own.

'Where's your magic?' she asked, looking me in the eye.

'Come here,' I said, and I took her to the window and showed her the world.

She said nothing but stared out of the window uncomprehendingly at first, and then with increasing interest. And after some time she turned around and smiled at me, and we were friends.

I only knew that her name was Koki, and that she had come with her aunt for the summer months; I didn't need to know any more about her, and she didn't need to know anything about me except that I wasn't really a ghost—not the frightening sort anyway . . .

She came up my steps nearly every day and joined me at the window. There was a lot of excitement to be had in our world, especially when the rains broke.

At the first rumblings, women would rush outside to retrieve the washing from the clothesline and if there was a breeze, to chase a few garments across the compound. When the rains came, they came with a vengeance, making a bog of the garden and a river of the path. A cyclist would come riding furiously down the path, an elderly gentleman would be having difficulty with an umbrella, naked children would be frisking about in the rain. Sometimes Koki would run out to the roof, and shout and dance in the rain. And the rain would come through the open door and window of the room, flooding the floor and making an island of the bed.

But the window was more fun than anything else. It gave us the power of detachment: we were deeply interested in the life around us, but we were not involved in it.

'It is like a cinema,' said Koki. 'The window is the screen, the world is the picture.'

Soon the mangoes were ripe, and Koki was in the branches of the mango tree as often as she was in my room. From the window I had a good view of the tree, and we spoke to each other from the same height. We ate far too many mangoes, at least five a day.

'Let's make a garden on the roof,' suggested Koki. She was full of ideas like this.

'And how do you propose to do that?' I asked.

'It's easy. We bring up mud and bricks and make the flower beds. Then we plant the seeds. We'll grow all sorts of flowers.'

'The roof will fall in,' I predicted.

But it didn't. We spent two days carrying buckets of mud up

the steps to the roof and laying out the flower beds. It was very hard work, but Koki did most of it. When the beds were ready, we had the opening ceremony. Apart from a few small plants collected from the garden below, we had only one species of seeds—pumpkin . . .

We planted the pumpkin seeds in the mud, and felt proud of ourselves.

But it rained heavily that night, and in the morning I discovered that everything—except the bricks—had been washed away.

So we returned to the window.

A myna had been in a fight—with a crow perhaps—and the feathers had been knocked off its head. A bougainvillea that had been climbing the wall had sent a long green shoot in through the window.

Koki said, 'Now we can't shut the window without spoiling the creeper.'

'Then we will never close the window,' I said.

And we let the creeper into the room.

The rains passed, and an autumn wind came whispering through the branches of the banyan tree. There were red leaves on the ground, and the wind picked them up and blew them about, so that they looked like butterflies. I would watch the sun rise in the morning; the sky all red until its first rays splashed the windowsill and crept up the walls of the room. And in the evening, Koki and I watched the sun go down in a sea of fluffy clouds; sometimes the clouds were pink and sometimes orange; they were always coloured clouds framed in the window.

'I'm going tomorrow,' said Koki one evening.

I was too surprised to say anything.

'You stay here for ever, don't you?' she said.

I remained silent.

'When I come again next year you will still be here, won't you?'

'I don't know,' I said. 'But the window will still be here.'

'Oh, do be here next year,' she said, 'or someone will close the window!'

In the morning the tonga was at the door, and the servant, the aunt and Koki were in it. Koki waved to me at my window. Then the driver flicked the reins, the wheels of the carriage creaked and rattled, the bell jingled. Down the path went the tonga, down the path and through the gate, and all the time Koki waved; and from the gate I must have looked like a ghost, standing alone at the high window, amongst the bougainvillea.

When the tonga was out of sight, I took the spray of bougainvillea in my hand and pushed it out of the room. Then I closed the window. It would be opened only when the spring and Koki came again.

A Job Well Done

DHUKI, THE GARDENER, was clearing up the weeds that grew in profusion around the old disused well. He was an old man, skinny and bent and spindly legged but he had always been like that. His strength lay in his wrists and in his long, tendril-like fingers. He looked as frail as a petunia but he had the tenacity of a vine.

'Are you going to cover the well?' I asked. I was eight, and a great favourite of Dhuki's. He had been the gardener long before my birth, had worked for my father until my father died and now worked for my mother and stepfather.

'I must cover it, I suppose,' said Dhuki. 'That's what the Major Sahib wants. He'll be back any day and if he finds the well still uncovered he'll get into one of his raging fits and I'll be looking for another job!'

The 'Major Sahib' was my stepfather, Major Summerskill. A tall, hearty, back-slapping man, who liked polo and pig-sticking. He was quite unlike my father. My father had always given me books to read. The major said I would become a dreamer if I read too much and took the books away. I hated him and did not think much of my mother for marrying him.

'The boy's too soft,' I heard him tell my mother. 'I must see that he gets riding lessons.'

But before the riding lessons could be arranged the major's regiment was ordered to Peshawar. Trouble was expected from some of the frontier tribes. He was away for about two months.

Before leaving, he had left strict instructions for Dhuki to cover up the old well.

'Too damned dangerous having an open well in the middle of the garden,' my stepfather had said. 'Make sure that it's completely covered by the time I get back.'

Dhuki was loath to cover up the old well. It had been there for over fifty years, long before the house had been built. In its walls lived a colony of pigeons. Their soft cooing filled the garden with a lovely sound. And during the hot, dry summer months, when taps ran dry, the well was always a dependable source of water. The bhisti still used it, filling his goatskin bag with the cool clear water and sprinkling the paths around the house to keep the dust down.

Dhuki pleaded with my mother to let him leave the well uncovered.

'What will happen to the pigeons?' he asked.

'Oh, surely they can find another well,' said my mother. 'Do close it up soon, Dhuki. I don't want the sahib to come back and find that you haven't done anything about it.'

My mother seemed just a little bit afraid of the major. How can we be afraid of those we love? It was a question that puzzled me then and puzzles me still.

The major's absence made life pleasant again. I returned to my books, spent long hours in my favourite banyan tree, ate buckets of mangoes and dawdled in the garden talking to Dhuki.

Neither he nor I were looking forward to the major's return. Dhuki had stayed on after my mother's second marriage only out of loyalty to her and affection for me. He had really been my father's man. But my mother had always appeared deceptively frail and helpless and most men, Major Summerskill included, felt protective towards her. She liked people who did things for her.

'Your father liked this well,' said Dhuki. 'He would often sit here in the evenings with a book in which he made drawings of birds and flowers and insects.'

I remembered those drawings and I remembered how they had all been thrown away by the major when he had moved into the house. Dhuki knew about it too. I didn't keep much from him.

'It's a sad business closing this well,' said Dhuki again. 'Only a fool or a drunkard is likely to fall into it.'

But he had made his preparations. Planks of sal wood, bricks and cement were neatly piled up around the well.

'Tomorrow,' said Dhuki. 'Tomorrow I will do it. Not today. Let the birds remain for one more day. In the morning, baba, you can help me drive the birds from the well.'

On the day my stepfather was expected back, my mother hired a tonga and went to the bazaar to do some shopping. Only a few people had cars in those days. Even colonels went about in tongas. Now, a clerk finds it beneath his dignity to sit in one.

As the major was not expected before evening, I decided I would make full use of my last free morning. I took all my favourite books and stored them away in an outhouse where I could come for them from time to time. Then, my pockets bursting with mangoes, I climbed up the banyan tree. It was the darkest and coolest place on a hot day in June.

From behind the screen of leaves that concealed me, I could see Dhuki moving about near the well. He appeared to be most unwilling to get on with the job of covering it up.

'Baba!' he called several times. But I did not feel like stirring from the banyan tree. Dhuki grasped a long plank of wood and placed it across one end of the well. He started hammering. From my vantage point in the banyan tree, he looked very bent and old.

A jingle of tonga bells and the squeak of unoiled wheels told me that a tonga was coming in at the gate. It was too early for my mother to be back. I peered through the thick, waxy leaves of the tree and nearly fell off my branch in surprise. It was my stepfather, the major! He had arrived earlier than expected.

I did not come down from the tree. I had no intention of confronting my stepfather until my mother returned.

The major had climbed down from the tonga and was watching his luggage being carried on to the veranda. He was red in the face and the ends of his handlebar moustache were stiff with Brilliantine. Dhuki approached with a half-hearted salaam.

'Ah, so there you are, you old scoundrel!' exclaimed the major, trying to sound friendly and jocular. 'More jungle than garden, from what I can see. You're getting too old for this sort of work, Dhuki. Time to retire! And where's the memsahib?'

'Gone to the bazaar,' said Dhuki.

'And the boy?'

Dhuki shrugged. 'I have not seen the boy today, sahib.'

'Damn!' said the major. 'A fine homecoming, this. Well, wake up the cook boy and tell him to get some sodas.'

'Cook boy's gone away,' said Dhuki.

'Well, I'll be double damned,' said the major.

The tonga went away and the major started pacing up and down the garden path. Then he saw Dhuki's unfinished work at the well. He grew purple in the face, strode across to the well, and started ranting at the old gardener.

Dhuki began making excuses. He said something about a shortage of bricks, the sickness of a niece, unsatisfactory cement, unfavourable weather, unfavourable gods. When none of this seemed to satisfy the major, Dhuki began mumbling about something bubbling up from the bottom of the well and pointed down into its depths. The major stepped on to the low parapet and looked down. Dhuki kept pointing. The major leant over a little.

Dhuki's hand moved swiftly, like a conjurer making a pass. He did not actually push the major. He appeared merely to tap him once on the bottom. I caught a glimpse of my stepfather's boots as he disappeared into the well. I couldn't help thinking of Alice in Wonderland, of Alice disappearing down the rabbit hole.

There was a tremendous splash and the pigeons flew up, circling the well thrice before settling on the roof of the bungalow.

By lunchtime—or tiffin, as we called it then—Dhuki had the well covered over with the wooden planks.

'The major will be pleased,' said my mother when she came home. 'It will be quite ready by evening, won't it, Dhuki?'

By evening the well had been completely bricked over. It was the fastest bit of work Dhuki had ever done.

Over the next few weeks, my mother's concern changed to anxiety, her anxiety to melancholy, and her melancholy to resignation. By being gay and high-spirited myself, I hope I did something to cheer her up. She had written to the colonel of the regiment and had been informed that the major had gone home on leave a fortnight previously. Somewhere, in the vastness of India, the major had disappeared.

It was easy enough to disappear and never be found. After seven months had passed without the major turning up, it was presumed that one of two things must have happened. Either he had been murdered on the train and his corpse flung into a river; or, he had run away with a tribal girl and was living in some remote corner of the country.

Life had to carry on for the rest of us. The rains were over and the guava season was approaching.

My mother was receiving visits from a colonel of His Majesty's 32nd Foot. He was an elderly, easy going, seemingly absent-minded man, who didn't get in the way at all but left slabs of chocolate lying around the house.

'A good sahib,' observed Dhuki as I stood beside him behind the bougainvillea, watching the colonel saunter up the veranda steps. 'See how well he wears his sola topi! It covers his head completely.'

'He's bald underneath,' I said.

'No matter. I think he will be all right.'

'And if he isn't,' I said, 'we can always open up the well again.'

Dhuki dropped the nozzle of the hose pipe and water gushed out over our feet. But he recovered quickly and taking me by the hand led me across to the old well now surmounted by a three-tiered cement platform which looked rather like a wedding cake.

'We must not forget our old well,' he said. 'Let us make it beautiful, baba. Some flower pots, perhaps.'

And together we fetched pots and decorated the covered well with ferns and geraniums. Everyone congratulated Dhuki on the fine job he'd done. My only regret was that the pigeons had gone away.

The Woman on Platform No. 8

IT WAS MY second year at boarding school, and I was sitting on platform no. 8 at Ambala station, waiting for the northern bound train. I think I was about twelve at the time. My parents considered me old enough to travel alone, and I had arrived by bus at Ambala early in the evening; now there was a wait till midnight before my train arrived. Most of the time I had been pacing up and down the platform, browsing through the bookstall, or feeding broken biscuits to stray dogs; trains came and went, the platform would be quiet for a while and then, when a train arrived, it would be an inferno of heaving, shouting, agitated human bodies. As the carriage doors opened, a tide of people would sweep down upon the nervous little ticket collector at the gate; and every time this happened I would be caught in the rush and swept outside the station. Now tired of this game and of ambling about the platform, I sat down on my suitcase and gazed dismally across the railway tracks.

Trolleys rolled past me, and I was conscious of the cries of the various vendors—the men who sold curds and lemon, the sweetmeat seller, the newspaper boy—but I had lost interest in all that was going on along the busy platform, and continued to stare across the railway tracks, feeling bored and a little lonely.

'Are you all alone, my son?' asked a soft voice close behind me.

I looked up and saw a woman standing near me. She was leaning over, and I saw a pale face and dark kind eyes. She wore no jewels, and was dressed very simply in a white sari.

'Yes, I am going to school,' I said, and stood up respectfully. She seemed poor, but there was a dignity about her that commanded respect.

'I have been watching you for some time,' she said. 'Didn't your parents come to see you off?'

'I don't live here,' I said. 'I had to change trains. Anyway, I can travel alone.'

'I am sure you can,' she said, and I liked her for saying that, and I also liked her for the simplicity of her dress, and for her deep, soft voice and the serenity of her face.

'Tell me, what is your name?' she asked.

'Arun,' I said.

'And how long do you have to wait for your train?'

'About an hour, I think. It comes at twelve o'clock.'

'Then come with me and have something to eat.'

I was going to refuse, out of shyness and suspicion, but she took me by the hand, and then I felt it would be silly to pull my hand away. She told a coolie to look after my suitcase, and then she led me away down the platform. Her hand was gentle, and she held mine neither too firmly nor too lightly. I looked up at her again. She was not young. And she was not old. She must have been over thirty, but had she been fifty, I think she would have looked much the same.

She took me into the station dining room, ordered tea and samosas and jalebis, and at once I began to thaw and take a new interest in this kind woman. The strange encounter had little effect on my appetite. I was a hungry school boy, and I ate as much as I could in as polite a manner as possible. She took obvious pleasure in watching me eat, and I think it was the food that strengthened the bond between us and cemented our friendship, for under the influence of the tea and sweets I began to talk quite freely, and told her about my school, my friends, my likes and dislikes. She questioned me quietly from time to time, but preferred listening; she drew me out very well, and I had soon forgotten that we were strangers. But she did not ask me about my family or where I lived, and I did not ask her where she lived. I accepted her for what she had been to me—a quiet, kind and gentle woman who gave sweets to a lonely boy on a railway platform . . .

After about half an hour we left the dining room and began walking back along the platform. An engine was shunting up and down beside platform no. 8, and as it approached, a boy leapt off the platform and ran across the rails, taking a short cut to the next platform. He was at a safe distance from the engine, but as he leapt across the rails, the woman clutched my arm. Her fingers dug into my flesh, and I winced with pain. I caught her fingers and looked up at her, and I saw a spasm of pain and fear and sadness pass across her face. She watched the boy as he climbed the platform, and it was not until he had disappeared in the crowd that she relaxed her hold on my arm. She smiled at me reassuringly and took my hand again, but her fingers trembled against mine.

'He was all right,' I said, feeling that it was she who needed reassurance.

She smiled gratefully at me and pressed my hand. We walked together in silence until we reached the place where I had left my suitcase. One of my schoolfellows, Satish, a boy of about my age, had turned up with his mother.

'Hello, Arun!' he called. 'The train's coming in late, as usual. Did you know we have a new headmaster this year?'

We shook hands, and then he turned to his mother and said: 'This is Arun, Mother. He is one of my friends, and the best bowler in the class.'

'I am glad to know that,' said his mother, a large imposing woman who wore spectacles. She looked at the woman who held my hand and said: 'And I suppose you're Arun's mother?'

I opened my mouth to make some explanation, but before I could say anything the woman replied: 'Yes, I am Arun's mother.'

I was unable to speak a word. I looked quickly up at the woman, but she did not appear to be at all embarrassed, and was smiling at Satish's mother.

Satish's mother said: 'It's such a nuisance having to wait for the train right in the middle of the night. But one can't let the child wait here alone. Anything can happen to a boy at a big station like this—there are so many suspicious characters hanging about. These days one has to be very careful of strangers.'

'Arun can travel alone though,' said the woman beside me, and somehow I felt grateful to her for saying that. I had already forgiven her for lying; and besides, I had taken an instinctive dislike to Satish's mother.

'Well, be very careful, Arun,' said Satish's mother looking sternly at me through her spectacles. 'Be very careful when your mother is not with you. And never talk to strangers!'

I looked from Satish's mother to the woman who had given me tea and sweets, and back at Satish's mother.

'I like strangers,' I said.

Satish's mother definitely staggered a little, as obviously she was not used to being contradicted by small boys. 'There you are, you see! If you don't watch over them all the time, they'll walk straight into trouble. Always listen to what your mother tells you,' she said, wagging a fat little finger at me. 'And never, never talk to strangers.'

I glared resentfully at her, and moved closer to the woman who had befriended me. Satish was standing behind his mother, grinning at me, and delighting in my clash with his mother. Apparently he was on my side.

The station bell clanged, and the people who had till now been squatting resignedly on the platform began bustling about.

'Here it comes,' shouted Satish, as the engine whistle shrieked and the front lights played over the rails.

The train moved slowly into the station, the engine hissing and sending out waves of steam. As it came to a stop, Satish jumped on the footboard of a lighted compartment and shouted,

'Come on, Arun, this one's empty!' and I picked up my suitcase and made a dash for the open door.

We placed ourselves at the open windows, and the two women stood outside on the platform, talking up to us. Satish's mother did most of the talking.

'Now don't jump on and off moving trains, as you did just now,' she said. 'And don't stick your heads out of the windows, and don't eat any rubbish on the way.' She allowed me to share the benefit of her advice, as she probably didn't think my 'mother' a very capable person. She handed Satish a bag of fruit, a cricket bat and a big box of chocolates, and told him to share the food with me. Then she stood back from the window to watch how my 'mother' behaved.

I was smarting under the patronizing tone of Satish's mother, who obviously thought mine a very poor family; and I did not intend giving the other woman away. I let her take my hand in hers, but I could think of nothing to say. I was conscious of Satish's mother staring at us with hard, beady eyes, and I found myself hating her with a firm, unreasoning hate. The guard walked up the platform, blowing his whistle for the train to leave. I looked straight into the eyes of the woman who held my hand, and she smiled in a gentle, understanding way. I leaned out of the window then, and put my lips to her cheek and kissed her.

The carriage jolted forward, and she drew her hand away.

'Goodbye, Mother!' said Satish, as the train began to move slowly out of the station. Satish and his mother waved to each other.

'Goodbye,' I said to the other woman, 'goodbye—Mother . . .'

I didn't wave or shout, but sat still in front of the window, gazing at the woman on the platform. Satish's mother was talking to her, but she didn't appear to be listening; she was looking at me, as the train took me away. She stood there on the busy platform, a pale sweet woman in white, and I watched her until she was lost in the milling crowd.

Running Away

AS THE BIG clock on the top of the school pavilion struck eleven, I crept out of bed, slipped on my gym shoes, and moved silently across the dormitory.

I stopped in the doorway and peered back into the dark room to make sure that no one else was awake; then I hurried along the corridor and down the stairs.

Daljit was already on the veranda. He was a Sikh and a good friend of mine—we studied in the same class. He had removed his turban for the night and his long hair was now bunched up on his head in a big knot. The white pyjama-suit he was wearing stood out like a beacon in the darkness. If any teachers were about, we would certainly be seen.

Daljit put a finger to his lips as soon as he saw me. This was quite unnecessary, since I was the cautious one; but Daljit was enjoying himself, and wanted to make everything seem mysterious.

Tiptoeing was not in Daljit's line; he had big feet, and was often teased about them. There is a saying in Punjab that if you have big feet you will be good only for manual work. Daljit denied this. Instead, he said that if you had big feet you would travel a lot, and he was now out to prove his theory.

We ran silently across the flat in front of the pavilion, while heavy monsoon clouds scurried overhead. Running down the pavilion steps, we entered the gymnasium. The gym door was usually left open, and it was in this huge damp room, smelling of coir-matting, varnish and perspiration, that we held our nocturnal meetings.

This was to be our final meeting before running away from school.

'Have you got everything ready?' asked Daljit, lighting a candle stub and placing it on the floor between us.

We sat cross-legged, facing each other. The candle cast a glow on Daljit's round, good-natured face. It left me in the shadows.

'Yes. Everything's ready,' I replied. 'A knife, two packets of biscuits, some bread, a tin of sardines and some sweets.'

The bread, which had been pocketed during the previous week's meals, was now quite stale and hard, but I wanted to make my list as long as possible.

'Not much,' commented Daljit. 'And how much money do you have?'

'Six rupees. That's two months' pocket-money.'

'Not bad, Rusty.' He knew I did not get much pocket-money from my guardian. 'Well, I've got about thirty rupees, so we don't have to worry too much about money—not yet, anyway. And I've got some cheese, jam, chocolate and pickle which I saved from my last parcel.'

'Pickle with chocolate?'

'No, of course not. But it will go with any stuff we'll get to eat on the way.'

Daljit frequently received food parcels from his father who was a businessman in East Africa. Part of Daljit's plan was to get back to Africa, because he was fed up with living in a boarding school in India. This was where we joined forces. My uncle Jim was the captain of a small tramp-steamer which sometimes plied between Mombasa in East Africa, and either Jamnagar or Dwarka, two small ports on the west coast of India. His ship, the *O.H. Iris*, was due to call at Jamnagar at the end of the month, and we hoped to persuade him to take us on board.

Daljit wanted to get back to Africa. He was certain his father would realize that if he could get back to Africa on his own from India, it might not be a good idea after all to send him to school in India once again.

I too wanted to get away—but for different reasons. True, school was one of them. Though not as grim as Dickens's Dotheboy's Hall, it was not a good school. The Principal ran the place more as a business enterprise than as a school. 'Give a little, take a lot,' was his motto. He charged his fees, and in return gave us bad teachers and worse food. At any rate, that's what we boys thought.

Daljit, of course, had only himself to blame for ending up in Arundel. He had refused to settle down in any of the other schools he had been sent to, and had, by a process of elimination, come to Arundel, where, after only three months of a diet consisting mostly of lentil soup and mutton fat, he was eager to get away.

'I'll have no more schools after this one,' he declared. 'I'll go straight into my father's business in Nairobi. I can read and write, and I know the difference between a profit and a loss. That's all I need. What about you, Rusty?'

'I want to be a writer,' I said. Gone were the days when I wanted to study plants and become a botanist. I was now fifteen years old. Big enough to make up my mind for once and for all. 'I don't mind going to a school, but I have been here for a year now, and I don't like it one bit, and I know my guardian won't send me to any other.'

Mr Harrison had sent me to Arundel because the Principal was a friend of his, and he had only to pay half-fees for me. Before coming to Arundel, I had attended a day school and stayed with my guardian and his wife. But they travelled often for business purposes and I think they found it very irksome to look after me as I grew older. I was inclined to be rebellious, to spend my time in the bazaars instead of at home, and to read books instead of taking an interest in manly pastimes like those enjoyed by my guardian, which consisted of shooting wild animals. I had never cared much for my guardian and he had been disappointed in me.

But the main reason for running away was not to get back to the bazaars or my guardian's house, but to reach my uncle's ship in Jamnagar.

Uncle Jim was another of my father's cousins. He had last seen me when I was a small boy of five and had written to me off and on throughout the years. His letters had been gay and came in envelopes that bore colourful stamps of different countries. They came from Valparaiso, San Diego, San Francisco, Buenos Aires, Dar-es-Salaam, Mombasa, Freetown, Singapore, Bombay, Marseilles, London . . . these were some of the places where Uncle Jim's ship called. He was seldom on the same route, and seemed to move leisurely across the oceans of the earth, calling at ports which had only the most romantic associations for me, for I had already read Stevenson, Captain Marryat, some Conrad and W.W. Jacobs.

In his letters, Uncle Jim often spoke of my joining him at sea— 'When you are a little older, Rusty.'

I felt I was old enough now. I was sick of school and sick of my guardian. But that was not all. I was in love with the world. I wanted to see the world, every corner of it, the places I had read about in books—the junks and sampans of Hong Kong, the palm-fringed lagoons of the Indies, the streets of London, the beautiful ebony-skinned people of Africa, the bright birds and exotic plants of the Amazon . . .

When Uncle Jim's last letter had arrived, telling me that his ship would call at Jamnagar towards the end of the month, I felt a deep thrill of anticipation. Here was my chance at last! True, Uncle Jim had said nothing about my joining him, but he was not to know that I was seriously considering it.

It was not simply a question of walking out of school and taking a quick ride down to the docks. Jamnagar, on the west coast, was at least *800 miles* from Paharganj, the hill station in northern India where Arundel was located. Eight hundred miles!

I doubt if I would have made the attempt if Daljit had not agreed to come too. It isn't much fun running away on your own. It is even worse if you have a companion who is full of enthusiasm at the beginning and who backs out at the last moment. This leaves one feeling defeated and crushed.

Daljit was not that kind of companion. He meant the things he said. About a month earlier, when I had told him of my uncle's ship and my wish to get to it, he had said, without a moment's hesitation: 'I'm coming too!'

Daljit lived impulsively. Sometimes he made mistakes. But he never went half-way and stopped. Someone had to stop him, otherwise he did whatever it was he set out to do.

We had become friends during the early monsoon marathon runs. I was much better at short races, and Daljit was a little too chubby to keep up with the other boys. Allowing the good athletes to forge ahead, I would sit down on a grassy knoll and read a comic or a chapter from *David Copperfield*. One evening, while I was making use of the run in this way, I saw Daljit strolling down the road, whistling cheerfully.

'Aren't you in the race?' I asked.

'Yes. Aren't you?'

'Yes,' I said, and returned to my book.

Daljit sat down beside me.

'They won't miss us if we're a little late,' he said. 'Why don't we go over to that stall and eat some hot pakoras? Don't worry about money. I have more than enough. I can't stop my mother from spoiling me.'

It was the beginning of a steady friendship. Based initially on pakoras, and a mutual aversion to long-distance races, it soon developed a stronger foundation. After several marathons together, we felt we had known each other for years.

Now, sitting together in the dark, high-ceilinged gymnasium, we felt we understood each other perfectly. I did not mind the fact that Daljit had more money. He did not mind the fact that I was more 'brainy', as he put it. He was impressed by the extent of my reading. But I was an impractical fellow, and in the ways of the world Daljit was more experienced.

He pulled a folder from his pyjama-suit, and opened it out on the floor. It was a railway map of India. We had purchased it during our last and final marathon run, a memorable occasion when we had cut off to the bazaar, and then, having made several purchases, taken a short cut back to school, arriving first and second respectively in the race. (We were, of course, disqualified when the judges came back and insisted that they had not seen us anywhere along the prescribed route: but we had our few moments of glory, with everyone congratulating us on our victory.)

With the map spread out before us, I took a red pencil and circled Paharganj in the Himalayan foothills. Then I circled Jamnagar, at the tip of the Kathiawar Peninsula, facing the Gulf of Kutch. What lay in between? First, hills and forests; then the flat, fertile plains of the Doab (the Ganga-Jamuna basin) stretching to a little beyond Delhi; then the bare brown hills and sand dunes of the Rajasthan desert; and finally the fertile coastal regions of Gujarat and Maharashtra. There were rivers and lakes. We would make what use we could of all available means of transport, as we did not have much time to lose. Uncle Jim's ship would not stay in port any longer than was necessary; it would sail again at the end of July, before the monsoon became too troublesome.

'We must get to Delhi as soon as possible,' I pointed out, 'otherwise we'll be caught easily. Once Delhi has been left behind, they won't know where to look. India's too big. It's easy to get lost.'

'Do you think they'd bother to look for us?'

'Yes, of course. Remember, my guardian is a friend of the

Principal. And your father will sue the school if anything happens to you. As soon as they find us missing, they'll start searching in Paharganj, and if they don't find us here or in Dehra, they'll inform the police, and we'll be on the Wanted list, like criminals. The railway stations and bus stands will be watched.'

'Does that mean we're going to walk to Delhi?' asked Daljit, looking dismayed. 'I can't walk 200 miles.'

'We'll walk only as far as Dehra. That's twenty miles, downhill. Can you manage that?'

'I suppose so, if it's all downhill.'

'From Dehra we'll have to get a train or a bus or a truck. We'll have to avoid the railway stations.'

'All right, Rusty. That's fine. Let's not plan too far ahead. Let's get to Delhi first. It's far enough. After that, we'll take our chances.'

We fell silent for a few minutes, busy with our own thoughts—thinking of the consequences if we were caught, of the dangers and difficulties we might encounter. The candle spluttered and went out. There was total darkness for a minute, then a thin light darted across the floor and over my feet.

'Do you like my pencil torch?' asked Daljit. 'Made in Japan, and designed by James Bond. I bought it in Nairobi last year. But we mustn't waste the battery; this size isn't available here.' He switched it off.

'You must have been terribly spoilt at home,' I said enviously. At times I felt that it was unfair that some children should enjoy being indulged by their family so much when I didn't even have a family to my name anymore.

'I was,' said Daljit with a chuckle. 'In fact, I'm still thoroughly spoilt!' He gave me his hand. 'It's tomorrow night, then?' he whispered. There was no need to whisper, but Daljit never let up a chance to dramatize things.

'Yes, tomorrow night,' I said.

'Where do we meet?'

'Down in the pine forest. Near the big rock. At ten. From there we'll follow the stream until we meet the bridle-path to Dehra.'

'Be on time,' said Daljit. 'I don't want to be waiting for you in the dark, in the middle of the forest. They say it's haunted.'

'Well, you have your torch,' I said reassuringly.

He gripped my hand again. 'We won't talk to each other in school tomorrow. No one must have any suspicion. Now let's go to bed, I'm sleepy.'

'Sleep well,' I said. 'There won't be much sleep for us from tomorrow.'

As we emerged from the gymnasium, we saw that the moon had risen. The flat, the pavilion and the dormitory building stood out clearly in the moonlight. The deodars threw ghostly shadows on the hillside. There were only a few clouds drifting overhead. It was a beautiful night.

'I hope we don't get spotted,' said Daljit.

'If you're caught, say you saw me sleep-walking, and followed to keep an eye on me.'

'That's a good idea. I suppose you get your brilliant ideas out of books.'

We flitted across the flat like a couple of ghouls, and ran swiftly upstairs to our dormitories.

At the entrance to his dormitory, Daljit turned and gave me a conspiratorial wave. I crept into my bed and tried to sleep. But sleep was elusive. I kept thinking of our coming adventure, imagining the kind of journey we would have, and visualizing my uncle's surprise when we turned up on his ship.

I would work for my passage, of course. Daljit and I could be deck-hands.

Yokohama, Valparaiso, San Diego, London!

∾

Running away from school! It is not to be recommended to everyone. Parents and teachers would disapprove. Or would they, deep down in their hearts? Everyone has wanted to run away, at some time in his life: if not from a bad school or an unhappy home, then from something equally unpleasant. Running away seems to be in the best of traditions. Huck Finn did it. So did Master Copperfield and Oliver Twist. So did Kim. Various enterprising young men have run away to sea. Most great men have run away from school at some stage in their lives; and if they haven't, then perhaps it is something they should have done.

Anyway, Daljit and I ran away from school, and we did it quite successfully too, up to a point. But then, all this happened in India, which, though it forms only two per cent of the world's land mass, has fifteen per cent of its population, and so it is an easy place to hide in, or be lost in, or disappear in, and never be seen or heard of again!

Not that we intended disappearing. We were headed for a particular place—Jamnagar—and as soon as I took my first step into the unknown, that first step on the slippery pine needles below the school, I knew quite definitely that I wasn't running away from anything, but that I was running towards something. Call it a dream, if you like. I was running towards a dream.

In bare feet and pyjamas, I slid down the steep slope of the hill, and was the first to reach the flat rock in the middle of the forest. There was a soft breeze sighing in the pine trees. The night was pleasant and cool. From the ravine below came the subdued murmur of the stream; it made a sound like a man humming rather tunelessly to himself. The full moon came out from behind massed monsoon clouds, and the trees, bushes and boulders emerged from the darkness.

Daljit arrived a few minutes later. Though still in his pyjamas, he was wearing his turban. Daljit's turban was a source of great pride to him as turbans are to most Sikhs. He removed it only at night, or for games, and he would never have dreamt of running away bareheaded. When going to bed that night he had taken it off without unwinding it, and on leaving bed he had put it on again like a hat, very neatly, without spoiling a single fold.

We had brought our gym clothes along in bundles and changed into them before going any further as our school clothes would be too conspicuous and our home clothes were packed away in the box room during the term. We had put on our gym shoes. Our haversacks were filled with our provisions; pyjamas, and a couple of books, went in with them. The bulk of our possessions—our clothes, bedding and boxes we had gaily left behind.

A narrow path ran downhill, and we followed it until it levelled out, running parallel with the small stream that rumbled down the mountainside. We followed the stream for a mile, walking swiftly and silently, until we met the bridle-path which was little more than a mule-track going steeply down the last hills to the valley.

The going was easy. We knew the road well. And by the time we reached the last foothills it was beginning to rain, not heavily, but as a light, thin drizzle.

We took shelter in a small dhaba on the outskirts of a village. The dhabawallah was sleeping, and his dog, a mangy pariah with only one ear, sniffed at us in a friendly way instead of chasing us off the premises.

We sat down on an old bench and watched the sun rising over the distant mountains.

This was something I have always remembered. Not because it was a more beautiful sunrise than on any other day, but because the special importance of that morning made me look at everything in a new way, hence the details still stand out clearly in my memory.

As the sky grew lighter, the pines and deodars stood out clearly, and the birds came to life. A blackbird started it all with a low, mellow call, and then the thrushes began chattering in the bushes. A barbet shrieked monotonously at the top of a spruce tree, and, as the sky grew lighter still, a flock of bright green parrots flew low over the trees.

The drizzle continued and there was a bright crimson glow in the east. And then, quite suddenly, the sun shot through a gap in the clouds, and the lush green monsoon grass sprang into relief. Both Daljit and I were wonderstruck. Never before had we been up so early. Hundreds of spider webs, which were spun in trees and bushes and on the grass, where they would not normally have been noticed, were now clearly visible, spangled with gold and silver raindrops. The strong silk threads of the webs held the light rain and the sun, making each drop of water look like a tiny jewel.

A great wild dahlia, its scarlet flowers drenched and heavy, sprawled over the hillside and an emerald-green grasshopper reclined on a petal, stretching its legs in the sunshine.

The dhabawallah was now up. His dog, emboldened by his master's presence, began to bark at us. The man lit a charcoal fire in a choolah, and put on it a kettle of water to boil.

'Would you like to eat something?' he asked conversationally in Hindi.

'No, just tea for us,' I said.

He placed two brass tumblers on a table.

'The milk hasn't yet been delivered,' he said. 'You're very early.'

'We'll take the tea without milk,' said Daljit, 'but give us lots of sugar.'

'Sugar is costly these days. But because you are schoolboys, and need more, you can help yourselves.'

'Oh, we are not schoolboys,' I said hurriedly.

'Not at all,' added Daljit.

'We are just tourists,' I lied unconvincingly.

'We have to catch the early train at Dehra,' offered Daljit.

'But there's no train before ten o'clock,' said the puzzled dhabawallah.

'It is the ten o'clock train we are catching!' said Daljit smartly. 'Do you think we will be down in time?'

'Oh yes, there's plenty of time . . .'

The dhabawallah poured out steaming hot tea into the tumblers and placed the sugar bowl in front of us. 'At first I thought you were schoolboys,' he said with a laugh. 'I thought you were running away.'

Daljit almost gave us away by laughing nervously.

'What made you think that?' he asked.

'Oh, I've been here many years,' the dhabawallah replied, gesturing towards the small clearing in which his little wooden stall stood, almost like a trading outpost in a wild country. 'Schoolboys always pass this way when they're running away!'

'Do many run away?' I asked. I felt a little downcast at the thought that Daljit and I were not the first to embark on such an adventure.

'Not many. Just two or three every year. They get as far as the railway station in Dehra and there they're caught!'

'It is silly of them to get caught,' said Daljit disgustedly.

'Are they always caught?' I asked.

'Always! I give them a glass of tea on their way down, and I give them a glass of tea on their way up, when they are returning with their teachers.'

'Well, you won't be seeing us again,' said Daljit, ignoring the warning look that I gave him.

'Ah, but you aren't schoolboys!' said the shopkeeper, beaming at us. 'And you aren't running away!'

We paid for our tea and hurried on down the path. The parrots flew over again, screeching loudly, and settled in a lichee tree. The sun was warmer now, and, as the altitude decreased, the temperature and humidity rose and we could almost smell the heat of the plains rising to meet us.

The hills levelled out into the rolling countryside, patterned with fields. Rice had been planted out, and the sugarcane was waist-high.

The path had become quite slushy. Removing our shoes and wrapping them in newspaper, we walked barefoot in the soft mud. All these little out-of-routine acts simply added to our excitement and thrill, making everything quite unforgettable for life.

'It's about three miles into Dehra,' I said. 'We must go round the town. By now, everyone in school will be up and they'll have found out we've gone!'

'We must avoid the Dehra station then,' said Daljit.

'We'll walk to the next station, Raiwala. Then we'll hop onto the first train that comes along.'

'How far must we walk?'

'About ten miles.'

'Ten miles!' Daljit looked dismayed. 'It'll take us all day!'

'Well, we can't stop here nor can we wander about in Dehra, neither can we enter the station. We have to keep on walking.'

'All right, Rusty. We'll keep on walking. I suppose the beginning of an adventure is always the most difficult part.'

ॐ

Already the fields were giving way to jungle. But there were still some fields of sugarcane stretching away from the railway lines.

'How much further do we have to walk?' asked Daljit impatiently. 'Is Raiwala in the middle of the jungle?'

'Yes, I think it is. We've covered about four miles I suppose. Six to go! It's funny how some miles seem longer than others. It depends on what one is thinking about, I suppose. If our thoughts are pleasant, the miles are not so long.'

'Then let's keep thinking pleasant thoughts. Isn't there a short cut anywhere, Rusty? You've been in these forests before.'

'We'll take the firepath through the jungle. It'll save us three or four miles. But we'll have to swim or wade across a small river. The rains have only just started, so the water shouldn't be too swift or deep.'

Heavy forests have paths cut through them at various places to prevent forest fires from spreading easily. These paths are not used much by people since they don't lead anywhere in particular, but they are frequently used by the larger animals.

We had gone about a mile along the path when we heard the sound of rushing water. The path emerged from the forest of sal trees and stopped on the banks of the small river I had mentioned earlier. The main bridge across the river stood on the main road, about three miles downstream.

'It isn't more than waist-deep anywhere,' I said. 'But the water is swift and the stones are slippery.'

We removed our clothes and tied everything into two bundles which we carried on our heads. Daljit was a well-built boy, strong in the arms and thighs. I was slimmer. But I had quick reflexes.

The stones were quite slippery underfoot, and we stumbled, hindering rather than helping each other. We stopped in midstream, waist-deep, hesitating about going any further for fear of being swept off our feet.

'I can hardly stand,' said Daljit.

'It shouldn't get worse,' I said hopefully. But the current was strong, and I felt very wobbly at the knees.

Daljit tried to move forward, but slipped and went over backwards into the water, bringing me down too. He began kicking and thrashing about in fear, but eventually, using me as a support, he came up spouting water like a whale.

When we found we were not being swept away, we stopped struggling and cautiously made our way to the opposite bank, but we had been thrust about twenty yards downstream.

We rested on warm sand, while a hot sun beat down on us. Daljit sucked at a cut in his hand. But we were soon up and walking again, hungry now, and munching biscuits.

'We haven't far to go,' I said.

'I don't want to think about it,' said Daljit.

We shuffled along the forest path, tired but not discouraged.

Soon we were on the main road again, and there were fields and villages on either side. A cool breeze came across the open plain, blowing down from the hills. In the fields there was a gentle swaying movement as the wind stirred the cane. Then the breeze came down the road, and dust began to swirl and eddy around us. Out of the dust, behind us, came the rumble of cart wheels.

'Ho! Heeyah! Heeyah!' shouted the driver of the cart. The bullocks snorted and came lumbering through the dust. We moved to the side of the road.

'Are you going to Raiwala?' called Daljit. 'Can you take us with you?'

'Climb up!' said the man, and we ran through the dust and clambered on to the back of the moving cart.

The cart lurched forward and rattled and bumped so much that we had to cling to its sides to avoid falling off. It smelt of grass and mint and cow-dung cakes. The driver had a red cloth tied round his head, and wore a tight vest and a dhoti. He was smoking a beedi, and yelling at his bullocks, and he seemed to have forgotten our presence. We were too busy clinging to the sides of the cart to bother about making conversation. Before long we were involved in the traffic of Raiwala—a small but busy market town. We jumped off the bullock-cart and walked beside it.

'Should we offer him any money?' I asked.

'No. He will be offended. He is not a taxi driver.'

'All right, we'll just say thank you.'

We called out our thanks to the cart driver, but he didn't look back. He appeared to be talking to his bullocks.

'I'm hungry,' declared Daljit. 'We haven't had a proper meal since last night.'

'Then let's eat,' I said. 'Come on, Daljit.'

We walked through the small Raiwala bazaar, looking in at

the tea and sweet shops until we found the cheapest-looking dhaba. A servant-boy brought us rice and dal and Daljit ordered an ounce of ghee which he poured over the curry. The meal cost us two rupees but we could have as much dal as we wanted, and between us we finished four bowls of it.

'We'll rest at the station,' I said, as we emerged from the dhaba. 'We'll buy second-class tickets, and rest in the first-class waiting room. No one will check on us. We look first class, don't we?'

'Not after that walk through the jungle,' replied Daljit.

But we did occupy the best waiting room and Daljit made himself comfortable in an armchair.

'Wake me when the train comes in,' he said drowsily.

We didn't have long to wait. I was leaning against the door, staring across the railway tracks, when I heard the whistle of the approaching train. It came in slowly, the big hissing engine sending out waves of steam. A crowd was waiting on the platform, and it surged forward as the train drew up. At the same time the carriage doors opened and passengers started pouring out.

I had to shake Daljit to wake him up, and we emerged on to the platform to join the fray. Men, women and children pushed and struggled, and bundles of belongings were passed through windows over the heads of people. Daljit and I, clinging to our bundles, were caught up in the general rush and confusion, and were conveniently swept into a compartment.

By the time we had settled down in a corner seat, the train was moving. One or two people still hung on to the doors and windows, worming their way in as opportunity offered.

I was near a window, and as the train gathered speed and mango groves and villages mingled with telegraph posts as we rushed past, I realized that we were now really on our way, moving into the mysterious unknown. In my excitement I gripped Daljit by the arm.

'We are on our way!' I said.

'That's obvious,' said Daljit, who was trying to extract his haversack from under a fat fellow passenger who had fallen asleep on it in the midst of all the commotion.

But Daljit knew what I meant, and after retrieving the haversack, he gave me a grin, and his eyes were alive with excitement.

∽

At Old Delhi Station we got down from the train like perfectly respectable people and moved confidently towards the exit, quite pleased at the prospect of handing over our tickets to the ticket-collector. The crowd was dense and movement slow. And this was a good thing, because when we were only about thirty feet from the exit, I spotted Mr Jain, our maths teacher, talking to the ticket-collector.

Mr Jain was the most efficient teacher we had at Arundel and he had obviously been sent after us. He was tubby and wore glasses, but he was a shrewd man and knew just where to intercept us. We had to get away from the exit right away.

'Let's get away from here,' I whispered fiercely, grabbing at Daljit.

'Why?' asked Daljit, who had not yet spotted our teacher.

'Can't you see?' I said. 'With the ticket-collector!'

Daljit almost tripped himself up in his hurry to vanish. The crowd was pushing towards the exit, and we were up against a human wall which would not give way at any point. Just then Mr Jain spotted us, and we heard him shout:

'Boys, come here! Rusty! Daljit!'

For a brief moment, I was on the verge of obeying the familiar voice of my teacher; and then I had a swift vision of classrooms and dormitories and the Principal's gloomy, rat-whiskered face, and I hated it all and wanted to get away as fast as I could; I wanted to keep running until I reached the sea and my uncle's ship.

Daljit did not hesitate for a moment. He plunged beneath the legs of a tall Jat farmer, and almost lost his turban as he went through. I headed for a narrow gap between two stout Punjabi women, but they closed their ranks before I was completely through, and the result was a tangle of legs and arms. Mr Jain was close behind me. And then a coolie sprinted across the platform to get to a compartment, and collided with Mr Jain.

Mr Jain rolled over and lost his glasses. I disengaged myself from the women and ran after Daljit who was far ahead, using his fists and elbows to cut a path through the crowd.

He stopped once, turned to see if I had freed myself, and shouted: 'Come on, Rusty! Across the railway tracks!'

He leapt down from the platform, and slipped between two carriages of a waiting train. I followed unwillingly. I have always had a superstitious dread of crossing railway lines, and sometimes I'd get nightmares in which I'd find myself lying helpless (though not bound) on a railway track, while a steam-engine thundered towards me. I'd somehow manage to get away all of a sudden in the nick of time—with the engine about three feet away, but sometimes I'd wonder what would happen if I failed to get up at the crucial moment!

Daljit had already crossed two sets of railway lines, and was climbing the railings on the other side. I looked left, and then right, and then left again, and saw a shunting engine in the distance. It was far away, and I had plenty of time in which to cross the lines and join Daljit. But I was overcome by an irrational fear and sweat broke out on my forehead and on the palms of my hands.

'Come on!' called Daljit urgently.

I took a deep breath, looked straight ahead and made a dash across the tracks. I was so nervous that I tripped and fell across the lines. A feeling of nausea swept over me and the ground seemed to be in the throes of an earthquake. Was my nightmare going to come true at last? I could still hear Daljit shouting; I could hear the puff-puff of the engine coming closer.

'Come on, Rusty, get up,' Daljit's voice was in my ear now, and I was surprised to find him beside me, tugging at my arm.

His presence gave me confidence. I scrambled to my feet, snatched up my haversack, and ran with him to the embankment. A fence made of corrugated iron sheeting blocked our way. It was about ten feet high and there were no footholds which would enable us to climb it. So we ran along the side of the fence until we found an opening which gave on to a goods yard.

We dashed through an open turnstile, and entered a small side street. We kept running, keeping to narrow lanes and alleys, where small mosques, temples, schools and shops jostled with each other, and then found ourselves on a wide thoroughfare, bustling with people and noisy with traffic.

We were in Chandni Chowk, Delhi's famed and historic street of silversmiths.

❧

Here, in the crowd of shoppers, pedlars, clerks, urchins, sadhus, jewellers, barbers and pickpockets, we felt fairly safe. The heart of a city is always a good place to get lost in. Fugitives usually make the mistake of fleeing into the countryside, where, being strangers, they are soon noticed. By sheer accident we had come upon the safest place in Delhi.

Tongas, bullock-carts, cycles, scooter-rickshaws, and cars new, old and ancient, all struggled for advantage on the road. Any vehicle that had a horn blew it and anything which had a bell jangled it; and if you had neither horn nor bell, you used your vocal chords.

We found a sweet stall, and while Daljit dropped syrupy brown gulab jamuns down his throat, I helped myself to some golden-spangled jalebies.

A sudden sharp shower drove us into the shelter of a veranda. As it began to rain quite heavily, the street rapidly emptied, and in no time at all the throng of people had melted away. A couple of cars churned their way through the rushing water and stray cows continued rummaging in the garbage heaps.

A group of small boys came romping along the street which was now like a river in spate. When they came to a gutter filled with rain water, they plunged in, screaming with laughter. A garland of marigolds came floating down the middle of the road.

And then the rain stopped suddenly. The sun came out. A paper boat came sailing between my legs.

'Where do we go now?' asked Daljit. 'The station isn't safe.'

'We must leave Delhi by some other way. Meanwhile, let's find a cheap hotel for the night.'

'Oh that's not a problem, I've still got over thirty rupees,' said Daljit.

'Even then, I don't think it will be enough for both of us, not if we are going to buy tickets.'

'Then we won't buy tickets,' said Daljit rather flippantly.

It didn't take us long to find a hotel. It was called the Great Oriental Hotel, and was just behind the police station. It didn't pretend to be even a third-class hotel, and for five rupees we were given a small back room which had a window overlooking the godown of an Afghan spice merchant. The powerful smell of asafoetida came up from the courtyard below.

We were tired and hot, so we tossed our belongings down on the floor and took turns at the bathroom tap. Then we stretched out on the only cot in the room and slept through the afternoon, oblivious to the noises from the street, the attentions of the insect population in the hotel mattress, and the creaking of the old fan overhead.

It was late evening when we woke up, and we were hungry again. Daljit opened the door and shouted. Presently a servant-boy appeared.

'Bring us tea, toast, two big omelettes, and a bottle of tomato sauce,' ordered Daljit with a confidence that I wished I had.

The omelettes, when they arrived twenty minutes later, were tiny. Both had obviously been made from one egg. The sauce had been diluted with water, and the toasts were burnt. The salt was damp, and we had to prise open the salt-cellar to get to it. The pepper, however, came out in a generous rush and made up the major portion of the meal. As our hunger had not been satisfied by this poor fare, we ordered eggs again, boiled eggs this time. No matter how tiny, they would have to be whole.

'Let's go out,' said Daljit after we had eaten the eggs. 'It's stuffy in here.'

'I'm still sleepy,' I said.

'Then I'll go out for a little while. I may go to the gurdwara.'

'All right, but don't get lost.'

Daljit left me, and I settled back on the cot, and opened Tagore's *The Gardener* but I didn't read for long because as the evening wore on, I found myself a witness to the great yearly flight of the insects into the cool brief freedom of the night.

Termites and white ants, which had been sleeping through the hot season, emerged from their lairs. Out of every hole, crevice and crack, huge winged ants emerged, at first fluttering about heavily, on this, the first and last flight of their lives. There was only one direction in which they could fly, towards the light—towards electric bulbs and street lamps and kerosene lanterns throughout the city. The street lamp beneath our room attracted a massive swarm of clumsy termites, which gave the impression of one thick, slowly revolving body.

It was the hour of lizards. They had their reward for weeks of patient waiting. Plying their sticky pink tongues, they devoured insects swiftly. For hours they crammed their stomachs, knowing that such a feast would not be theirs again till the next season. Throughout the entire hot season the insect world prepares for this flight out of darkness into light, but not one survives its bid for freedom.

Drowsy, I closed my eyes, but the sounds of the city's unceasing traffic came through the window. Ships and distant ports seemed very far away but so did hills and mountain streams.

I fell asleep and woke up only when Daljit returned.

'I've solved our problem!' he said, beaming. 'We won't bother with the train. I got friendly with a truck driver, and he has offered to take us as far as Jaipur. That's nearly 300 miles. It will be quite safe to take a train from Jaipur.'

'When can your friend take us?'

'The truck leaves at four o'clock in the morning.'

'There's no rest for the wicked,' I said. 'Still, the less time we lose the better. It's Wednesday, and my uncle's ship might sail on Saturday. What will we have to pay?'

'Nothing. It's a free ride. The driver is a Sikh, and I persuaded him that we are related to each other through the marriage of my brother-in-law to his sister-in-law's niece!'

છ

At four the next morning we made our way towards the Red Fort, its ramparts dark against the starry sky. The streets which had been teeming with so much life the previous evening were now deserted. The street lamps shed lonely pools of light on the pavements. The occasional car glided silently past, but it belonged to another kind of world altogether.

Near the Fort we found a couple of dhabas which were still open. They did business with the truck drivers who slept by day and drove by night.

Our driver, a tall, bearded Sikh, loomed over us out of the darkness. He had a companion with him, also a Sikh, who was still in his underwear.

'You can get in at the back,' said the driver in his thick Punjabi which I could follow sufficiently well. 'We'll be off in a few minutes.'

The truck was parked beneath a peepul tree. We pulled

ourselves up into the back of the open truck, only to find our way barred by what seemed at first to be a prehistoric monster.

The monster snorted once, stamped heavily on the boards, and sent us tumbling backwards.

'Bhaiyyaji!' cried Daljit to the driver. 'There's some kind of animal in here!'

'Don't worry, it's only Mumta,' said our friend.

'But what is it doing in here?'

'She is going with us. I am taking her to the market in Jaipur. So get in with her boys, and make yourselves comfortable.'

There was now enough light to enable us to take a closer look at our travelling companion. She was a full-grown buffalo from the Punjab.

'An excellent buffalo,' said Daljit, who appeared to be familiar with the finer points of these animals. 'Notice her blue eyes!'

'I didn't know buffaloes had blue eyes,' I said dryly.

'Only the best buffaloes have them,' said Daljit. 'Blue-eyed buffaloes give more milk than brown-eyed ones.'

Fortunately for us, the Sardarji started the truck and an early morning breeze, blowing across the river, swept away some of the stench so typical of buffaloes.

We were soon out of Delhi and bowling along at a fair speed on the road to Jaipur. The recent rain had waterlogged low-lying areas, and the herons, cranes and snipe were numerous. Fields and trees were alive with strange, beautiful birds: the long-tailed king crow, bluejays and weaver birds, and occasionally the great white-headed kite, which is said to be Garuda, God Vishnu's famous steed.

As we travelled further into Rajasthan, the peacocks became more numerous; so did the camels loping along the side of the road in straight, orderly lines. And, as the vegetation grew less and the desert took over, the people themselves grew more colourful, as though to make up for the absence of colour in the landscape. The women wore wide red skirts, and gold and silver ornaments. They were handsome, tall, fair and strong. The men were tall too and the older among them had flowing white beards.

As the day grew older, and the sun rose higher in the sky, the traffic on the road increased; but our truck driver, instead of slowing down, drove faster.

Perhaps he was in a hurry to dispose of the buffalo. Soon he was trying to overtake another truck.

The truck in front was moving fast too, and its driver had no intention of giving up the middle of the road. It was piled high with stacks of sugarcane.

'It's going to be a race!' cried Daljit excitedly, standing up against the buffalo, in order to get a better view.

The road was not wide enough to take two large vehicles at once, and as the other truck wouldn't make way, ours had to fall in behind it, almost suffocating us with the exhaust fumes. We were thrown to the floor-boards as the truck lurched over the ruts in the rough road, and Mumta, getting nervous, almost trampled upon us. Then there was a tremendous bump, a grinding of brakes, and we came to a stop.

As the dust cleared, we made out our driver's bearded face gazing anxiously down at us.

'Are you all right?' he asked gruffly.

'I think so,' I said.

'Did you overtake the other truck?' asked Daljit.

'No,' grunted our friend. 'He would not give way. He was a Sikh, too. You had better come in front.'

We agreed without any hesitation and his assistant rather grudgingly joined the buffalo.

After a few miles, the driver became friendly and told us that his name was Gurnam Singh.

'Would you like to hear my new horn?' he asked in Punjabi.

'Have we not been hearing it all this time?' I asked rather pointedly in Hindi. We got along well enough.

'You can't hear it well in the back,' he said, quite oblivious to what I meant. 'That's why I've brought you here in front. What do you think of it?' he asked, as a shattering sound filled the cabin of the truck.

'It is a fine horn,' I said, fingers in my ears. 'It could not be louder.'

'You can hear it half a mile ahead,' said Gurnam Singh proudly, and he blasted off at two young men who were sharing a bicycle. They moved out of the way with alacrity.

'It makes a lot of noise in here, too,' I said, and added hastily, for fear of offending him, 'not that it matters, of course . . .'

'Doesn't your horn have more than one tone of voice?' asked Daljit.

I thought this was a bit rude, but Gurnam Singh seemed to welcome the question.

'Two!' he exclaimed. 'Male and female. See.' And he produced a high note and then a low note, both equally ear-shattering. Ahead of us, a camel ran off the road and into the fields.

'This is a terrific horn,' said Gurnam Singh. 'I've had it made specially for this truck. No foreign horns for me. They are not loud enough. Indian horns are the best!'

In an interval of comparative quiet, I found myself reflecting on the nature of sound—the unpleasantness of some sounds, and the sweetness of others, and why certain sounds (like those made by monster-horns) can be sweet to some and terrible to others.

'It was made in Old Delhi,' continued Gurnam Singh, interrupting my thoughts with further comment on his horn. 'Seventy-five rupees only. Made by hand, to my own specifications. There is only one drawback—it mustn't get wet!'

As his fist came down on the horn again, I thought of praying for rain; but the sky was quite clear and I decided that such a prayer would be an unreasonable and ungrateful demand considering the huge kindness this man was showing us by letting us ride with him so far.

'Ah, but you don't know what it is to have a horn like mine. Try it, friend. Why don't you try it for yourself?'

The question was addressed to me, as I was sitting beside him, Daljit being near the door.

'Oh, that is quite all right,' I said. 'You have already proved its excellence.'

'No, you must try it. I insist that you try it!' He was like a big boy, suddenly generous, determined to share a new toy with a younger brother.

He grabbed my right hand and placed it on the horn, and, as I felt it give a little, a thrill of pleasure rushed up my arm. I pressed hard, and a stream of music flowed in and out of the truck. And as I kept pressing down, I experienced the driver's happiness; for, with a horn like his, one felt the power and glory that belongs to the kings of the road.

ॐ

It was getting dark by the time we reached Jaipur, so we were not able to see much of the city. We spent the night in the truck, sleeping in the back with Gurnam Singh. Mumta had been disposed of on the way. Jaipur nights can be chilly, even in summer, so Gurnam Singh considerately shared his bedding with us. Because he was accustomed to sleeping in the body of the truck, he was soon asleep, snoring loudly and rhythmically. Daljit and I tossed and turned restlessly. He kicked me several times in the night. The floor of the truck was hard, and retained various buffalo smells.

We had hardly fallen asleep (or so it seemed), when Gurnam Singh woke us up, saying that it was almost four o'clock and that he had to start on his return journey, this time with a load of red sandstone.

'What a life!' exclaimed Daljit, sleepily rubbing his eyes with one hand. 'I'd hate to be a truck driver.'

'One has to live somehow,' philosophized Gurnam Singh. 'I like driving. I knew how to drive when I was merely six or seven. The money is not so bad, either. Now, when I get back to Delhi, I will have two days off, which I will spend with my wife and children. Goodbye friends, and if you pass through Delhi again, you will find me near the walls of the Red Fort.'

We waved to him as he shot off in his truck, throwing up huge clouds of dust, making a great noise and probably waking the local inhabitants. Dogs barked, and a cock began to crow.

We were on the outskirts of the city, facing a large lake. On the other side was open country, bare hills and desert. We could also make out the ruins of a building—probably a palace or a hunting lodge—among some thorn bushes and babul trees.

'Let's go out there,' suggested Daljit. 'We can bathe in the lake and rest. Then later in the morning we can come into the city and find out about trains.'

We set out along the shores of the lake, and it was a good half hour before we reached the opposite bank.

There was no one in the fields, but a camel was going round and round a well, drawing up water in small trays. Smoke rose from houses in a nearby village, and the notes of a flute floated over to us on the still morning air.

It took us about twenty minutes to reach the ruin, which seemed like an old hunting lodge put up by some Rajput prince when game must have been plentiful.

The gate of the lodge was blocked with rubble, but part of the wall had crumbled apart and we climbed through the gap and found ourselves in a stone-paved courtyard in the centre of which stood a dry, disused stone fountain. A small peepul tree was growing from the cracks in the floor of the fountain.

We crossed the courtyard to the main structure, and then Daljit stopped and asked: 'Do you smell something, Rusty?'

'Yes,' I said, 'Curry.'

This was the last thing we expected to find. It meant the ruin was inhabited. I wondered if it would be better to turn around and leave, but curiosity got the better of us—curiosity, and the tantalizing aroma of curry! So Daljit and I moved forward, out of the sun and into the shade of a covered veranda. A door led into a dark chamber from which the curry smells appeared to be wafting across, and there we stood, hesitating on the brink of the unknown.

'Well, go ahead,' prompted Daljit.

'I was waiting for you,' I said, feeling a bit apprehensive for no clear reason.

Smiling at each other in mutual understanding, we stepped into the room together and found it empty.

There was a choolah in one corner, and on it stood a pot in which something delicious was cooking. Of the cook there was no sign.

I moved warily towards the fire, lifted the lid off the pot, and sniffed. Chicken curry! Chicken curry in a ruined hunting lodge in the middle of nowhere! We didn't stop to wonder how or why it had got there. There weren't any utensils about, so we dipped our fingers into the curry and I had just sunk my teeth into a fleshy bit when a pair of strong arms came around from behind and lifted me off my feet.

I was so startled that I dropped the piece of chicken. I struggled to get free from the other's grip but his arms were very powerful. That they were a man's arms and not a ghost's I could tell by the black hair on his forearm. I struggled and kicked about wildly, and then someone, another man, loomed up in front of me and grabbed me by the legs. I could hear Daljit struggling with someone else, and tried to shout to him, but the man who held me by my legs stuck an oily rag into my mouth. He caught my hands and held them while my feet were tied together with a length of rope. I was dumped on the ground, face downwards, with my hands and feet in ropes. Daljit, I saw, was in much the same position at the other end of the room. There wasn't much we could do. There were at least three men with us.

'He's only a boy,' said one of the men, in the local dialect of Hindi (which to my surprise I found I understood), bending over and examining my face. In the darkness of the room I could not make out his features; but I knew he had a beard, because I had felt it on my neck, and his breath smelt strongly of garlic.

'Boy, man or girl,' said another, 'whoever tries to make off with our food deserves a good thrashing.'

'He is quite fair, this one,' said the bearded man.

'Is he a foreigner?'

'Yes, he looks like one. Let us take them into the courtyard. We'll be able to see them better outside.'

'No, we mustn't show ourselves! If the villagers spot us in here, word would soon get around. We want to use this place again, don't we?'

'Light the lamp, then.'

The man who set to work lighting a kerosene lantern was the tallest man in the group. As the flame in the lantern shot up, it cast a huge shadow on the wall. This man was a giant, several inches over six feet. He was bare-chested, and his hair was close-cropped. His muscles stood out like lumps of iron. Another man behind the bearded one appeared to be the one giving the orders; I could not see him as yet.

'Turn him over so that we can have a good look,' he said.

The giant rolled me over on the ground, so that I was staring helplessly at the blackened ceiling. A few moments later three faces were staring down at me. At their mercy in that dark, dark room, tied, gagged and trussed up, I was quaking with fear. They looked like criminals. Probably they were dacoits, using the ruin as a hide-out.

The bearded man had high cheekbones and slanting eyes. The giant did not have a cruel face, inspite of his broad nose and thick, heavy lips. It was the third man who frightened me most. He wasn't big and he wasn't ugly. He was, in fact, rather short, and he was smiling down at me; but it was a smile that sent a shiver down my spine.

'It wasn't very nice of you to help yourself to our chicken,' he said in a smooth voice. 'Not after Bhambiri here went to so much trouble to steal it.'

'Yes, in the middle of the night,' said the giant, who had the quaint name of Bhambiri, which means spinning top. 'I had three dogs and half the village chasing me through the fields. But I gave them the slip!' And he chuckled hugely to himself.

'It's all very well to make a joke of it,' said the bearded one with a look of gloom. 'The chicken isn't important. Why did they really come here? What do you think they know?'

'Let's ask this one,' said the short, sinister man. He bent down, stared hard into my eyes and then pulled the rag out of my mouth. No sooner had the gag gone than I felt something cold and hard against my lower teeth. It was like a dentist making a preliminary examination of his patient's teeth, but this short, sinister man was doing it with the point of a dagger.

'Don't talk or shout except when we tell you,' he warned. Then, taking the knife away he stood back. 'Let him sit up a little. Do you understand me?'

I nodded. Bhambiri came forward, and lifting me with ease, set me up against the wall.

'My wrists are hurting,' I said.

Bhambiri made as if to untie my hands, but his leader said, 'Don't untie him, you fool,' and the giant moved away.

'Now. Tell us what you are doing here.'

'We were just looking for a place to rest,' I said, deciding that there was no harm in telling the truth.

'Twist his arm, Bhambiri.'

I don't think the giant meant to twist my arm very hard, but even the slight wrench he gave it made me cry out. He had obviously been a wrestler at some point in his career.

'Don't lie!' spat out the leader. 'It's very painful to lie. You've been spying on us.'

'We do not know anything about you,' I said desperately. 'We have only been in Jaipur one night.'

'They're only boys.'

'We are on our way to the coast,' I said. 'We do not have much money.'

'So you were about to steal our food,' said Bhambiri sternly. A lost meal concerned him more than the possibility of our being police spies.

'Let's see if they have any money on them,' said the short one. He went through my pockets and produced the few notes and loose change that I possessed. Then he went over to Daljit, still gagged and helpless, took his wallet, examined it and said: 'There's thirty or forty here.' He put everything into his own pockets. I was dismayed. Now what were we to do?

'Shall I let them go now?' asked Bhambiri.

'No, you idiot, they'll set up an alarm. We should just finish what's left of the food, and then be off.'

So we lay there, trussed up for about fifteen minutes, while the dacoits finished their meal. I could see that Daljit, like me, was itching to be set free and leave this horrible place for ever. Meanwhile, it looked as if the dacoits had no intention of leaving anything behind, and when they finished, they licked their fingers and belched. I couldn't help thinking that Bhambiri had a wonderful belch. It came from deep down in his belly, gathered volume as it rose to the surface, and then resounded round the chamber as though a gong had been struck. The short one belched very quietly, in his mean way.

'We'll leave them here,' he said, giving me a narrow sly smile. 'They can have as much rest as they like. They won't be found for a day or two, perhaps. Close the fair boy's mouth again, Bhambiri.'

The giant bent over me, shutting off the light from the lantern and though it was dark I thought I had detected a glimmer of sympathy in his eyes. He thrust the dirty rag back into my mouth and made it fast with a strip of cloth. And then, while he still had me away from the light, he slipped his hands behind my back and swiftly loosened the knot of the rope that bound my hands.

'All right, let's go,' said the leader.

He walked out of the chamber, followed by the others. Bhambiri went out last but he did not look back at us. I waited until I could no longer hear their footsteps and then I slipped my hands out of the rope that Bhambiri had loosened, and wrenched the gag off my mouth. I managed to free my feet, and then crawled over to Daljit. I removed his gag, then started on the rope round his wrists.

'How did you get loose?' he asked, as soon as he was able to find his voice.

'Don't talk too loudly,' I said. 'They might return. Their cooking pots are still here, though they probably belong to someone else.'

'But how did you get loose, Rusty?'

'The big fellow freed my hands when the others weren't looking. I think he felt sorry for us.'

'God bless his soft heart,' said Daljit fervently. 'We might have been lying here for days starving to death. Or dying of thirst, whichever happens first.'

He sat up as soon as his limbs were free, and began stretching his arms and legs. Then he brought his knees up to his chin and gave me an anxious look.

'What do we do now, Rusty? They've taken our money. We can't go anywhere, forward or backward. We'll have to give ourselves up at the nearest police station.'

'They have taken our haversacks, too. Well, if they're dacoits, I suppose it's their business to take what they can. I suppose we should consider ourselves lucky. They might have murdered us.'

'We wouldn't have been their first victims. That short fellow . . .' Daljit, with a scowl on his face, was considering the possibilities; then, his hands in his pockets, his face brightened, 'They weren't so clever, Rusty. They forgot my watch, just imagine, and there's still some change in one of my pockets!'

'Well, that's something,' I said. 'We won't starve. We can always sell the watch. But if we can get to Jamnagar somehow without selling it ... We should keep it in case of a real emergency.'

'Isn't this an emergency?'

'I suppose so. Still . . .'

'And you think we can go on? You haven't given up yet?'

'What about you?'

'Do you think I'm likely to give up before you? Come on, Rusty, let's get out of here. It's Saturday tomorrow and we have to get to that ship!'

∿

Daljit and I lay stretched out on the floor of a goods wagon, which was open to the sky. The train jogged slowly through the desert, and hot winds blew the sand in upon us. The gritty sand got in our hair and into our eyes and mouths. There was no escape from it. Daljit's face, caked with sand, was the same colour as mine. The sun beat down on us mercilessly and there was only a small corner of the wagon which gave us some shade. We had bought some bananas with what was left of our money, and we took bites on them from time to time.

'We'll be half starved by morning,' I said. 'I think we should save something of these bananas.'

'Morning comes tomorrow,' said Daljit. 'I'm hungry today. Besides, we'll reach Jamnagar in the morning.'

'And if the ship has gone?' I couldn't help wondering about all the possible situations we might find ourselves in—even if they weren't what we hoped for.

'The ship will be there.' Daljit was, as usual, confident about everything.

'How do you know?' I asked.

'I don't. I'm just an optimist.'

'It will sail any day now. Perhaps it has left already. Daljit, we'll be stuck without any money; what will we do then?'

'Stop worrying, Rusty. Don't be so nervous. If we're in trouble, we'll sell the watch and go back to school and be expelled. No, they won't expel us—they'll lose all my father's money—but if you like, we can run away again.'

'That ship had better be there,' I muttered.

'It will be there. We'll be off in it tomorrow. I hope you will come and live with me in Mombasa for some time.'

'Oh, I'll probably be too busy travelling with my uncle,' I said.

'How wonderful! No more school. I may come with you, Rusty. I don't think business will be very interesting.'

'We could see the world together,' I said. 'What dreamers we are!'

'Well, we are on our way somewhere. As my grandfather used to say (he was the grandfather who travelled round the world selling cloth made in the Punjab), "The best reason for going from one place to another is to see what's in between."'

'He sold cloth in between,' I said. 'He wasn't dreaming like us.'

'You're giving up, Rusty.'

'No, I'm not.'

But it was a hard night's journey. The train was agonizingly slow and stopped at many places. At one small station, a number of sacks filled with what must have been cattle-fodder were tossed into the wagon, almost burying us in our fitful sleep. But we found they were comfortable to rest on and lay stretched out on top of them until the first light of morning.

As the sky cleared, we knew we were not far from our journey's end. The landscape had undergone a complete change. We had left the desert for the coastal plain.

The tall waving palms parted, and then I spotted the sea.

It was the sea as I had always dreamt of it ever since my days in Kathiawar with my father. It was vast, lonely and blue, blue as the sky was blue, and the first ship I saw was a sailing-ship, an Arab dhow, listing slightly in the mild breeze that blew onto the shore.

The train stopped at a small bridge spanning a stream which wound its way across the plain down to the sea.

We got down here, and waved our thanks to the brakesman who had tolerated our presence on the train. Then we slid down the banks of the stream, and hid beneath the bridge until the train moved off again. We didn't want the guard to see us; he might not be as tolerant as the brakesman.

Seeing that no one was about, we removed our dusty, travel-stained clothes, and waded out into the stream, pushing our way through a tangle of water-lilies. The current was sluggish unlike the swift streams in the hills and the warm water was not as invigorating as the water we were used to from the mountain springs, but it was fresh enough for our purpose, and brought new life into our weary bodies. We thrashed about, splashing away and ducking each other, and Daljit, trying to swim underwater, came up with a water-lily clinging to his long hair, which had come undone.

We stayed in the water for about fifteen minutes, and by then had lost all awareness of our surroundings. When we finally climbed back on the bank, we got a rude shock: our clothes were missing. Daljit's turban was all that remained.

Higher up the bank, three boys clad only in loincloths, stood staring down at us. The biggest of them held out our clothes teasingly.

'Please bring us our clothes,' said Daljit goodnaturedly in Hindi. 'It is kind of you to leave my turban, but I do not wear a turban anywhere except on my head!'

The three boys burst into laughter and turned on their heels, ambling away through the fields.

'Come back!' shouted Daljit.

'Let's go after them,' I said.

It was almost a matter of life and death for us. All that Daljit had on his person was his turban and his watch, but I didn't even have that much. We scrambled up the bank and ran in desperate pursuit of the boys. But they had had a good start, and knew their way through the fields. They had reached the village while we were still struggling through the field, tripping over culverts and irrigation ditches. A shower of pebbles, thrown at us from behind a wall, brought us to a stop.

'Let's try persuasion,' I suggested. Cupping my hands to my mouth, I shouted: 'Please give us back our clothes, we do not have any others!' I took the trouble to use my best Hindi.

The only response was a large stone, which flew past my ear.

'I don't think they speak Hindi here,' I told Daljit.

'Shall I try English? I don't know any other language.'

'Not English! It will only result in more stones. I suppose they speak Gujarati . . . and I don't know any.'

A man appeared at the edge of the field, waving a stick at us and shouting incomprehensibly.

'What do you think he's saying?' asked Daljit.

'How should I know? He probably wants us to get off his land.'

'Well, we're not going without our clothes.'

'I think we are,' I said. 'Here come the dogs!'

Several village dogs, baying like the hounds of the Baskervilles, came bounding towards us, followed by two men with sticks and several boys with stones. Daljit and I lost no time in presenting them with a rear view, and we made off through the fields as fast as our weary limbs would take us. It wasn't until we had crossed the stream again that we paused for breath. The villagers did not follow us across, so we concluded that we were now on someone else's land. The village men shook their sticks at us and we shook our fists at them; but we were still without our clothes. We left the stream and took shelter in a grove of mango trees. There, we were left alone.

'And now what do we do?' Daljit wanted to know.

'Wearing nothing, you mean?'

'Why not? We'll wait until it gets dark.'

'And when morning comes?'

'Oh, we'll find something. We can sell my watch and buy some clothes.'

'I can't imagine walking into a shop wearing nothing but a watch, which we then offer for sale.'

'We can pretend to be sadhus,' he said. 'Or at least the disciples of sadhus, chelas. It's the fashion these days. Only the best sadhus go about naked. We might even be given free board and lodging for the night.'

'And by the morning we'd find the ship has sailed without us.'

'I hadn't thought of that . . .'

But as we sat there discussing our predicament we saw two men, probably railway workers, walking down to the stream on our side of it. They wore trousers and shirts and shoes unlike the farmers who wore dhotis. At first I thought they were going to the stream to drink water, but when I saw them removing their clothes, I sat up with a wild hope.

'Daljit,' I said urgently, 'do you see them?'

'Of course I see them.' He was not slow in grasping what I meant. 'Yes, this is our only chance, Rusty. We must show no mercy, remember! This world is no place for gentlemen like us. We must change our ways, and do as the local people do! They will probably blame the villagers. But move quietly.

Let's keep to the bushes. They mustn't see us!'

Crawling along on all fours, heedless of the thorns that scratched our bare flesh, we approached the stream again, at the approximate place where the men were bathing. They were making a fair noise as they romped about in the water like boys (bathing in the open seems to make adults quite skittish, I've noticed, perhaps because they are back in the element from which mankind first emerged as playful amoebae!) and did not see or hear us. Their clothes lay in an untidy heap a few yards away.

'I'll get them,' whispered Daljit. 'If they see me, they'll mistake me for a boy from the village. But if they see you, we've had it!'

He dashed out from the bushes with great speed (and if he had shown the same spirit in school, he would have made a good athlete), swept up all the clothes in his arms, and scrambled back to me.

'Brilliant!' I whispered. 'They didn't see a thing.'

We didn't wait for them to discover their loss (though we were sorely tempted to do so), but took to our heels and fled back through the mango grove.

We crossed the railway tracks and ran across the open countryside until we got to an old well; and there, in the generous shade of an ancient banyan tree, we got into our new clothes, which were several sizes too big for us. But who cared about that anyway? At least we were not naked anymore!

ॐ

Two hours later we were at Jamnagar.

We stopped near a small tea-shop and watched other people eating laddoos and bhelpuri. We couldn't even afford a coconut.

'Where is the harbour?' I asked the shopkeeper.

'Two miles from here,' he replied.

'Are there any ships in the port?' I asked, relieved yet anxious.

'What do you want with a ship?'

'What does anyone want with a ship?'

'Well there's only one and it sails today, so you had better hurry if you want to go away on it.'

'Let's go,' said Daljit.

'Wait!' said a young man who was lounging against the counter. 'It will take you almost an hour to get there if you walk. I will take you in my cart.' He pointed to a shabby pony-cart close by. The pony did not look as though it wanted to go anywhere.

'My pony is fast!' said the young man, following our glances. 'Never go by appearances. She may look tired but she runs like a champion! Get in friends, I will charge you only one rupee.'

'We don't have any money,' I said. 'We'll walk.'

'Fifty paisa, then,' he said. 'Fifty paisa and a glass of tea. Jump in my friends!'

'All right,' agreed Daljit. 'There's no time to lose. Fifty paisa and buy your own tea.'

We climbed into the cart, and the youth jumped up in front and cracked his whip. The pony lurched forward, the wheels rattled and shook, and we set off down the bazaar road at a tremendous trot.

'I didn't know you had fifty paisa left,' I said.

'I don't,' Daljit replied. 'But we'll worry about that later. Your uncle can pay!'

As soon as we were out of the town and on the open road to the sea, the pony went faster. She couldn't help doing so, as the road was downhill. The wind blew my hair across my eyes, and the salty tang of the sea was in the air.

Daljit shook me in his excitement.

'We will soon be at the harbour,' he yelled joyfully. 'And then away at last!'

The driver called out endearments to his pony, and, exhilarated by the sea breeze and the comparative speed of his carriage, he burst into song. As we turned a bend in the road, the sea-front came into view. There were several small dhows close to the shore, and fishing-boats were beached on the sand. The fishermen were drying their nets while their children ran naked in the surf. A steamer stood out on the sea and though I could not make out its name from that distance, I was sure it was the Iris.

The cart stopped at the beginning of the pier, and we tumbled out and began running along the pier. But even as we ran, it became clear to me that the ship was moving away from us, moving out to the sea. Its propeller sent small waves rippling back to the pier.

'Captain!' I shouted. 'Uncle Jim! Wait for us!'

A lascar standing in the stern waved to us; but that was all. I stood at the end of the pier, waving my hands and shouting into the wind.

'Captain! Uncle Jim! Wait for us!'

Nobody answered. The seagulls, wheeling in the wake of the steamer, seemed to take up the cry—'Captain, Captain . . .'

The ship drew further away, gaining speed. And still I called to it in a hoarse, pleading voice.

Yokohama, San Diego, Valparaiso, London, all slipping away for ever . . .

We stood by ourselves on the pier, in the late afternoon, with gulls wheeling around us, mocking us with their calls. A phrase from one of Uncle Jim's letters ran through my head. 'First call Aden, then Suez and up the Canal . . .' But for me there was only the long journey back, the indignation of my guardian, the boredom of the classroom and the misery of boarding school.

Daljit had been silent. When at last I forced myself to look at him, I was surprised to see him smiling. He did not seem at all downcast.

'We've arrived too late,' I said. 'We've come hundreds of miles, and we're five minutes too late!'

'Never mind!'

'Everything has been for nothing, Daljit. All our plans . . . All our dreams!'

'What's wrong with dreams? Nothing. As long as they don't come true, we can keep on dreaming. We'll go back to school and we'll have other dreams.'

'I didn't know you were a philosopher, Daljit. And how do you think we are going to get back to school? Even if you sell your watch, it won't be enough. I'm fed up. I don't want to go anywhere. I'll sit on this pier until my uncle returns.'

'How long will you have to wait?'

'One or two years,' I said, smiling.

'Don't worry about getting back.' said Daljit reassuringly. 'When we ran away, it had to be secret, but it isn't a secret any more. We'll sell the watch, pay the cart driver, and send a telegram!'

'To the Principal?'

'No. To an uncle of mine in Bombay. He can come and fetch us in his car. And he can take us back to school too by car. We'll travel in comfort this time! We'll eat chicken and have ice-cream all the way. We'll enjoy ourselves for a few days!'

'Yes,' I said gloomily. 'We won't have anything to enjoy when we get back.'

I didn't say much else as we walked back to the cart.

My thoughts were far away. I told myself that next year, some time, Uncle Jim would return in the Iris, and then I wouldn't make another mistake. I'd be on the ship long before it sailed.

And so I stopped and stared out at the sea for the last time. The steamer looked very small in that vast expanse of ocean.

This year, next year, some time ... Yokohama, Valparaiso, San Diego, London ...

The Hills and Beyond

KISHEN AND SOMI had become my friends when I had left my guardian's home and gone to live on my own in Dehra. When Kishen lost his mother he had looked to me for comfort and companionship. This part of my life is described in my first novel, *The Room on the Roof* (Puffin Classics).

THE HOMELESS

It was December and the sun was up, pouring into the banyan tree at the side of the road to Dehra where Kishen and I were sitting on the great tree's gnarled, protruding roots. A boy played on a flute as he drove his flock of sheep down the road. He was barefoot and his clothes were old. A faded red shawl was thrown across his shoulders.

The flute player passed the banyan tree and glanced at us, but did not stop playing. Presently he was only a speck on the dusty road, and the flute music was thin and distant, subdued by the tinkle of sheep-bells.

We left the shelter of the banyan tree and began walking in the direction of the distant hills.

The road stretched ahead, lonely and endless, towards the low ranges of the Siwalik hills. The dust was in our clothes and in our eyes and in our mouths. The sun rose higher in the sky, and as we walked, the sweat trickled down our armpits and down our legs.

I walked with my hands in the pockets of my thin cotton pyjamas, with my eyes on the road. My hair was matted with dust, and my cheeks and arms were scorched red by the fierce sun. Kishen was in the same state as me, but walked with an air of nonchalance, whistling to himself. For a change, he wasn't chewing gum.

'We will be in Raiwala soon,' I told him. 'Would you like to rest?'

Kishen shrugged his thin shoulders. 'We'll rest when we get to Raiwala. If I sit down now, I'll never be able to get up. I suppose we have walked about ten miles this morning.'

'From Raiwala we'll take the train,' I said. 'It will cost us about five rupees.'

'Never mind,' said Kishen. 'We've done enough walking. And we've still got twelve rupees. Is there anything in our old room in Dehra that we can sell?'

'Let me see . . . The table, the bed and the chair are not mine. There's an old tiger-skin, a bit eaten by rats, which no one will buy. There are one or two shirts and trousers.'

'Which we will need. These are all torn.'

We were quiet for a few minutes, wondering how we would sustain ourselves once we were back in Dehra.

'Somi!' said Kishen. 'Somi will be in Dehra—he'll help us! He got you a job once, he can do it again.'

I was silent. I didn't want to dishearten Kishen by telling him that we would be pretty much without anyone to help us, for Somi too had left Dehra.

Now a cool breeze came across the plain, blowing down from the hills. In the fields there was a gentle swaying movement as the wind stirred the wheat. Then the breeze hit the road, and the dust began to swirl and eddy about the footpath. We moved into the middle of the road, holding our hands to our eyes, and stumbling forward.

Finally we reached Raiwala after an exhausting, seemingly endless walk.

'I'm hungry,' said Kishen. 'We haven't eaten since last night.'

'Then we must eat,' I said. 'Come on, Kishen, let's eat.'

We walked through the narrow Raiwala bazaar, looking in at the tea and sweet shops until we found a place that looked dirty enough to be cheap. A servant boy brought us chappatis and dal and Kishen ordered an ounce of butter; this was melted and poured over the dal. The meal cost us a rupee, and for this amount we could eat as much as we liked. The butter was an extra, and cost six annas. At the end of the meal we were left with a little over ten rupees.

When we came out, the sun was low in the sky and the day was cooler.

'We can't walk tonight,' I said. 'We'll have to sleep at the railway station. Maybe we can get on the train without a ticket.'

'And if we are caught, we'll spend a month in jail. Free board and lodging.'

'And then the social workers will get us, or they'll put us in a remand home and teach us to make mattresses.'

'I think it's better to buy tickets,' said Kishen.

'I know what we'll do,' I said. 'We won't get the train till past midnight, so let's not buy tickets. We'll get to Harrawala early in the morning. Then it's only about eight miles by road to Dehra.'

Kishen agreed, and we found our way to the railway station, where we made ourselves comfortable in a first-class waiting-room. It didn't matter that we didn't own any tickets—we just wanted to rest in some comfort.

Kishen settled down in an armchair and covered his face with a handkerchief. 'Wake me when the train comes in,' he said drowsily.

I went to the bathroom and put my head under a tap to let cold water play over my neck. I washed my face, drying it with a handkerchief before returning to the waiting-room.

A man entered, setting out his belongings on the big table in the centre of the room. He seemed to be in his thirties. The man was white, but he was too restless to be a European. He looked smart, but tired; he had a lean, sallow face, and pouches under the eyes. I sat down on the edge of Kishen's armchair.

'Going to Delhi?' asked the stranger. His accent, though not very pronounced, was American.

'No, the other way,' I replied. 'We live in Dehra.'

'I've often been there,' said the man. 'I've been trying to popularize a new steel plough in northern India, but without much success. Are you a student?'

'Not now. I finished with school two years ago.'

'And your friend?' He inclined his head towards Kishen.

'He's with me,' I said vaguely. 'We're travelling together.'

'Buddies.'

'Yes.'

The American took a flask from his bag and looked enquiringly at me. 'Will you join me for a drink while we're waiting? There's almost an hour left for my train to arrive.'

'Well,' I said hesitantly, 'I don't drink.' I wanted to forget that day when I drank whisky neat from Mr Kapoor's bottles.

'A small one won't harm you. Just to keep me company.'

He took two small glasses from his bag, wiped them with a clean white handkerchief and set them down on the table. Then he poured some dark brown stuff from his flask.

'Brandy,' I said, sniffing.

'So you recognize it. Yes, it's brandy.'

I reached across the table and took the glass.

'Here's luck!' said the stranger.

'Thank you,' I replied, and gulped down a mouthful of neat liquor. I coughed and tears sprang to my eyes.

'You've come a long way,' said the American looking at my clothes.

'On foot,' I answered. 'From Hardwar. Since morning.'

'Hardwar! That's a long walk. What made you do that?'

I emptied my glass and set it down. The friendly stranger

poured out more brandy. This is the way they do things in America, I thought. When you meet a stranger, offer him a drink. I decided to go there one day.

'What made you walk?' asked the stranger again.

'Tomorrow we'll walk some more,' I replied evasively, not wanting to reveal that we were actually penniless.

'But why?'

'Because we have the time. We have all the time in the world.'

'How come?'

I felt tired. 'Because we have no money,' I said. 'You can't have both time and money.'

'Oh, I agree. You are quite a philosopher. But what happened?' asked the American, looking at Kishen again. 'What is he to you?'

'He's with me,' I said, ignoring the question. I was beginning to feel sleepy. The American seemed to be getting further and further away and his voice came from a great distance.

I must have dozed off. I woke to the sound of a bell clanging on the station platform. The stranger looked at his watch and said it was almost time for his train to arrive. He wiped the glasses with his handkerchief and returned them to his bag, then went outside and stood on the platform, waiting for the Delhi train.

I leant against the waiting-room door, staring across the railway tracks. I could hear the shriek of the whistle as the front light of an engine played over the rails. The train came in slowly, the hissing engine sending out waves of steam. At the same time, the carriage doors opened and people started pouring out.

There was a jam on the platform while men, women and children pushed and struggled, and it was several minutes before anyone could get in or out of the carriage doors. The American had been swallowed up by the crowd. After a few minutes, the train pulled out of the station. Then a calm descended on the platform. A few people waiting for the morning train to Dehra still slept near their bundles. Vendors selling soda-water, lemons, curds and cups of tea pushed their barrows down the platform, still calling out their wares in desultory, sleepy voices.

I returned to the chairs in the waiting-room. Kishen was sound asleep in the armchair.

I turned off the light switch, but the light from the platform streamed in through the gauze-covered doors. I sat down beside Kishen.

'Kishen, Kishen,' I whispered, touching the boy's shoulder.

Kishen stirred. 'What is it?' he mumbled drowsily. 'Why is it dark?'

'I put the light off,' I told him. 'You can sleep now.'

'I was sleeping,' said Kishen. 'But thank you all the same.'

THE FOREST ROAD

At Doiwala next morning, we had to get off the train for an inspector came round checking tickets. Kishen and I slipped out of the carriage from the side facing the jungle.

Doiwala stood just outside the Siwalik range, and already the fields were giving way to jungle. But there were maize fields stretching away from the bottom of the railway banking, and we went in amongst the corn and waited in the field until the train had left. Kishen broke three or four corn-cobs from their stalks, stuffing them into his pockets.

'We might not get anything else to eat,' he said. 'Rusty, have you got matches so that we can light a fire and roast the corn?'

'We'll get some at the station.'

We bought a box of matches at Doiwala station, but we did not roast the corn until we had walked two miles up the road, into the jungle. Kishen collected dry twigs, and when we sat down at the side of the road he made a small fire. He turned the corn-cobs over the fire until they were roasted a dark brown, burnt black in places. We dug our teeth into them, relishing the juicy corn.

'I wish we had some salt,' said Kishen.

'That would only make us thirsty, and we have no water. I hope we find a spring soon.'

'How far is Dehra now?'

'About twelve miles, I think. It's funny how some miles seem longer than others. It depends on what you are thinking about, I suppose. What you are thinking and what I am thinking. If our thoughts agree, the miles are not so long. We get on better when we are thinking together rather than when we are talking together!'

'All right then Rusty, stop talking.'

After our light meal, we began to walk once again. We walked in silence; speaking only when we stopped to rest.

I had realized by then that once we were back in Dehra I would have to take on the responsibility of looking after both Kishen and myself as Kishen was too young to look after himself. He would only get into trouble. I did not like to leave him alone even for a little while because of this. Maybe I could get an English tuition. Or if I could write a story, a really good story, and sell it to a magazine, perhaps an American magazine . . .

Suddenly we heard the sound of rushing water. The road emerged from the jungle of sal trees and ended beside a river. There was a swift stream in the middle of the river bed, coursing down towards the Ganges. Perhaps a bridge had crossed this once and had been swept away during heavy monsoon rains. That must have been the reason why the road ended at the river-bank.

We walked over sand and sharp rocks until we reached the water's edge. We stood there, looking at the frothy water as it swirled below us.

'It's not deep,' said Kishen. 'I don't think it's above the waist anywhere.'

'It's not deep, but it's swift,' I pointed out. 'And the stones are slippery.'

'Shall we go back?'

'No, let's carry on—if it's too fast, we can turn back.'

We removed our shoes, tying them together by the laces and hanging them about our necks, then holding hands for security, we stepped into the water gingerly.

The stones were slippery underfoot, and we stumbled, hindering rather than helping each other. When we were halfway across, the water was up to our waists. We stopped in midstream, unwilling to go further for fear of being swept away.

'I can hardly stand,' said Kishen. 'It will be difficult to swim against the current.'

'It won't get deeper now,' I said hopefully.

Just then, Kishen slipped and went over backwards into the water, bringing me down on top of him. He began kicking and thrashing about, but eventually—by clinging on to my right foot—came spluttering out of the water.

When we found we were not being swept away by the current, we stopped struggling and dragged ourselves cautiously across to the opposite bank. When we emerged from the water we were about thirty yards downstream.

The sun beat down on us as we lay exhausted on the warm sand. Kishen sucked at a cut in his hand, spitting the blood into the stream with a contemptuous gesture.

After some time we were walking again, though Kishen kept on bringing up mouthfuls of water.

'I'm getting hungry now,' he said, when he had emptied himself of water.

'We'll be in Dehra soon,' I said. 'And then never mind the money, we'll eat like pigs.'

'Gourmets!' put in Kishen. 'I suppose there are still eight or ten miles left. Now I'm not even thinking. Are you?'

'I was thinking we should visit that river again one day, when we have plenty of food and nothing to worry about.'

'You won't get me coming here again,' he declared.

We shuffled along the forest path, tired and hungry, but quite cheerful. Then we rounded a bend and found ourselves face to face with a tiger.

Well, not quite face to face. The tiger was about fifteen yards away from us, occupying the centre of the path. He seemed as surprised to see us as we were to see him. He lifted his head, and his tail swished from side to side, but he made no move towards us.

We stood absolutely still in the middle of the path as we were too astonished to do anything else. This was just as well, because had we run or shouted or shown fear, the tiger might well have been provoked into attacking us. After a moment's hesitation, he crossed the path and disappeared into the forest without so much as a growl.

We were still rooted to the spot and tongue-tied. Finally Kishen found his voice.

'You didn't tell me there were tigers here,' he said in a hoarse whisper.

'I didn't think about it,' I said rather apologetically.

'Shall we go forward or backward?'

'Do you want to cross the stream again? Anyway, the tiger didn't seem to worry about us. Let's go on.'

And we walked on through the forest without seeing the tiger again, though we saw several splendid peacocks and a band of monkeys. It was not until we had left the forest behind and were on an open road with fields and villages on either side that we relaxed and showed our relief by bursting into laughter.

'I think we frightened that tiger more than it frightened us,' said Kishen. 'Why, it didn't even roar!'

'And a good thing it didn't, otherwise we might not have been here.'

The danger we had shared helped revive our drooping spirits, and we walked happy and carefree into the fertile valley that lay between the Siwaliks and the Himalayan foothills. Spreading over the valley were wheat and maize and sugar-cane fields, tea gardens and orchards of guava, litchee and mango.

There was a small village on the outskirts of Dehra, and the village lamps were lit when we, dusty and dishevelled, walked through with dragging feet. Now that our journey was almost over, we were acutely conscious of our weariness and our aches, and the town which had been our home suddenly seemed strange and heartless, as though it did not recognize us any more.

A PLACE TO SLEEP

When we got to the Tandoori Fish Shop, Kishen and I were too hungry and tired to think of going any further, so we sat down and ordered a meal. The fish came hot, surrounded by salad and lemon, and when we finished it, we ate the same dish once again, and drank glasses of hot, spiced tea.

'The best thing in life is food,' said Kishen. 'There is nothing to equal it.'

'I agree,' I said. 'You are absolutely right.'

Afterwards, we walked through the noisy, crowded bazaar which we knew so well, past the Clock Tower, up the steps of our old room. We were ready to flop down on the string cot and sleep for a week. But when we reached the room we found the door locked. It was not our lock, but a heavy, unfamiliar padlock, and its presence was ominous.

'Let's smash it!' said Kishen.

'That's no use,' I said. 'The landlord doesn't want us to have the room. He's shut us out at the first opportunity. Well, let's go and see his agent. Perhaps he'll let us have the room back. Anyway, our things are inside.'

Standing at the top of the steps, looking at the grounds—the gravel path, the litchee and mango trees, the grass badminton court, now overgrown with weeds—I half-expected to hear Meena calling to Kishen from below, calling to him to go down and play, while Mr Kapoor, in his green dressing-gown, sat on the steps clutching a bottle. They had gone now, and would never come back. Now, I was not so sure if I wanted to stay in the old room anymore.

'Would you like to wait here while I get the key?' I asked.

'No, Rusty,' said Kishen. 'I'd be afraid to wait here alone.'

'Why?'

'Because,' he looked to me for understanding, 'because this was our house once, and my mother and father lived here, and I'm afraid of the house when they are no longer in it. I'll come with you. I'd like to break the munshi's neck, anyway.'

The munshi met us at the door of his house. He was a slow, bent, elderly man, dressed in a black coat and white dhoti, a pair of vintage spectacles balanced precariously on his nose. He was in the service of the seth who owned a great deal of property in town, and his duties included the collection of rents, eviction of tenants and seeing to the repair and maintenance of the seth's property.

'Your room has been rented out,' explained the munshi.

'What do you mean, mister?' said Kishen, bristling.

'Why has it been rented when we haven't given it up?' I asked.

'You were never a tenant,' said the munshi, with a shrug that almost unsettled his spectacles. 'Mr Kapoor let you use one of the rooms. Now he has vacated the house. When you went away, I thought you had gone permanently.' The munshi made a helpless gesture with his hands, and prevented the imminent fall of his spectacles by taking them off and wiping them on his shirt.

Finally he said: 'Sethji ordered me to let the room immediately.'

'But how could I have gone permanently when my things are still in the room?' I argued.

The munshi scratched his head. 'There were not many things, I thought you had no need for them. I thought you were going to England. You can have your things tomorrow. They are in the storeroom, and the key is with the seth. But I cannot let you have the room again.'

Uncertain as to what to do next, I continued to stand where I was. Kishen stepped forward.

'Give us another room, then,' he said belligerently.

'I cannot do that now,' said the munshi. 'It is too late. You will have to come tomorrow, and even then I cannot promise you anything. All our rooms are full. Just now I cannot help you. There must be some place where you can stay . . .'

'We'll find a place,' I said, tired of the whole business. 'Come on, Kishen. There's always the railway platform.'

Kishen hesitated, scowling at the munshi, before following me out of the gate.

'What now?' he grumbled. 'Where do we go now?'

'Let's sit down somewhere,' I suggested. 'Then we can think of something. We can't come to a decision simply by standing stupidly on the road.'

'We'll sit in some tea shop,' said Kishen. 'We've had enough tea, but let's go anyway.'

We found a tea shop at the end of the bazaar, a makeshift wooden affair built over a gully. There were only two tables in the shop, and most of the customers sat outside on a bench where they could listen to the shopkeeper who was a popular storyteller.

Sitting on the ground in front of the shop was a thick-set youth with his head shaved, wearing rags. I had seen him around tea shops often. He was dumb—and was called Goonga—and the customers at these shops often made sport of him, abusing him goodnaturedly, and clouting him over the head from time to time. Goonga did not seem to mind this; he made faces at the others, and chuckled derisively at their remarks. He could say only one word, 'Goo', and he said it often. This kept the customers in fits of laughter.

'Goo!' he said, when he saw Kishen and me enter the shop. He pointed at us, chuckled, and said 'Goo!' again. Everyone laughed. Someone got up from the bench and with the flat of his hand, whacked Goonga over his head. Goonga sprang at the man, making queer, gurgling noises. Someone else tripped him and sent him sprawling on the ground, and there was more laughter.

Kishen and I sat at a table inside the shop. Everyone, except Goonga, was drinking tea.

'Give Goonga a glass of tea,' said Kishen to the shopkeeper.

The shopkeeper grinned and made the tea. Goonga looked at us and said, 'Goo!'

'Now how much money is left?' asked Kishen, getting down to business.

'About Rs 9. If we are careful, it will last us a few days.'

'More than a week,' said Kishen. 'We can get enough food for a rupee a day, as long as we don't start eating chicken. But you should find some work in a day or two.'

'Don't be too optimistic about that.'

'Well, it's no use worrying as yet.'

There was an interesting story being told by the shopkeeper, about a jinn who used his abnormally long reach to steal sweets, and we forgot about our 'conference' and worries until the story was finished.

'Now it's someone else's turn,' said the shopkeeper.

'The fair boy will tell us one,' said a voice, and everyone turned to look at me.

The person who had made the request was one of the boys who served tea to the customers. He could not have been more than twelve years old, but he had a worldly look about him, in spite of the dimples in his cheeks and the mischievous glint in his eyes. His fair complexion and high cheekbones showed that he came from the hills, from one of the border districts. 'I don't know any stories,' I protested.

'That isn't possible,' said the shopkeeper. 'Everyone knows at least one story, even if it is his own.'

'Yes, tell us,' said the boy from the hills.

'You find us a room for the night,' said Kishen, always ready to bargain in true Punjabi fashion, 'and he'll tell you a story.'

'I don't know of any place,' said the shopkeeper, 'but you are welcome to sleep in my shop. You won't sleep much, because there are people coming and going all night, especially the truck drivers.'

'Don't worry,' said the boy. 'I know of many places where you can stay. Now tell us the story.'

So I embarked on a ghost story which had been popular in school.

Mr Oliver, an Anglo-Indian teacher, was returning to the school, which lay on the outskirts of the hill station of Simla, late one night. From before Kipling's time, the school had been run on English public school lines and the boys, most of them from wealthy Indian families, wore blazers, caps and ties. Mr Oliver had been teaching in the school for several years.

The Simla Bazaar, with its cinemas and restaurants, was about three miles from the school and Mr Oliver, a bachelor, usually strolled into the town in the evening, returning after dark, when he would take a short cut through the pine forest.

When there was a strong wind the pine trees made sad, eerie sounds that kept most people to the main road. But Mr Oliver was not a nervous or imaginative man. He carried a torch and its gleam—the batteries were running down—moved fitfully down the narrow forest path. When its flickering light fell on the figure of a boy, who was sitting alone on a rock, Mr Oliver stopped. Boys were not supposed to be out after dark.

'What are you doing out here?' asked Mr Oliver sharply, moving closer so that he could recognize the miscreant. But even as he approached the boy, Mr Oliver sensed that something was wrong. The boy appeared to be crying. His head hung down, he held his face in his hands, and his body shook convulsively. It was a strange, soundless weeping and Mr Oliver felt distinctly uneasy.

'Well, what's the matter?' he asked, his anger giving way to concern. 'What are you crying for?' The boy would not answer or look up. His body continued to be racked with silent sobbing. 'Come on, boy, you shouldn't be out here at this hour. Tell me the trouble. Look up!' The boy looked up. He took his hands from his face. The light from Mr Oliver's torch fell on the boy's face—if you could call it a face.

It had no eyes, ears, nose or mouth. It was just a round smooth head—with a school cap on top of it! And that's where the story could have ended. But for Mr Oliver it did not end here.

The torch fell from his trembling hand. He turned and scrambled down the path, running blindly through the trees and calling for help. He was still running towards the school buildings when he saw a lantern swinging in the middle of the path. Mr Oliver stumbled up to the watchman, gasping for breath. 'What is it, sahib?' asked the watchman. 'Has there been an accident? Why are you running?'

'I saw something—something horrible—a boy weeping in the forest—and he had no face!'

'No face, sahib?'

'No eyes, nose, mouth—nothing!'

'Do you mean it was like this, sahib?' asked the watchman and raised the lamp to his own face. The watchman had no eyes, no ears, no features at all—not even an eyebrow! And that's when the wind blew the lamp out.

'All right, now tell us,' I said, after my story was over and the audience had drifted away, 'where are we going to sleep tonight? You can't get a hotel room for less than Rs 2.'

'It's not too cold,' said Kishen. 'We can sleep in the maidan. There's shelter there.'

I couldn't help feeling pity on my own plight. A year ago when I had run away from my guardian's house I had slept in the maidan, and now again I was going to sleep in the maidan. That summed up how much 'progress' I had made in life.

'Kishen,' I said, 'The last time I slept in the maidan, it rained. I woke up in a pool of mud.'

'But it won't rain today,' said Kishen cheerfully. 'There isn't a cloud in the sky.'

We looked out at the night sky. The moon was almost at the full, robbing the stars of their glory.

With no other choice before us, we left the shop and began walking towards the open grassland of the maidan. The bazaar was almost empty now, the shops closed, lights showing only from upper windows. I became conscious of the sound of soft footfalls behind us, and looking over my shoulder, saw that we were being followed by Goonga.

'Goo,' said Goonga, on being noticed.

'Damn!' said Kishen. 'Why did we have to give him tea? He probably thinks we are rich and won't let us out of sight again.'

'He'll change his mind about us when he finds us sleeping in the maidan.'

'Goo,' said Goonga once again from behind, quickening his step.

We turned abruptly down an alleyway, trying to shake Goonga off, but he padded after us, chuckling ghoulishly to himself. We cut back to the main road, but he was behind us at the Clock Tower. At the edge of the maidan I turned and said: 'Go away, Goonga. We've got no money, no food, no clothes. We are no better off than you. Go away!'

'Yes, buzz off!' said Kishen, a master of Indo-Anglian slang.

But Goonga merely said, 'Goo!' and took a step forward, his shaved head glistening in the moonlight. I shrugged and led Kishen to the maidan. Goonga stood at the edge, shaking his head and chuckling. His dry black skin showed through his rags, and his feet were covered with mud. He watched us as we walked across the grass, watched us until we lay down, and then he shrugged his shoulders and said, 'Goo,' and went away.

THE OLD CHURCH

'Let us leave our things with the munshi,' I said. 'It's no use collecting them until we have somewhere to stay. But I would like to change my clothes.'

It had been cold in the maidan until the sun threw its first pink glow over the hills. On the grass lay yesterday's remnants—a damp newspaper, a broken toy, a kite hanging helplessly from the branches of a tree. We were sitting on the dewsodden grass, waiting for the sun to seep through to our skin and drive the chill from our bones. We had not slept much, and our eyes were ringed and heavy. Kishen's legs were covered with mosquito bites.

'Why is it that you haven't been bitten as much as I have?' complained Kishen.

'No doubt you taste better,' I replied. 'We had better split up now, I suppose.'

'But why?'

'We will get more done that way. You go to the munshi and see if you can persuade him to let us have another room. But don't pay anything in advance! Meanwhile, I'll call at the schools to see if I can get any English tuitions.'

'All right, Rusty. Where do we meet?'

'At the Clock Tower. At about twelve o'clock.'

'Then we can eat,' said Kishen with enthusiasm. I couldn't help smiling at that.

'Eating is something we always agree upon,' I said.

We washed ourselves at the public tap at the edge of the maidan, where the wrestlers were usually to be found. They had not assembled that morning, and the wrestling pit was empty, otherwise I might have encountered a friend of mine, called Hathi, who often came there to wrestle and use the weights. Scrubbing my back and shoulders at the tap, I realized that I needed a haircut and, worse still, a shave.

'I will have to get a shave,' I said ruefully. 'You're lucky to have only a little fluff on your cheeks so far. I have to shave at least once a week, do you know that?'

'How extravagant!' exclaimed Kishen. 'Can't you grow a beard? A shave will cost four annas.'

'Nobody will give me a tuition if they see this growth on my face.'

'Oh, all right,' grumbled Kishen, stroking the faint beginning of a moustache. 'You take four annas and have your shave, but I will keep the rest of the money with me in case I have to give the munshi something. It will be all right to let him have a rupee or two in advance if he can give us a room.'

I went to the barber's shop and had my shave for four annas. And the barber, who was a friend of mine, and took great pleasure in running his fingers through my hair, gave me a head massage into the bargain.

It was a wonderful massage and included not only my head, but my eyes, neck and forehead as well. The barber was a dark, glistening man, with broad shoulders and a chest like a drum; he wore a fine white Lucknow shirt through which you could see his hard body. His strong fingers drummed and stroked and pressed, and with the palms and sides of his hands he thumped and patted my forehead. I felt the blood rush to my temples, and when the massage was finished, I was hardly conscious of having a head, and walked into the street with a peculiar, elated, headless feeling.

I then made a somewhat fruitless round of the three principal schools. At each of them I was told that if anything in my line turned up, they would certainly let me know. But they did not ask me where I could be found if I was wanted. The last school asked me to call again in a day or two.

On the outskirts of the town I found the old church of St. Paul's, which had been abandoned for over a year due to meagre parish resources and negligible attendance. The Catholics of Dehra had been able to afford the upkeep of their church and convent, but nobody outside Dehra had bothered about St. Paul's, and eventually the padre had locked the building and gone away. I regretted this, not because I had been fond of church-going—I had always disliked large gatherings of people— but because the church was old, with historic and personal associations and I hated to see old things, old people, suffer lonely deaths. The plaster was crumbling, the paint peeling off the walls, moss growing in every crack. Wild creepers grew over the stained-glass windows. The garden, so well-kept once, was now a jungle of weeds and irrepressible marigolds.

I leaned on the gate and gazed at the church. There had been a time when I hated visiting this place, for it had meant the uncomfortable presence of my guardian, the gossip of middle-aged women, the boredom of an insipid sermon. But, now, seeing the neglected church, I felt sorry for it—not only for the people who had been there, but for the place itself, and for those who were buried in the graves that kept each other silent company in the grounds. People I had known lay there, and some of them were people my father had known.

I opened the creaking wooden gate and walked up the overgrown path. The front door was locked. I walked around trying the side doors, finding them all closed. There was no lock on the vestry door, though it seemed to be bolted from within. Two panes of glass were set in the top portion of the door. Standing on my toes, I reached up to them, pressing my fingers against the panes to test the thickness of the glass. I stood back from the door, took my handkerchief from my pocket and wrapped it round my hand. Standing on my toes again, I pushed my fist through one of the panes.

There was a tinkle of falling glass. I groped around and found the bolt. Then I stepped back and kicked at the door.

The door opened. The handkerchief had fallen from my hand and one of my knuckles was bleeding. I picked up the handkerchief and wrapped it round the cut. Then I stepped into the vestry.

The place was almost empty. A cupboard door hung open on one hinge and a few old cassocks lay on a shelf in a dusty pile. An untidy heap of prayer books and hymnals was stacked in a packing-case, and a mouse sat on top of a half-eaten hymnal, watching my intrusion.

I went through the vestry into the church hall, where it was lighter. Sunlight poured through a stained-glass window, throwing patches of mellow orange and gold on the pews and on the frayed red carpet that ran down the aisle. The windows were full of cobwebs. As I walked down the aisle, I broke through cordons of cobwebs, sending the frightening spiders scurrying away across the pews.

I left the church by the vestry door, closing it behind me, and removing the splintered glass from the window, I threw the pieces into the bushes.

Kishen met me at the Clock Tower, and together we went to the chaat shop to have a cheap meal of spiced fruits and vegetables. On the way, Kishen told me that he had been to the munshi again.

'The munshi wouldn't give me a room without an advance of fifteen rupees,' he said. 'But I got our clothes anyway.'

'It doesn't matter about the room. I've found a place to stay.'

'Oh, good! What is it like?'

'Wait till you see it. I had no luck at the schools, though there may be something for me in a day or two. How much money did you say was left?'

'Eight rupees,' said Kishen, looking guilty and stuffing his mouth with potatoes to hide his confusion.

'I thought it was nine rupees,' I said.

'It was nine,' said Kishen. 'But I lost one rupee. I was sure I could win, but those fellows had a trick I didn't know!'

'What!' I was aghast. How could Kishen have been so careless with our meagre funds? 'How did you manage to find company for a game of cards?' I asked, trying not to shout in anger.

'Well,' said Kishen sheepishly, 'it wasn't so difficult. After I left you, I went straight to the munshi's house, but had no luck there. He was only the seth's servant, he insisted, and he had to carry out orders. I made a few insulting remarks about the seth and left.

'I went off into the alleyways behind the bazaar. There were two hours ahead of me before I had to meet you so I was looking for some way to pass time.

'In a courtyard off one of the alleyways were three young men, playing cards. I watched them for a while, until one of the players beckoned to me, inviting me to join the game.

'I was with the card players till twelve o'clock. As you know Rusty, only a Punjabi can make and lose a fortune with both speed and daring. And being a Punjabi myself, I have only proved that I too could do this, in my own, small way.'

'I see,' I said resignedly. 'From now on I'll keep everything.'

Showing no sign of shame Kishen put the notes and coins on the table. I separated the money into two piles, put the notes in my pocket, and pushed six annas across the table to Kishen.

Kishen grinned. 'So you are letting me keep something, after all?'

'That's to pay for the chaat,' I retorted, and his grin turned into a grimace.

We walked to the church, Kishen grumbling a little. However, I felt very cheerful. 'I want a bath,' said Kishen unreasonably. 'How far is this place where you've got a room?'

'I didn't say anything about a room, and there's no place for a bath. But there's a stream not far away, in the jungle behind the road.'

Kishen looked puzzled and scratched his fuzzy head, but he did not say anything, reserving judgement till later.

'Hey, where are you going, Rusty?' he said, when I turned in at the church gate.

'To the church,' I replied.

'What for—to pray?' asked Kishen anxiously. 'I did not know that you were religious.'

'I'm not. This is where we're going to stay.'

Kishen slapped his forehead in astonishment, then burst into laughter. 'The places we stay at!' he exclaimed. 'Railway stations. Maidans. And now cathedrals!'

'It's not a cathedral, it's a church.'

'What's the difference? It's the same religion. A mosque can be different from a temple, but how is a cathedral different from a church?'

I did not try to explain, but led Kishen in through the vestry door. He crept cautiously into the quiet church, looking nervously at the dark, spidery corners, at the high windows, the bare altar; the gloom above the rafters.

'I can't stay here,' he said. 'There must be a ghost in the place.' He ran his fingers over the top of a pew, leaving tracks in the thick dust.

'We can sleep on the benches or on the carpet,' I said, ignoring his protests. 'And we can cover ourselves with those old cassocks.'

'Why are they called cassocks?'

'I haven't the slightest idea.'

'Then don't lecture me about cathedrals. If someone finds out we are staying here, there will be trouble.'

'Nobody will find out. Nobody comes here any more. The place is not looked after, as you can see.

Those who used to come have all gone away. Only I am left, and I never came here willingly.'

'Up till now,' said Kishen. 'Let some air in.'

I climbed on a bench and opened one of the high windows. Fresh air rushed in, smelling sweet, driving away the mustiness of the closed hall.

'Now let's go to the stream,' I said.

We left the church by the vestry door, passed through the unkempt garden and went into the jungle. A narrow path led through the sal trees, and we followed it for about a quarter of a mile. The path had not been used for a long time, and we had to push our way through thorny bushes and brambles. Then we heard the sound of rushing water.

We had to slide down a rock face into a small ravine, and there we found the stream running over a bed of shingle. Removing our shoes and rolling up our trousers, we crossed the stream. Water trickled down from the hillside, from amongst ferns and grasses and wild flowers; and the hills, rising steeply on either side, kept the ravine in shadow. The rocks were smooth, almost soft, and some of them were grey and some yellow. A small waterfall fell across them, forming a deep, round pool of apple-green water.

We removed our clothes and jumped into the pool. Kishen went too far out, felt the ground slipping away from beneath his feet, and came splashing back into the shallows.

'I didn't know it was so deep,' he said.

Soon we had forgotten the problem of making money, had forgotten the rigours of our journey. We swam and romped about in the cold mountain water. Kishen gathered our clothes together and washed them in the stream, beating them out on the smooth rocks, and spreading them on the grass to dry. When we had bathed, we lay down on the grass under a warm afternoon sun, talking spasmodically and occasionally falling into a light sleep.

'I am going to wire to Somi,' I said, 'but I don't know his address.'

'Isn't his mother still here?' said Kishen.

I sat up suddenly. 'I never thought of her. Somi said he was the only one leaving Dehra. She must be here.'

'Then let us go and see her,' said Kishen. 'She might be able to help us.'

'We'll go now.'

We waited until our clothes were dry, and then we dressed

and went back along the forest path. The sun was setting when we arrived at Somi's house, which was about a mile from the church, in the direction of the station.

I missed Sómi's welcoming laughter as I walked up the veranda steps. I found Somi's mother busy in the kitchen. Grey-haired, smiling, and dressed in a simple white sari, she put her hands to her cheeks when she saw us.

'Master Rusty!' she exclaimed. 'And Kishen! Where have you been all these weeks?'

'Travelling,' I said. 'We have been doing a world tour.'

'On foot,' added Kishen.

We sat in cane chairs on the veranda, and I gave Somi's mother an account of our journey, deliberately omitting to mention that we were without work or money. But she had sensed our predicament.

'Are you having any trouble about your room?' she asked.

'We left it,' I said. 'We are staying in a bigger place now.'

'Yes, much bigger,' said Kishen.

'What about that book you were going to write—is it published?'

'No, I'm still writing it,' I said.

'How much have you done?'

'Oh, not much as yet. These things take a long time.'

'And what is it about?'

'Oh, everything I suppose,' I answered, feeling guilty and changing the subject, for my novel had not progressed beyond the second chapter. 'I'm starting another tuition soon. If you know of any people who want their children to learn English, please pass them on to me.'

'Of course I will. Somi would not forgive me if I did not do as you asked. But why don't you stay here? There is plenty of room.'

'Oh, we are quite comfortable in our place,' I lied.

'Oh, yes, very comfortable,' said Kishen, glaring at me.

Somi's mother persuaded us to stay for dinner, and we did not take much persuading, for the aroma of rich Punjabi food had been coming to us from the kitchen. We were prepared to sleep in churches and waiting-rooms all our lives, provided there was always good food to be had—rich, non-vegetarian food, for we scorned most vegetables . . .

We feasted on tandoor bread and buffalo's butter, meat cooked with spinach, vegetables with cheese, a sour pickle of turnip and lemon, and a jug of lassi. We did full justice to the meal, under the watchful eyes of Somi's mother.

'Do you need any money?' she asked, when we had finished.

'Oh, no,' I lied yet again, 'we have plenty of that.'

A painful kick on my right leg from Kishen made me jump up from my seat.

'Enough for a week, anyway,' I continued.

After the meal, I took Somi's address in Amritsar with the intention of writing to him the next day. I also stuffed my pockets with pencils and writing-paper. When we were about to leave, Somi's mother thrust a ten-rupee note into my hand, and I blushed, unable to refuse the money.

Once on the road, I said: 'We didn't come to borrow money, Kishen.' I knew he was smouldering with rage at my refusal to take more money from Somi's mother.

'But you can pay it back in a few days. What's the use of having friends if you can't go to them for help?'

'I would have gone when there was nothing left. Until there is nothing left, I don't want to trouble anyone.'

We walked back to the church, buying two large candles on the way. I lit one candle at the church gate and led the way down the dark, disused path.

NEW ENCOUNTERS

'It's creepy here,' said Kishen, keeping close to me. 'So quiet. I think we should go back and stay at Somi's house. Also, it must be wrong to sleep in a church.'

'It is no more wrong than sleeping in a tree.'

Once we were inside, I placed the burning candle on the altar steps. A bat swooped down from the rafters and Kishen ducked under a pew. 'I would rather sleep in the maidan,' he said.

'It's better here,' I insisted. I brought out a bundle of cassocks from the vestry and dumped them on the floor. 'Now, I'll do some writing,' I declared, sitting down near the candle and producing pencil and paper from my pocket.

Kishen sat down on a bench and removed his shoes, rubbing his feet and playing with his toes. When he had got used to the bats diving overhead, he stood up and undressed. Long and bony in his vest and underpants, he sat down on the pile of cassocks, and with his elbows resting on his knees, and his chin cupped in the palms of his hands, he watched me write.

I was rudely awakened by a yelp from Kishen in the early hours of the morning.

'I've been bitten,' he said urgently as I tried to surface from the cassocks. 'I've been bitten on my toes by a church mouse.'

'At least it isn't a cathedral rat,' I said. 'I've had one crawling over me all night.' I shook out the cassocks, and with a squeak, a mouse leapt from the clothes and made a dash for safety.

Kishen put out his hand and touched my shoulder. He looked reassured by my presence, and he drew nearer and went to sleep with his arm around me.

We rose before the sun was up, and went straight to the pool. It was a cold morning. The water was startlingly ice cold. As we swam about, the sun came striking through the sal trees, making emeralds of the dewdrops, and pouring through the clear water till it touched the yellow sand. I felt the sun touch my skin, felt it sink deep into my blood and bones and marrow, and, exulting in it, I hurled myself at Kishen. We tumbled over in the water, going down with a wild kicking of legs, and came spluttering to the surface, gasping and shouting. Then we lay on the rocks till we were dry.

We then left the pool and walked to the maidan.

Every morning a group of young men wrestled at one end of the maidan, in a pit of soft, newly-dug earth. Hathi was one of the wrestlers. He was like a young bull, with a magnificent chest and great broad thighs. His light brown hair and eyes were quite a contrast to the rest of his dark body.

We found him at the tap, washing the mud and oil from his body, pummelling himself with resounding slaps. Obviously, he had just finished his bout of wrestling for the morning. When he looked up and saw us, he left the tap running, and gave me an exuberant wet hug, transferring a fair amount of mud and oil on to my already soiled shirt.

'My friend! Where have you been all these weeks? I thought you had forgotten me. And Kishen bhaiya, how are you?'

Kishen received the bear-hug with a grumble: 'I've already had my bath, Hathi.'

But Hathi continued talking while he put on his shirt and pyjamas. 'You are just in time to see me, as I am going away in a day or two,' he said.

'Where are you going?' I asked.

'I'm going to my village in the hills. I have land there, you know—I am going back to look after it. Come and have tea with me—come!'

He took us to the tea shop near the Clock Tower, where he mixed each of us a glass of hot milk, honey and beaten egg. The morning bath had refreshed us and we were feeling quite energetic.

'How do you get to your village?' I asked. 'Is there a motor road?'

'No. The road ends at Landsdowne. From there one has to walk about thirty miles. It is a steep road, and you have to cross two mountains, but it can be done in a day if you start out early enough. Why don't you come with me?' he asked suddenly. 'There you will be able to write many stories. That is what you want to do, isn't it? There will be no noise or worry.'

'I can't come just now,' I replied. 'Maybe later, but not now.'

'You come too, Kishen,' pressed Hathi. 'Why not?'

'Kishen would be bored by mountains,' I said teasingly.

'How do you know?' said Kishen, looking annoyed.

'Well, if you want to come later,' said Hathi, 'you have only to take the bus to Lansdowne, and then take the north-east road for the village of Manjari. You can come whenever you like. I will be living alone.'

'If we come,' I said, 'we should be of some use to you there.'

'I will make farmers of you!' exclaimed Hathi, slapping himself on the thigh.

'Kishen is too lazy.'

'And Rusty too clumsy.'

'Well, maybe we will come,' I said. 'But first I must see if I can get some sort of work here. I'm going to one of the schools again today. What will you do, Kishen?'

Kishen shrugged. 'I'll wait for you in the bazaar.'

'Stay with me,' said Hathi. 'I have nothing to do except recover money from various people. If I don't get it now, I will never get it.'

The school to which I had been (the visit proved fruitless) stood near the dry river-bed of the Rispana, and on the other side of the river-bed lay mustard fields and tea gardens. As I had more than an hour left before meeting Kishen, I crossed the sandy river-bed and wandered through the fields. A peacock ran along the path with swift, ungainly strides.

A small canal passed through the tea gardens, and I followed the canal, counting the horny grey lizards that darted in and out of the stones. I picked a tea leaf from a bush and holding it to my nose, found the smell sweet and pleasant. When I had walked about a mile, I came to a small clearing. There was a house in the clearing, surrounded by banana and poinsettia trees, the poinsettia leaves hanging down like long red tongues of fire. Bougainvillaea and other creepers covered the front of the house.

Sitting in a cane chair on the veranda was an Englishman. At least, he seemed to be an Englishman. He may have been a German or an American or a Russian, but the only Europeans I had known in Dehra were Englishmen, so I immediately took the white-haired gentleman in the cane chair to be English.

He was elderly, red-faced, dressed in a tweed coat and flannel shorts and thick woollen stockings. An unlit pipe was held between his teeth, and on his knees lay a copy of the *Times Literary Supplement*.

The last Englishman I had interacted with had been my guardian, and I had hated him. But the old man in the chair seemed, somehow, bluff and amiable. Cautiously I advanced up the veranda steps, then waited for the old man to look up from his paper.

The old man did not look up, but he said, 'Yes, come in, boy. Pull up a chair and sit down.'

'I hope I'm not disturbing you,' I said.

'You are, but it doesn't matter. Don't be so self-effacing.' He looked up at me, and his grey eyes softened a little, but he did not smile; it must have been too much trouble to remove the pipe from his mouth.

I pulled up a chair and sat down awkwardly, twiddling my thumbs. The old man looked me up and down, said, 'Have a drink, I expect you're old enough,' and producing another glass from beneath the table, poured out two fingers of Solan whisky into my glass. He poured three fingers into his own glass. Then, from under the table, he produced two soda-water bottles and an opener. The bottle-tops flew out of the veranda with loud pops, and the golden liquid rose fuzzily to the top of the glass.

'Cheers,' he said, tossing down most of his drink. 'Pettigrew is the name. They used to call me Petty, though, down in Bangalore.'

'I'm pleased to meet you, Mr Pettigrew,' I said politely. 'Is this your house?'

'Yes, the house is mine,' said Mr Pettigrew, knocking out his pipe on the table. 'It's all that is still mine—the house and my library. These gardens were mine once, but I only have a share in them now. It's third-grade tea, anyway. Only used for mixing.'

'Isn't there anyone to look after you?' I asked, noticing the emptiness of the house.

'Look after me!' exclaimed Pettigrew indignantly. 'Whatever for? Do you think I'm a blooming invalid! I'm seventy, my boy, and I can ride a horse better than you can sit a bicycle!'

'I'm sure you can,' I replied hastily. 'And you don't look a year older than sixty. But I suppose you have a servant.'

'Well, I always thought I had one. But where the blighter is half the time, I'd like to know. Running after some wretched woman, I suppose.' A look of reminiscence passed over his face. 'I can remember the time when I did much the same thing. That was in the Kullu valley. There were two things Kullu used to be famous for—apples and pretty women!' He spluttered with laughter, and his face became very red. I was afraid the old man's big blue veins were going to burst.

'Did you ever marry anyone?' I asked.

'Marry!' exclaimed Pettigrew. 'Are you off your head, young fellow? What do you think a chap like me would want to marry for? Only invalids get married, so that they can have someone look after them in their old age. No man's likely to be content with one woman in his life.'

He stopped then, and looked at me in a peculiar defiant way, and I gathered that the old man was not really as cynical as he sounded.

'You're Harrison's boy, aren't you?' he asked suddenly.

'He was my guardian,' I replied. 'How did you know?'

'Never mind, I know. You ran off on your own a year ago, didn't you? Well, I don't blame you. Never could stand Harrison myself. Awful old bounder. Never bought a man a drink if he could help it. Guzzled other people's though. Don't blame you for running away. But what made you do it?'

'He was mean and he thrashed me and didn't allow me to make Indian friends. I was fed up. I wanted to live my own life.'

'Naturally. You're a man now. Your father, too, was a fine man.'

'Did you know him?' I was quite surprised to find someone who claimed to be acquainted with my father.

'Of course I knew him. He managed this estate for me once. I wanted to meet you before, but Harrison never gave me the opportunity.'

'It was just chance that brought me this way.'

'I know. That's how everything happens.'

'Tell me whatever you can about my father,' I said.

'Well, he was a good friend of mine, and we saw quite a lot of each other. He was interested in birds and insects and wild flowers—in fact, anything that had to do with natural history. Both of us were great readers and collectors of books, and that was what brought us together. But what I've been wanting to tell you is this: before he passed away, he had spent a couple of months with an aunt and uncle of yours in the hills—near some village in Garhwal. He was ill with malaria then. And it was probably malaria which caused his death a few months later. Well, I may be wrong, but I think that your father probably guessed that he had not much time to live. So if there was anything of value that your father may have wanted you to have, he'd have left it in the keeping of this couple. He trusted them—he trusted them a great deal. It was only recently that I heard of your uncle's death. But perhaps that aunt of yours still lives in that house.'

'What is her name?' I asked.

'I don't remember. I never saw her myself. But I do know she lived in the hills, where she had some land of her own.'

'Do you think I should look for her?' I asked, surprised at my growing interest and enthusiasm.

'It might be a good idea,' replied Mr Pettigrew, 'She must be about fifty-five now. I think she lived in a small house on the banks of the river, about forty miles from Lansdowne. You'll have to walk much of the way from Lansdowne.'

'I'm used to walking. I have a Garhwali friend; perhaps he can help me.' I was thinking of Hathi. I rose to go, anxious to tell Kishen and Hathi about this new development.

'Don't be in a hurry,' said Mr Pettigrew. 'Have you got any money?'

'A little.'

'Well, if you need any help, remember I'm here. I was your father's friend, you know.'

'Thank you, Mr Pettigrew. I'll see you again before I leave.'

PROSPECT OF A JOURNEY

I waited at the Clock Tower for almost an hour, until it was nearly one o'clock. I had been feeling slightly impatient, not because I was anxious about Kishen, but because I wanted to tell him about Mr Pettigrew and the aunt in the hills. I presumed Kishen was loafing about somewhere in the bazaar with Hathi, or spending money at the Sindhi Sweet Shop. This did not worry me as I had kept most of the money; but one never knew what indiscretions Kishen might indulge in.

I leant against the wall of the Clock Tower, watching the peddlars move lazily about the road, calling out their wares in desultory, afternoon voices; the toy-seller, waiting for the schools to close for the day and spill their children out into the streets; the fruit-vendor, with his basket of papayas, oranges, bananas and Kashmiri apples, which he continually sprinkled with water to make them look fresh; a cobbler drowsing in the shade of the tamarind tree, occasionally fanning himself with a strip of uncut leather. I saw them all, without being very conscious of their existence, for my thoughts were far away, visualizing a strange person in the mountains.

A tall Sikh boy with a tray hanging by a string from his

shoulders, approached me. He stopped near me, but did not ask me if there was anything I wanted to buy. He stopped only to look at me, I think.

We stared at each other for a minute with mutual interest. He wore a bright red turban, broad white pyjamas and black Peshawari chappals which had been left unbuckled. He stood tall and upright, and his light brown eyes were friendly and direct. In the tray hanging from his neck lay an assortment of goods—combs, buttons, key-rings, reels of thread, bottles of cheap perfume, soaps and hair oils. It was the first time we had set eyes on each other, but there was a compelling expression in the stranger's eyes, a haunting, half-sad, half-happy quality that held my attention, appealing to some odd quirk in my nature. The atmosphere was charged with this quality of sympathy.

A crow flapped down between us, and the significance of the moment vanished, and the bond of sympathy was broken.

I turned away, and the Sikh boy wandered on down the road.

After waiting for another ten minutes, I left the Clock Tower and began walking in the direction of the church, thinking that perhaps Kishen had gone there instead. I had not walked far when I found the Sikh boy sitting in the shade of a mango tree with his tray beside him and a book in his hands. I paused to take a look at the book. It was Goldsmith's *The Traveller*. That gave me enough confidence to start a conversation with the boy.

'Do you like the book?' I asked.

The Sikh looked up with a smile. 'It is in my Intermediate course. My exams begin next month. But I read other books too,' he added.

'But when do you go to school?' I asked, looking at the tray which was obviously his means of livelihood.

'In the evening there are classes. During the day I sell this rubbish. I make enough to eat and to pay for my tuition. My name is Devinder.'

'My name is Rusty.'

I leant against the trunk of the mango tree. 'What about your parents, Devinder?' By now I was well versed with the formalities of Indian life. I knew that it was a common and accepted practice for strangers to know each other's personal history before they became friends.

'My parents are dead,' said Devinder. He spoke bluntly. 'They were killed during Partition in 1947, when we had to leave the Punjab. I was looked after in the refugee camp. But I prefer to be on my own, like this. I am happier this way.'

'And where do you stay?'

'Anywhere,' he replied, closing the book and standing up. 'In somebody's kitchen or veranda, or in the maidan. During the summer months it doesn't matter where I sleep, and in the winter people are kind and find some place for me.'

'You can sleep with us,' I said impulsively. 'But I live in a church. I've been there since yesterday. It isn't very comfortable, but it's big.'

'Are you a refugee too?' asked Devinder with a smile.

'Well, I'm a displaced person all right.'

We began walking down the road. We walked at a slow, easy pace, stopping now and then to sit on a wall or lean against a gate as we were not in a hurry to get anywhere.

Soon I began to tell Devinder all about myself. I also told him about Kishen who might be waiting for me at the church. But I did not find Kishen at the church. I began to really worry, but there was nothing I could do except wait for him. Devinder left his tray in the church and we went to the pool. We bathed and lay in the sun.

Goonga must have been following me again, for he was sitting on the vestry steps when Devinder and I returned to the church. 'Goo,' he said, chuckling at his own cunning.

'Now I suppose he'll stay here too,' I said, a little exasperated.

Night fell, but there was no sign of Kishen. I felt it would be pointless to go out in the dark to search for him, so after laying some cassocks on the floor, Devinder and I made ourselves comfortable. Goonga had appeared yet again. 'Goo!' we heard him say in excitement.

I looked up from the book that I was reading as a shadow fell across the page.

'You!'

It was Kishen finally.

Kishen seemed to be taken aback to find a stranger with me. Devinder had removed his turban, and his long hair fell over his shoulders, giving him a wild, rather dangerous look.

'Where have you been, Kishen?' I asked sternly. 'You did not tell me you would be so late.'

'I was kidnapped,' said Kishen, sitting down on a bench and looking suspiciously at Devinder.

'He is our new member,' I told him. 'He, too, will be staying here from now on. His name is Devinder.'

Kishen gave Devinder a hostile nod. He was inclined to be possessive in his friendships, so he probably resented anyone else being too close to me.

'Is Goonga staying here too?' he asked.

'He followed me again. We can use him as a chowkidar. But tell me, what happened to you?'

'Oh, it's a long story; but let me give you the gist of it.

'While Hathi was engaged at the Sindhi Sweet Shop, arguing with a man about a certain amount of money, I wandered off on my own, lounging about in front of the shops. I was standing in front of a clothes shop when I saw an old family friend, Mrs Bhushan, with her vixenish, fifteen-year-old daughter, Aruna, an old playmate of mine. They were in the shop, haggling with the shopkeeper over the price of a sari. Mrs Bhushan, from what Mummy once told me, has the irksome habit of going from shop to shop, like a bee sampling honey; today she had bales of cloth unfurled for inspection, but she hardly bought anything. Aruna is a dark, thin girl. She has pretty green eyes, and a mischievous smile. I wanted to speak to her, but did not relish the prospect of meeting Mrs Bhushan, who would make things awkward for me, so I turned my back on the shop and looked around for Hathi. I was about to walk away when I felt a heavy hand descend on my shoulder, and turning, found myself looking into the large, disagreeable eyes of Mrs Bhushan.

'Mrs Bhushan is an imposing woman of some thirty-five years and she walks with a heavy determination that keeps people, and even bulls, out of her way. Her dogs, her husband and her servants are all afraid of her and submit to her dictates without a murmur. A masculine woman, she bullies men and children and lavishes most of her affection on dogs. Suri once told me that her cocker spaniels sleep on her bed, and her husband sleeps in the drawing-room.

'"Kishen!" exclaimed Mrs Bhushan, pouncing upon me. "What are you doing here?" And at the same time Aruna saw me, and her green eyes brightened, and she cried, "Kishen! What are you doing here? We thought you were in Hardwar!"

'I felt confused. To have Mrs Bhushan towering over me was like experiencing an eclipse of the sun. Moreover, I did not know how to explain my presence in Dehra. I contented myself with grinning sheepishly at Aruna.

'"Where have you been, boy?" demanded Mrs Bhushan, getting business-like. "Your clothes are all torn and you're a bundle of bones!"

'"Oh, I've been on a walking-tour," I said, though I'm sure I sounded really unconvincing.

'"A walking-tour! Alone?"

'"No, with a friend . . . "

'"You're too young to be wandering about like a vagrant. What do you think relatives are for? Now get into the car and come home with us."

'And she walked with determination towards the pre-war Hillman that stood beneath the tamarind tree. It had once belonged to a British magistrate, who had sold it cheap when he went away after Indian independence. I am sure that Mrs Bhushan's aggressive ways will only serve to shorten the car's life.

'I felt unhappy at the way things were getting out of my control. "What about my friend?" I asked as a last bid to foil Mrs Bhushan's plans.

'"You can see him later, can't you? Come on, Aruna, get in. There's something fishy about this walking-tour business, and I mean to get to the bottom of it!" And she trod on the accelerator with such ferocity that a lame beggar, who had been dawdling in the middle of the road, suddenly regained the use of both legs and sprang nimbly on to the pavement.'

'Can't you cut out the frills and just give us an idea of what happened, Kishen?' I was beginning to feel sleepy yet I wanted to hear about Kishen's experience with the Bhushans.

Kishen grinned and Devinder inched forward to hear the rest. Kishen did know how to keep his audience engrossed.

'When I arrived at Mrs Bhushan's smart white bungalow, I was placed in an armchair and subjected to Mrs Bhushan's own brand of third-degree, which consisted of snaps and snarls and snorts of disapproval. The cocker spaniel, disapproving of my ragged condition, snapped at me.

'Before long, I had told them the whole story of my journey from Hardwar with you, Rusty. Aruna listened to every word, full of admiration for the two of us, but Mrs Bhushan voiced her disapproval in strong terms.

'"Well, this is the end of your wanderings, young man," she said. "You're staying here in this house. I won't have you wandering about the country with a lot of loafers."

'Obviously Mrs Bhushan, who is given to exaggeration, had visualized you not as one person, but as several—an entire gang of tramps . . .!' Kishen said, chuckling to himself.

'And when she saw that I was still hesitant about staying with her, she gave me an ultimatum.

'"Who would you rather stay with?" she demanded. "Your father or me? For, if you don't want to stay with me, I'll see to it that your father comes to fetch you back to Hardwar. It won't be much of a problem to find him and inform him of your whereabouts, your latest activities and the strange company you are keeping these days."

'I had no choice. "I'd like to stay with you," I said.

'Then I spent half an hour under a hot shower, luxuriating in its warmth. It was weeks since I had used soap as I had no proper bath in Hardwar ever since I left my father's house. I lathered myself from head to foot, and watched the effect in the bathroom mirror. My skin began to glow.

'Mrs Bhushan had been nice enough to lend me a pair of Mr Bhushan's pyjamas—strangely though, Mr Bhushan himself was nowhere to be seen. Anyway, I was glad to have his clothes as I couldn't even bear the thought of getting into my dusty old clothes once again.

'Aruna was alone in the dining room, reclining on the carpet. She pulled me down beside her and held my hand.

'"I wish I had been with you," she said.

'"Have you ever slept with a rat?" I asked, wanting to spoil her excitement. "Because I did, last night."

'"What about your friend Rusty? I can ask Mummy to let him stay with us for some time."

'"He won't come."

'"Why not?"

'"He just won't come."

'"Is he too proud?"

'"No, but you are proud. That's why he won't come."

'"Then let him stay where he is."

'"But Aruna, I must go and tell him what has happened. He'll be waiting for me at the Clock Tower."

'"Not today, you won't," said Mrs Bhushan, marching back into the room with a pink pyjama over her shoulder. "You can see him tomorrow when we drive you over in the car. I'm sure he can look after himself all right. If he had any sense, he'd have taken you home when he found you. The fellow must be an absolute rogue!" And with that compliment to you the argument ended.

'So, for the rest of the day, I was held prisoner in Mrs Bhushan's comfortable drawing-room where Aruna kept me company, feeding me chicken curry and soft juicy papayas.

'In Aruna's company for a few hours, I managed to forget my desire to meet you. We played carrom and listened to the radio. Forgetting—or pretending to forget—that we are almost grown-up people, we began wrestling on the white Afghan carpet until Mrs Bhushan, who had been visiting the neighbours to tell them about me (no doubt), came home and lifted us off the carpet by the scruffs of our necks.

'Aruna had to do her school homework, so she got me to help her with arithmetic.'

Kishen paused abruptly. He seemed to be at a loss for words. Ignoring the curious Devinder, he smiled a little foolishly and said, 'You know what, Rusty? As I leant over Aruna, explaining sums which I did not understand, I became acutely conscious of the scent of her hair and the proximity of her right ear, and the sum gradually lost its urgency. The right ear with its soft creamy lobe, was excruciatingly near. I . . . I was tempted to bite it.'

I burst out laughing. It was too funny to see Kishen (who was usually so shameless and nonchalant) now squirming in embarrassment. Devinder smiled.

'So what happened next, Kishen?' I asked. 'Did you succumb to that temptation?'

'All I could manage to say was, "You have a nice ear, Aruna," and Aruna smiled—not at me, but at the sum.'

I burst out laughing again. This time, Devinder too laughed.

'But at night,' continued Kishen, to put an end to our laughter, 'I was plagued by the intolerable vision of you sitting alone in the empty church, waiting for me.

'I was sleeping in a separate room. Mrs Bhushan and Aruna slept together in the big bedroom. (Mr Bhushan, I learnt later, was in Delhi, enjoying a week's freedom.) I had only to open my window and slip out into the garden.

'I crept quietly out of bed and went slowly to the bedroom door. Opening it slowly, I peered into the other room. Mrs Bhushan lay flat on her back, her bosom heaving as though it were in the throes of a minor earthquake, her breath making strange, whistling sounds. There was no likelihood of her waking up. But Aruna was wide awake. She sat up in bed, staring at me.

'I put a finger to my lips and approached the bed.

'"I'm going to see Rusty," I whispered. "I will come back before morning."

'I found her hand, and gave it a squeeze. Then I left the room, climbing out of the window and running down the path to the gate. I kept running until I reached this church. That's how I happened to pass my day. But Rusty, Mrs Bhushan will be sure to arrive here in the morning. What should I do then?'

'You never trouble to make up your own mind, do you, Kishen?'

'I don't want to live with relatives.'

'But we can't wander about aimlessly for ever.'

'We have stopped wandering now,' he argued.

'You have. I think I must go away again. There is a relative of mine living in the hills. Perhaps she can help me.'

'Then I am definitely going with you!' exclaimed Kishen.

'And if I do not find her, what happens? We will both be stuck on a mountain without anything. If you stay here, you might be able to help me later.'

'Well, when you are going?' he asked impatiently.

'As soon as I collect some money.'

'I will try to get some from Mrs Bhushan, she has plenty, but she is a miser. Will he go with you?' said Kishen, looking at Devinder.

'I cannot go,' said Devinder. 'I have my examinations in a month.'

Kishen kicked off his shoes and made himself comfortable on a pew. I began reading aloud from *The Traveller*, and everyone listened—Kishen, with his feet stuck upon a pew-support; Devinder, with his chin resting on his knees; and Goonga (not understanding a word) grinning in the candlelight.

Next morning Devinder, Kishen and I went down to the pool to bathe. The smell of the neem trees, the sound of the water, the touch of the breeze intoxicated us, filled us with a zest for living. We ran over the wild wood-sorrel, over the dew-drenched grass down to the water.

Goonga, who on principal refused to bathe, was already there and now sat on top of the rocks, looking on with detached amusement at us swimming in the pool and wrestling in the shallow water.

Devinder could stand in the deepest part of the pool and still have his head above water. To keep his long hair out of the way, he tied it in a knot, like a bun, on top of his head. His hair was almost auburn in colour, his skin was a burnished gold. He slipped about in the water like a long glistening fish.

Kishen began making balls from loose mud, which he threw at Devinder and me. A mud fight ensued. It was like playing with snowballs, but more messy.

We were a long time at the pool. When we returned to the church a Hillman had been parked at the gate and an impatient and irate Mrs Bhushan was sitting at the wheel. She looked determined to be belligerent, but seeing Kishen accompanied not only by me but by two other dangerous-looking youths, her worst fears must have been confirmed. So she visibly changed her tactic; she must have felt that discretion would be the better part of valour.

'Kishen, my son,' she pleaded, 'we have been worrying about you very much. You should not have left without telling us! Aruna is very unhappy.'

Kishen stood sulkily near us.

'You had better go, Kishen,' I said. 'You will be of more help to me if you stay with Mrs Bhushan.'

'But when will I see you?'

'As soon as I come back from the hills.'

Once Kishen was in the car, I confronted Mrs Bhushan and said, 'He won't leave you now. But if he is not happy with you, we will come and take him away.'

'We are his friends,' said Mrs Bhushan.

'No, you are like a relative. We are his friends.'

Kishen said, 'If you don't come back soon, Rusty, I will start looking for you.' He scowled affectionately at me and waved to Devinder and Goonga as the car took him away.

'He might run back again tonight,' said Devinder.

'He will get used to Mrs Bhushan's house,' I replied. 'Soon he will be liking it. He will not forget us, but he will remember us only when he is alone. We are only something that happened to him once upon a time. But we have changed him a little. Now he knows there are others in the world besides himself.'

'I could not understand him,' said Devinder. 'But still I liked him a little.'

'I understood him,' I said, 'and still I liked him.'

THE LAFUNGA

'If you have nothing to do,' said Devinder, 'will you come with me on my rounds?'

'Sure, but first we will see Hathi. If he has not left yet, I can accompany him to Lansdowne.'

I set out with Devinder in the direction of the bazaar. As it was early morning, the shops were just beginning to open. Vegetable vendors were busy freshening their stock with liberal sprinklings of water, calling their prices and their wares. Children dawdled in the road on their way to school, playing hopscotch or marbles. Girls going to college chattered in groups like gay, noisy parrots.

Men cycled to work, and bullock-carts came in from the villages, laden with produce. The dust, which had taken all night to settle, rose again like a mist.

We stopped at the tea shop to eat thickly buttered buns and drink strong, sweet tea. Then we looked for Hathi's room, and found it above a clothes shop, lying empty, with its doors open. The string bed was propped up against a wall. On shelves and window-ledges, in corners and on the floor, lay little coloured toys made of clay—elephants and bulls, horses and peacocks and images of Krishna and Ganesha—a blue Krishna, with a flute to his lips, a jolly Ganesha with a delightful little trunk. Most of the toys were rough and unfinished, more charming than the completed pieces. The finished products would probably go on sale in the bazaar.

It came as a surprise to me to discover that Hathi, the big wrestler, made toys for a living. I had not imagined there would be delicacy and skill in my friend's huge hands. The pleasantness of the discovery offset my disappointment at finding Hathi had gone.

'He has left already?' I said. 'Never mind. I know he will welcome me even if I arrive unexpectedly.'

I left the bazaar with Devinder, making for the residential part of the town. As I would be leaving Dehra soon, there was no point in my visiting the school again. Later, though, I would see Mr Pettigrew.

When we reached the Clock Tower, someone whistled to us from across the street, and a tall young man came striding towards us.

He looked taller than Devinder, mainly because of his long legs. He wore a loose-fitting bush-shirt that hung open in front. His face was long and pale, but he had quick, devilish eyes, and he smiled disarmingly.

'Here comes Sudheer the Lafunga,' whispered Devinder. 'Lafunga means loafer. He probably wants some money. He is the most charming and the most dangerous person in town.' Aloud, he said, 'Sudheer, when are you going to return the twenty rupees you owe me?'

'Don't talk that way, Devinder,' said the Lafunga, looking offended. 'Don't hurt my feelings. You know your money is safer with me than it is in the bank. It will even bring you dividends, mark my words. I have a plan that will come off in a few days, and then you will get back double your money. Please tell me, who is your friend?'

'We stay together,' said Devinder, introducing me. 'And he is bankrupt too, so don't get any ideas.'

'Please don't believe what he says of me,' said the Lafunga with a captivating smile that showed his strong teeth. 'Really, I am not very harmful.'

'Well, completely harmless people are usually dull,' I said.

'How I agree with you! I think we have a lot in common.'

'No, he hasn't got anything,' put in Devinder.

'Well then, he must start from the beginning. It is the best way to make a fortune. You will come and see me, won't you, Mr Rusty? We could make a terrific combination, I am sure. You are the kind of person people trust! They take only one look at me and then feel their pockets to see if anything is missing!'

Instinctively I put my hand to my own pocket, and all three of us laughed.

'Well, I must go,' said Sudheer, now certain that Devinder was not likely to produce any funds. 'I have a small matter to attend to. It may bring me a fee of twenty or thirty rupees.'

'Go,' said Devinder. 'Strike while the iron is hot.'

'Not I,' said the Lafunga, grinning and moving off. 'I make the iron hot by striking.'

'Sudheer is not too bad,' said Devinder as we walked away from the Clock Tower. 'He is a crook, of course—a 420—but he would not harm people like us. As he is quite well educated, he manages to gain the confidence of some well-to-do-people, and acts on their behalf in matters that are not always respectable. But he spends what he makes, and is too generous to be successful.'

We had reached a quiet, tree-lined road, and walked in the shade of neem, mango, jamun and eucalyptus trees. Clumps of tall bamboo grew between the trees. Some marigolds grew wild on the footpath, and Devinder picked two of them, giving one to me.

'There is a girl who lives at the bottom of the road,' he said. 'She is pretty. Come with me and see her.'

We walked to the house at the end of the road and while I stood at the gate, Devinder went up the path. He stood at the bottom of the veranda steps, a little to one side, where he could be seen from a window, and whistled softly.

Presently a girl came out on the veranda. When she saw Devinder she smiled. She had a round, fresh face and long black hair, and she was not wearing any shoes.

Devinder gave her the marigold. She took it in her hand and not knowing what to say, ran indoors.

That morning we walked about four miles. Devinder's customers ranged from decadent maharanis and the wives of government officials to gardeners and sweeper women. Though his merchandise was cheap, the well-to-do were more finicky about the price than the poor. And there were a few who bought things from Devinder because they knew his circumstances and liked what he was doing.

A small girl with flapping pigtails came skipping down the road. She stopped to stare at me as though I were something quite out of the ordinary, but not unpleasant.

I took the marigold from my pocket and gave it to her. It was a long time since I had been able to make anyone a gift.

After some time we parted, Devinder going back to the town, while I crossed the river-bed. I walked through the tea gardens until I found Mr Pettigrew's bungalow.

The old man was not on the veranda, but a young servant gave me a salaam and asked me to sit down.

Apparently Mr Pettigrew was having his bath.

'Does he always bathe in the afternoon?' I asked.

'Yes, the sahib likes his water to be put in the sun to get warm. He does not like cold baths or hot baths. The afternoon sun gives his water the right temperature.'

I walked into the drawing-room and nearly fell over a small table. The room was full of furniture and pictures and bric-a-brac. Tiger-heads, stuffed and mounted, snarled down at me from the walls. On the carpet lay several cheetal skins, a bit worn at the sides. There were several shelves filled with books bound in morocco or calf. Photographs adorned the walls—one of a much younger Mr Pettigrew standing over a supine leopard, another of Mr Pettigrew perched on top of an elephant, with his rifle resting on his knees . . . I wondered how such an active shikari ever found time for reading. While I was gazing at the photographs, Pettigrew himself came in, a large bathrobe wrapped round his thin frame, his grizzly chest looking very raw and red from the scrubbing he had just given it.

'Ah, there you are!' he said. 'The bearer told me you were here. Glad to see you again. Sit down and have a drink.'

Mr Pettigrew found the whisky and poured out two stiff drinks. Then, still in his bathrobe and slippers, he made himself comfortable in an armchair. I said something complimentary about one of the mounted tiger-heads.

'Bagged it in Assam,' he said. 'Back in 1928, that was. I spent three nights on a machan before I got a shot at it.'

'You have a lot of books,' I observed.

'A good collection, mostly flora and fauna. Some of them are extremely rare. By the way,' he said, looking around at the wall, 'did you see the picture I have of your father?'

'Where is it?' I asked.

'He's in that group photograph over there,' said Mr Pettigrew, pointing to a picture on the wall.

I went over to the picture and saw three men dressed in white shirts and flannels, holding tennis rackets and looking very self-conscious.

'He's in the middle,' said Pettigrew. 'I'm on his right.'

I didn't need him to point out my father. Of course, he looked much younger in the picture and he was the only player who was smiling. Mr Pettigrew, sporting a fierce moustache, looked as though he was about to tackle a tiger with his racket. The third person was bald and uninteresting.

'Of course, he's very young in that photo,' said Pettigrew. 'It was taken long before you were ever thought of—before your father married.'

I did not reply. I was trying to imagine Father in action on a tennis court, and wondered if he was a better player than Pettigrew.

'Who was the best player among you?' I asked.

'Ah, well, we were both pretty good, you know. Except for poor old Wilkie on the left. He got in the picture by mistake.'

'Did my father talk much those days?' I asked. As far as I knew him, he had been quiet and thoughtful, yet he had been the one who taught me all about trees, nature, social history in a way that made everything seem so interesting.

'Well, we all talked a lot, you know, especially after a few drinks. He talked as much as any of us. He could sing, when he wanted to. His rendering of the "Kashmiri Love Song" was always popular at parties, but it wasn't often he sang, because he didn't like parties . . . Do you remember it? "Pale hands I loved beside the Shalimar . . ."'

Pettigrew began singing in a cracked, wavering voice, and I was forced to take my eyes off the photograph. Half-way through the melody, Pettigrew forgot the words, so he took another gulp of whisky and began singing 'The Rose of Tralee'. The sight of the old man singing love songs in his bathrobe, with a glass of whisky in his hand, made me smile.

'Well,' he said, breaking off in the middle of the song, 'I don't sing as well as I used to. Never mind. Now tell me, boy, when are you going to Garhwal?'

'Tomorrow, perhaps.'

'Have you any money?'

'Enough to travel with. I have a friend in the hills with whom I can stay for some time.'

'And what about money?'

'I have enough.'

'Well, I'm lending you twenty rupees,' he said, thrusting an envelope into my hands. 'Come and see me when you return, even if you don't find what you're looking for.'

'I'll do that, Mr Pettigrew.'

The old man looked at me for some time, as though summing me up.

'You don't really have to find out much about your father,' he said. 'You're just like him, you know.'

The next day—the day of my departure—Devinder handed me twenty rupees. I was too surprised to say anything. How Devinder had managed to get me this sum I could not understand. Seeing the bewildered look on my face, he smiled. 'Don't worry, Rusty. I haven't robbed anyone, or anything like that. The Lafunga—I wrangled this amount out of him.'

'But how, Devinder? And when? Besides, did you not tell me that Sudheer only takes money, and never gives any?'

'Well, it wasn't easy. Yesterday when I returned to the bazaar, I found Sudheer at a paan shop, his lips red with betel juice. I went straight to the point.

'"Sudheer," I said, "you owe me twenty rupees. I need that money back, not for myself, but for Rusty, who has to leave Dehra very urgently. You must get me the money by tonight."

'"It will be difficult," he said, scratching his head, "but perhaps it can be managed. He really needs the money? It is not just a trick to get your own money back?"

'"He is going to the hills. There may be money for him there, if he finds the person he is looking for."

'"Well, that's different," said the Lafunga, brightening up. "That makes Rusty an investment. Meet me at the Clock Tower at six o'clock, and I will have the money for you. I am glad to find you making useful friends for a change."

'He stuffed another roll of paan into his mouth, and strolled leisurely down the bazaar road.

'Do you know, as far as appearances go, Sudheer has little to do but loll around in the afternoon sunshine, frequenting tea shops and gambling with cards in small back rooms. All this he does very well—but it does not make him a living.

'To say that he lives on his wits would be an exaggeration. He lives a great deal on other people's wits. The seth, for instance, Rusty—your former landlord, who owns much property and dabbles in many shady transactions—is often represented by the Lafunga in affairs of an unsavoury nature.

'Sudheer came originally from the Frontier, where little value is placed on human life; and while still a boy, he had wandered, a homeless refugee, over the border into India. A smuggler adopted him (or so he says), taught him something of the trade, and introduced him to some of the best hands in the profession. But in a border-foray with the police, Sudheer's foster-father was shot dead, and he was once again on his own. By this time anyway he was old enough to look after himself. With the help of his foster-father's connections, he soon attained the service and confidence of the seth.

'Sudheer is no petty criminal. He practises crime as a fine art, and believes that thieves, and even murderers, have to have certain principles. If he steals, then he steals from a rich man who can afford to be robbed, or from a greedy man who deserves to be robbed. And if he did not rob poor men, it is not because of any altruistic motive—it is because the poor are not worth robbing.

'He is good to friends like me, who are good to him. Perhaps his most valuable friends (according to local gossip), as sources of both money and information, are two dancing girls who practise their profession in an almost inaccessible little road in the heart of the bazaar. Their names are Hastini and Mrinalini. He borrows money from them very freely, and seldom pays back more than half of it.

'I am sure that even this twenty rupees, which he gave me today, has been taken by him from either Hastini or Mrinalini. He has a way with them—probably plays one against the other—and in their eagerness to win his love, I am sure each of these girls would help him generously.'

'Well, that may be true, but it may also be pure speculation on our part, couldn't it?' I asked. 'Anyway, thanks for the money, Devinder. I hope I don't have to spend it, or else we'll have to find a way to either pay the Lafunga or to outwit him!'

TO THE HILLS

In the church, I was suddenly feeling the sadness of one leaving a familiar home and familiar faces. Till now I had been with friends, people who had given me help and comradeship; but now once again I would be on my own, without Kishen or Devinder.

That was the way it had always turned out.

I gave my spare clothes to Goonga because I did not feel like carrying them with me. And I left my books with Devinder.

'Stay here, Devinder,' I said. 'Stay here until I come back. I want to find you in Dehra.'

A breeze from the open window made the light from the candles flicker, and the shadows on the walls leapt and gesticulated; but Devinder stood still, the candle-light playing softly on his face.

'I'm always here, Rusty,' he said.

The northern-bound train was not crowded, because in

December few people went to the hills. I had no difficulty in finding an empty compartment.

It was a small compartment with only two lower berths. Lying down on one of them, I stared out of the far window at the lights across the railway tracks. I fell asleep, and woke only when the train jerked into motion.

Looking out of the window, I saw the station platform slipping away, while the shouts of the coolies and vendors grew fainter until they were lost in the sound of the wheels and the rocking of the carriage. The town lights twinkled, grew distant and were swallowed up by the trees. The engine went panting through the jungle, its red sparks floating towards the stars.

There were four small stations between Dehra and Hardwar, and the train stopped for five or ten minutes at each station. At Doiwala I was woken from a light sleep by a tap at the window. It was dark outside, and I could not make out the face that was pressed against the glass. When I opened the door, a familiar, long-legged youth stepped into the carriage suddenly out of the dark, swiftly shutting the door behind him. It was Sudheer, the Lafunga. Before sitting down, he dropped all the shutters on the side facing the platform.

'We meet again,' he said, sitting down opposite me as the train began to move. 'Don't you remember me? I'm Sudheer. I met you at the Clock Tower with Devinder.'

'Of course I remember you,' I said. 'But what are you doing on this train?'

'I'm going to Hardwar,' said Sudheer, a smile playing about the corners of his mouth. 'On business. Don't ask me for details.'

'Why didn't you get on the train at Dehra?'

'Because I have to use strategy, my friend.' He kicked off his shoes and put his feet up on the opposite bunk. 'And where are you going now?'

'I'm going to the hills to see an aunt.' I wasn't sure if I should confide my plans to Sudheer, but if Devinder could trust him, why not?

'And when will you come back? I suppose you will come back.'

'I'm not sure what I'll do. I want to give myself a chance to be a writer, because I may succeed. It is the only kind of work I really want to do—if you can call it work.'

'Yes, it is work. Real work is what you want to do. It is only when you work for yourself that you really work. I use my eyes and my fingers and my wits. I have no morals and no scruples . . .'

'But you have principles, I think.'

'I don't know about that.'

'You have feelings?'

'Yes, but I pay no attention to them.'

'I cannot do that.'

'You are too noble! Why don't you join me? I can guarantee money, excitement, friendship—my friendship, anyway . . .'

Sudheer leant forward and took my hand. There was earnestness in his manner, and also a challenge.

'Come on. Be with me. I wanted you to be with me since the day I met you. I'm a crook, and I don't have any real friends. I don't ask you to be a crook. I ask you to be my friend.'

'I will be your friend,' I said, taking a sudden liking to Sudheer. I almost said, 'I will be a crook, too,' but thought better of it.

'Why not get down at Hardwar?' asked Sudheer.

'Why not come with me to Lansdowne?'

'I have work in Hardwar.'

'And I in the hills.'

'That is why friends are so difficult to keep.' Sudheer smiled and leant back in the seat. 'All right, then. We will join up later. I will meet you in the hills. Wait for me, remember me, don't put me out of your mind.'

The train drew into a tunnel, and both of us fell silent. Sudheer looked preoccupied; as for myself, I was engrossed in memories of a past and another such tunnel I went through long ago, in the days when my father was alive.

THE LEOPARD

It was almost noon, and the jungle was very still, very silent. Heat waves shimmered along the railway embankment where it cut a path through the tall evergreen trees. The railway lines looked like two straight black serpents disappearing into the tunnel in the hillside.

I stood near the cutting, waiting for the mid-day train. It wasn't a station and I wasn't catching a train. I was waiting so I could watch the steam-engine come roaring out of the tunnel.

I had cycled out of town and taken the jungle path until I had come to a small village. I left the cycle there, and walked over a low, scrub-covered hill and down to the tunnel exit.

I looked up. I could hear in the distance the shrill whistle of the engine. But I couldn't see anything, because the train was approaching from the other side of the hill. But presently a sound like distant thunder came from the tunnel, and I knew the train was coming through. A second or two later the steam-engine shot out of the tunnel, snorting and puffing like some green, black and gold dragon, some beautiful monster out of my dreams. Showering sparks right and left, it roared a challenge to the jungle.

Instinctively I stepped back a few paces. Waves of hot steam struck me in the face. Even the trees seemed to flinch from the noise and heat. And then the train had gone, leaving only a plume of smoke to drift lazily over the tall shisham trees.

The jungle was still again. Nothing moved.

I turned from watching the drifting smoke and began walking along the embankment towards the tunnel. It grew darker the further I walked, and when I had gone about twenty yards it became pitch black. I had to turn and look back at the opening to make sure that there was a speck of daylight in the distance.

Ahead of me, the tunnel's other opening was also a small round circle of light.

The walls of the tunnel were damp and sticky. A bat flew past. A lizard scuttled between the lines. Coming straight from the darkness into the light, I was dazzled by the sudden glare. I put a hand up to shade my eyes and looked up at the scrub-covered hillside, and I thought I saw something moving between the trees.

It was just a flash of gold and black, and a long swishing tail. It was there between the trees for a second or two, and then it was gone.

About fifty feet from the entrance to the tunnel stood a hut. Marigolds grew in front of the hut, and I could see a small vegetable patch at the back.

A man was just settling down on his cot in the small yard in front of the house, perhaps for an afternoon nap. He saw me come out of the tunnel and waited until I was only a few feet away and then said, 'Welcome, welcome. I don't often get visitors. Sit down for a while, and tell me why you were inspecting my tunnel.'

'Is it your tunnel?' I asked.

'It is,' he replied. 'It is truly my tunnel, since no one else will have anything to do with it. I have only lent it to the government. I am the watchman of this tunnel and it is my duty to inspect it and keep it clear of obstacles. Every day, before the train comes through, I walk the length of the tunnel. If all is well, I return to my hut and take a nap. If something is wrong, I walk back up the line and wave a red flag and the engine-driver slows down.

'At night too, I light an oil-lamp and make a similar inspection. If there is any danger to the train, I'd go back up the line and wave my lamp to the approaching engine. If all is well, I'd hang my lamp at the door of my hut and go to sleep.'

I sat down on the edge of the cot.

'I wanted to see the train come through,' I said. 'And then, when it had gone, I decided to walk through the tunnel.'

'And what did you find in it?'

'Nothing. It was very dark. But when I came out, I thought I saw an animal—up on the hill—but I'm not sure, it moved off very quickly.'

'It was a leopard you saw,' said the watchman. 'My leopard.'

'Do you own a leopard too?'

'I do.'

'And do you lend it to the government?'

'I do not.'

'Is it dangerous?'

'Not if you leave it alone. It comes this way for a few days every month, because there are still deer in this jungle, and the deer is its natural prey. It keeps away from people.'

'Have you been here a long time?' I asked.

'Many years. My name is Raghu Singh.'

'Mine is Rusty.'

'There is one train during the day. And there is one train during the night. Have you seen the Night Mail come through the tunnel, Rusty?'

'No. At what time does it come?'

'About nine o'clock, if it isn't late. You could come and sit here with me, if you like. And, after it has gone, I will take you home.'

'I'll ask my father,' I said. 'Will it be safe?'

'It is safer in the jungle than in the town. No rascals out here. Only last week, when I went into the town, I had my pocket picked! Leopards don't pick pockets.'

Raghu Singh stretched himself out on his cot. 'And now I am going to take a nap, my friend. It is too hot to be up and about in the afternoon.'

'Everyone goes to sleep in the afternoon,' I complained. 'My father lies down as soon as he's had his lunch.'

'Well, the animals also rest in the heat of the day. It is only the tribe of boys who cannot, or will not, rest.'

Raghu Singh placed a large banana-leaf over his face to keep away the flies, and was soon snoring gently. I stood up, looking up and down the railway tracks. Then I began walking back to the village.

The following evening, towards dusk, as the flying-foxes swooped silently out of the trees, I made my way to the watchman's hut.

It had been a long hot day, but now the earth was cooling and a light breeze was moving through the trees. It carried with it the scent of mango blossom, and the promise of rain.

Raghu Singh was waiting for me. He had watered his small garden and the flowers looked cool and fresh. A kettle was boiling on an oil-stove.

'I am making tea,' he said. 'There is nothing like a glass of hot sweet tea while waiting for a train.'

We drank our tea, listening to the sharp notes of the tailor-bird and the noisy chatter of the seven-sisters. As the brief twilight faded, most of the birds fell silent. Raghu Singh lit his oil-lamp and said it was time for him to inspect the tunnel. He moved off towards the dark entrance, while I sat on the cot, sipping tea.

In the dark, the trees seemed to move closer. And the night life of the forest was conveyed on the breeze—the sharp call of a barking-deer, the cry of a fox, the quaint tonk-tonk of a nightjar.

And there were some sounds that came from the trees. Creakings, and whisperings, as though the trees were coming alive, stretching their limbs in the dark, shifting a little, flexing their fingers.

Raghu Singh stood outside the tunnel, trimming his lamp. The night sounds were obviously familiar to him for he did not pay them any attention; but like me, he too heard a new sound at that moment. It made him stand still for a few seconds, peering into the darkness. Then, humming softly, he returned to where I was waiting. Ten minutes remained for the Night Mail to arrive.

As the watchman sat down on the cot beside me, that sound reached both of us; quite distinctly this time—a rhythmic sawing sound, as of someone cutting through the branch of a tree.

'What's that?' I whispered. I felt a bit uneasy.

'It's the leopard,' said Raghu Singh. 'I think it's in the tunnel.'

'The train will soon be here.'

'Yes, my friend. And if we don't drive the leopard out of the tunnel, it will be run over by the engine.'

'But won't it attack us if we try to drive it out?' I asked, beginning to share the watchman's concern.

'It knows me well. We have seen each other many times. I don't think it will attack. Even so, I will take my axe along. You had better stay here, Rusty.'

'No, I'll come too. It will be better than sitting here alone in the dark.'

'All right, but stay close behind me. And remember, there is nothing to fear.'

Raising his lamp, Raghu Singh walked into the tunnel, shouting at the top of his voice to try and scare away the animal. I followed close behind, but I found myself unable to do any shouting; my throat had gone quite dry.

We had gone about twenty paces into the tunnel when the light from the lamp fell upon the leopard. It was crouching between the tracks, only fifteen feet away from us. Baring its teeth and snarling, it went down on its belly, tail twitching. I felt sure it was going to spring at us.

Raghu Singh and I both shouted together. Our voices rang through the tunnel. And the leopard, uncertain as to how many terrifying humans were there in front of him, turned swiftly and disappeared into the darkness.

To make sure it had gone, the watchman and I walked the length of the tunnel. When we returned to the entrance, the rails were beginning to hum. The train was coming.

I put my hand to one of the rails and felt its tremor. I heard the distant rumble of the train. And then the engine came round the bend, hissing at us, scattering sparks into the darkness, defying the jungle as it roared through the steep sides of the cutting. It charged straight into the tunnel, thundering past me like the beautiful dragon of my dreams.

And when it had gone, the silence returned and the forest seemed to breathe, to live again. Only the rails still trembled with the passing of the train.

They trembled again to the passing of the same train, almost a week later, when Father and I were both travelling in it.

Father was scribbling in a notebook, doing some accounts. How boring of him, I thought, as I sat near an open window staring out at the darkness. Father was going to Delhi on a trip and had decided to take me along.

The Night Mail rushed through the forest with its hundreds of passengers. The carriage wheels beat out a steady rhythm on the rails. Tiny flickering lights came and went as we passed small villages on the fringe of the jungle.

I heard the rumble as the train passed over a small bridge. It was too dark to see the hut near the cutting, but I knew that we were approaching the tunnel. I strained my eyes, looking out into the night; and then, just as the engine let out a shrill whistle, I saw the lamp.

I couldn't see Raghu Singh, but saw the lamp, and I knew that my friend was out there.

The train went into the tunnel and out again, it left the jungle behind and thundered across the endless plains. And I stared out at the darkness, thinking of the lonely cutting in the forest, and the watchman with the lamp who would always remain a firefly for those travelling thousands, as he lit up the darkness for steam-engines and leopards.

However, that was not my first encounter with leopards. When I was around ten years old, my father had taken me to Mussoorie, where he had an assignment. We spent a couple of months there. While Father and his friend discussed books and politics, I spent most of my time exploring Mussoorie.

I first saw the leopard when I was crossing the small stream at the bottom of the hill.

The ravine was so deep that for most of the day it remained in shadow. This encouraged many birds and animals to emerge from cover during the daylight hours. Few people ever passed that way: only milkmen and charcoal-burners from the surrounding villages. As a result, the ravine had become a little haven of wildlife, one of the few natural sanctuaries left near Mussoorie.

Our host Mr Thatcher lived all by himself. He had been my father's friend since their schooldays, and had recently written to Father, expressing his wish to meet him. Father had felt that this would be a good break for the two of us, as he was just preparing to leave Kathiawar (where he worked as a teacher) to go to Delhi where he was to join the RAF.

Below Mr Thatcher's cottage was a forest of oak and maple and Himalayan rhododendron. A narrow path twisted its way down through the trees, over an open ridge where red sorrel grew wild, and then steeply down through a tangle of wild raspberries, creeping vines and slender bamboo. At the bottom of the hill the path led on to a grassy verge, surrounded by wild dog roses.

The stream ran close by the verge, tumbling over smooth pebbles, over rocks worn yellow with age, on its way to the plains and to the little Sone River and finally to the sacred Ganges.

Nearly every morning, and sometimes during the day, I heard the cry of the barking deer. And in the evening, walking through the forest, I disturbed parties of pheasant. The birds went gliding down the ravine on open, motionless wings. I saw pine martens and a handsome red fox, and I recognized the footprints of a bear.

As I had not come to take anything from the forest, the birds and animals soon grew accustomed to my presence; or possibly they recognized my footsteps.

After some time, my approach did not disturb them.

The langurs in the oak and rhododendron trees, who would at first go leaping through the branches at my approach, now watched me with some curiosity as they munched the tender green shoots of the oak. The young ones scuffled and wrestled with each other while their parents groomed each other's coats, stretching themselves out on the sunlit hillside.

But one evening, as I passed, I heard them chattering in the trees, and I wondered about the cause of their excitement. As I crossed the stream and began climbing the hill, the grunting and chattering increased, as though the langurs were trying to warn me of some hidden danger. A shower of pebbles came rattling down the steep hillside, and I looked up to see a sinewy, orange-gold leopard poised on a rock about twenty feet above me.

It was not looking towards me but had its head thrust attentively forward, in the direction of the ravine. But it must have sensed my presence because it slowly turned its head and looked down at me.

It seemed a little puzzled at my presence there; so I felt a little bold and clapped my hands sharply. Immediately the leopard sprang away into the thickets, making absolutely no sound as it melted into the shadows.

I felt as if I had done some wrong. Perhaps I had disturbed the animal in its quest for food. But a little later I heard the quickening cry of a barking deer as it fled through the forest. The hunt was still on.

When I returned home I told my father about the leopard and its hunt for the deer. 'Probably the deforestation that's been taking place in the surrounding hills has driven the deer into this green valley; the leopard, naturally, followed,' said Father.

It was some weeks before I saw the leopard again, although I was often made aware of its presence. A dry, rasping cough sometimes gave it away. At times I felt almost certain that I was being followed.

Once, when I was late getting home, and the brief twilight gave way to a dark moonless night, I was startled by a family of porcupines running about in a clearing. I looked around nervously and saw two bright eyes staring at me from a thicket. I stood still, my heart banging away against my ribs. Then the eyes danced away and I realized that they were only fireflies.

Soon, I realized that the stream had at least one other regular visitor, a spotted forktail, and though it did not fly away at my approach it became restless if I stayed too long, and then it would move from boulder to boulder uttering a long complaining cry.

I spent an afternoon trying to discover the bird's nest, which I was certain contained young ones, because I had seen the forktail carrying grubs in her bill. The problem was that when the bird flew upstream I had difficulty in following her rapidly enough as the rocks were sharp and slippery.

Eventually I decorated myself with bracken fronds and, after slowly making my way upstream, hid myself in the hollow stump of a tree at a spot where the forktail often disappeared. I had no intention of robbing the bird. I was simply curious to see its home.

By crouching down, I was able to command a view of a small stretch of the stream and the side of the ravine; but I had done little to deceive the forktail, who continued to object strongly to my presence so near her home.

I summoned up my reserves of patience and sat perfectly still for about ten minutes. The forktail quietened down. Out of sight, out of mind. But where had she gone? Probably into the walls of the ravine where, I felt sure, she was guarding her nest.

I decided to take her by surprise and stood up suddenly, in time to see not the forktail on her doorstep but the leopard bounding away with a grunt of surprise! Two urgent springs, and it had crossed the stream and plunged into the forest.

I was as astonished as the leopard, and forgot all about the forktail and her nest. Had the leopard been following me again? I got a little scared and headed back home, trying not to rush back because of fear. 'Do you think the leopard is after me, Father?' I asked my father as soon as I got him alone.

'No Rusty,' said Father. 'Only man-eaters follow humans and, as far as I know, there has never been a man-eater in the vicinity of Mussoorie.'

One day I found the remains of a barking deer which had only been partly eaten. I wondered why the leopard had not hidden the rest of his meal, and decided that it must have been disturbed while eating.

Then, climbing the hill, I met a party of hunters resting beneath the oaks. They asked me if I had seen a leopard. I said I had not. They said they knew there was a leopard in the forest.

Leopard skins, they told me, were selling in Delhi at over 1000 rupees each. Of course there was a ban on the export of skins, but they gave me to understand that there were ways and means . . . I thanked them for their information and walked on, feeling uneasy and disturbed.

The hunters too had seen the carcass of the deer, and they had seen the leopard's pug-marks, so they kept coming to the forest. Almost every evening I heard their guns banging away; for they were ready to fire at almost anything.

'There's a leopard about,' they always told me. 'You shouldn't be walking alone in these parts. You are a small boy, you can't even protect yourself with a gun. Go home now.'

The presence of the hunters caused a few disturbances in a short span of time. There were fewer birds to be seen, and even the langurs had moved on. The red fox did not show itself; and the pine martens, who had become quite bold, now dashed into hiding at my approach. The smell of one human is like the smell of any other, I guess, and how were these innocent creatures supposed to know the difference between the hunters and me?

Then the rains were over and I could lie in the sun, on sweet-smelling grass, and gaze up through a pattern of oak leaves into a blinding blue heaven. And I would delight in the leaves and grass and the smell of things—the smell of mint and bruised clover—and the touch of things—the touch of grass and air and sky, the touch of the sky's blueness.

I thought no more of the men. My attitude towards them was similar to that of the denizens of the forest. These were men, unpredictable, and to be avoided if possible.

On the other side of the ravine rose Pari Tibba, Hill of the Fairies, a bleak, scrub-covered hill where no one lived.

It was said that in the previous century Englishmen had tried building their houses on the hill, but the area had always attracted lightning, due to either the hill's location or due to its mineral deposits; after several houses had been struck by lightning, the settlers had moved on to the next hill, where the town now stands.

To the hillmen it is Pari Tibba, haunted by the spirits of a pair of ill-fated lovers who perished there in a storm; to others it is known as Burnt Hill, because of its scarred and stunted trees.

One day, after crossing the stream, I climbed Pari Tibba—a stiff undertaking, because there was no path to the top and I had to scramble up a precipitous rock-face with the help of rocks and roots that were apt to come loose in my groping hand.

But at the top was a plateau with a few pine trees, their upper branches catching the wind and humming softly. There I found the ruins of what must have been the houses of the first settlers—just a few piles of rubble, now overgrown with weeds, sorrel, dandelions and nettles.

As I walked though the roofless ruins, I was struck by the silence that surrounded me, the absence of birds and animals, the sense of complete desolation.

The silence was so absolute that it seemed to be ringing in my ears. But there was something else of which I was becoming increasingly aware: the strong feline odour of one of the cat family. I paused and looked about. I was alone. There was no movement of dry leaf or loose stone.

The ruins were for the most part open to the sky. Their rotting rafters had collapsed, jamming together to form a low passage like the entrance to a mine; and this dark cavern seemed to lead down into the ground. The smell was stronger when I approached this spot, so I stopped again and waited there, wondering if I had discovered the lair of the leopard, wondering if the animal was now at rest after a night's hunt.

Perhaps he was crouching there in the dark, watching me, recognizing me, knowing me as the boy who walked alone in the forest without a weapon.

I liked to think that he was there, that he knew me, and that he acknowledged my visit in the friendliest way: by ignoring me altogether.

Perhaps I had made him confident—too confident, too careless, too trusting of the humans around him. I did not venture any further; I was too scared to do so. I did not seek physical contact, or even another glimpse of that beautiful sinewy body, springing from rock to rock. It was his trust I wanted, and I think he gave it to me.

But did the leopard, trusting one human, make the mistake of bestowing his trust on others? Did I, by casting out all fear—my own fear, and the leopard's protective fear—leave him defenceless?

Because the next day, coming up the path from the stream, shouting and beating drums, were the hunters. They had a long bamboo pole across their shoulders; and slung from the pole, feet up, head down, was the lifeless body of the leopard, shot in the neck and in the head.

'We told you there was a leopard!' they shouted, in great good humour. 'Isn't he a fine specimen?'

'Yes,' I said. 'He was a beautiful leopard.'

I walked home through the silent forest. It was very silent, almost as though the birds and animals knew that their trust had been violated.

Now, sitting in the train as I remembered all these things, the lines of a poem by D.H. Lawrence sprang to my mind. With each clickety-clack of the train's wheels, the words beat out their rhythm in my mind: 'There was room in the world for a mountain lion and me.'

A NOTE FROM SUDHEER

When the train drew into Hardwar, Sudheer got up and stood near the door.

'I have to go quickly,' he said. 'I will see you again.'

As the engine slowed down and the station lights became brighter, Sudheer opened the carriage door and jumped down to the railway banking.

Alarmed, I ran to the open door and shouted, 'Are you all right, Sudheer?'

'Just worry about yourself!' he called, his voice growing faint and distant. 'Good luck!'

He was hidden from view by a signal box, and then the train drew into the brightly lit, crowded station, and pilgrims began climbing into the compartments.

Two policemen came down the platform, looking in at carriage windows and asking questions. They stopped at my window and asked me if I had a companion during the journey, and gave me an unmistakable description of Sudheer.

'He got off the train long ago,' I lied. 'At Doiwala, I think. Why, what do you want him for?'

'He has stolen one thousand rupees from a seth in Dehra,' said one of the policemen. 'If you see him again, please pull the alarm cord.'

It was only after they left that I noticed a small black notebook lying under the seat on which Sudheer had been sitting. I took it and put it into my pocket, intending to return it to the Lafunga the next time we met.

Two days later, I was in Hathi's house, sitting on a string cot out in the courtyard. There was snow on the tiled roof and in the fields, but the sun was quite warm. The mountains stretched away, disappearing into sky and cloud. I felt as if I belonged there, to the hills and the pine and deodar forests, and the clear mountain streams.

There were about thirty families in the village. There were not many men about, and the few that could be found were either old or inactive. Most young men joined the army or took jobs in the plains, for the village economy was poor. The women remained behind to do the work. They fetched water, kept the houses clean, cooked meals, and would soon be ploughing the fields. The old men just sat around and smoked hookahs and gossiped the morning away.

It had been a long, lonely walk from the bus terminus at Lansdowne to Hathi's village. I had walked fast, because there had been no one to talk to, and no food to be had on the way. But I had met a farmer coming from the opposite direction, and had shared his meal. All the farmer had were some onions and a few chappatis; but I was hungry so I enjoyed the meal. When I had finished, I said goodbye and we went our different ways.

At first I walked along a smooth slippery carpet of pine needles; then the pine trees gave way to oak and rhododendron. It was cool and shady, but after I had done about fifteen miles, the forest ended, the hills became bare and rocky, and the earth the colour of copper. I was thirsty, but there was nothing to drink. My tongue felt thick and furry and I could barely move my lips. All I could do was walk on mechanically, hardly conscious of my surroundings or even of walking.

When the sun went down, a cool breeze came whispering across the dry grass. And then, as I climbed higher, the grass grew greener, there were trees, water burst from the hillsides in small springs, and birds swooped across the path—bright green parrots, tree-pies and paradise flycatchers. I was walking beside a river, above the turbulent water rushing down a narrow gorge. It was a steep climb to Hathi's village; and as it grew dark, I had to pick my way carefully along the narrow path.

As I approached Hathi's house on the outskirts of the village, I was knocked down by a huge Tibetan mastiff. I got up, and Hathi came out of the house and ran to greet me and knocked me over again. Then I was in the house, drinking hot milk. And later I lay on a soft quilt, and a star was winking at me from the skylight.

The house was solid—built of yellow granite—and it had a black-tiled roof. There was an orange tree in the courtyard, and though there were no oranges on it at this time of the year, the young leaves smelt sweet. When I looked around, I saw mountains, blue and white-capped, with dark clouds drifting down the valleys. Pale blue woodsmoke climbed the hill from the houses below, and people drifted about in the warm winter sunshine.

When Hathi and I walked in the hills, we sometimes went barefoot. Once we walked a few miles upstream, and found a waterfall dashing itself down on to smooth rocks fifty feet below. Here the forest was dark and damp, and at night bears and leopards roamed the hillsides. Apparently, when the leopards were hungry, they did not hesitate to enter villages and carry off stray dogs.

Leopards had been on my mind, and I was to encounter one here too. One day I heard the unmistakable hunting-cry of a leopard on the prowl. It was evening, and I was close to the village when I heard the harsh, saw-like cry, something between a grunt and a cough. Then the leopard appeared to my right, slinking through the trees, crouching low, a swift black shadow . . .

There was only one shop in the village, and it also served as the post office—it sold soap and shoes and the barest necessities. When I passed by it, I was hailed by the shopkeeper who was brandishing a postcard. I was surprised to see it addressed to me.

I was even more surprised when I discovered that the card was from Sudheer, the Lafunga.

It said: 'Join me at Lansdowne. I have news of your aunt. We will travel together. I have money for both of us, as I consider you a good investment.'

RUM AND CURRY

Sudheer and I left Lansdowne early one morning, and by the time we reached the oak and deodar forests of Kotli we were shivering with the cold.

'I am not used to this sort of travel,' complained Sudheer. 'If this is a wild goose chase, I will curse you, Rusty. At least we should have had mules to sit on.'

'We are sure to find a village soon,' I said. 'We can spend a night there. As for it being a wild goose chase, it was you who told me that my aunt lived somewhere here. If she is not in this direction, it is all your fault, Lafunga.'

There was little light in the Kotli forest, for the tall, crowded deodars and oaks kept out the moonlight. The road was damp and covered with snails.

It was a relief to find a few small huts clustered together in an open clearing. Light showed from only one of the houses. I rapped on the hard oak door and called out: 'Is anyone there? We want a place to spend the night.'

'Who is it?' asked a nervous, irritable voice.

'Travellers,' said Sudheer. 'Tired, hungry and poor.'

'This is not a dharamsala,' grumbled the man inside. 'This is no place for pilgrims.'

'We are not pilgrims,' said Sudheer, trying a different approach. 'We are road inspectors, servants of the government—so open up, my friend!'

Much ill-natured muttering could be heard before the door opened, revealing an old and dirty man who had stubble on his chin, warts on his feet, and grease on his old clothes.

'Where do you come from?' he asked suspiciously.

'Lansdowne,' I replied. 'We have walked twenty miles since morning. Can we sleep in your house?'

'How do I know you are not thieves?' asked the old man, who did not look very honest himself.

'If we were thieves,' said Sudheer impatiently, 'we would not stand here talking to you. We would have cut your throat and thrown you to the vultures, and carried off your beautiful daughter.'

'I have no daughter here.'

'What a pity! Never mind. My friend and I will sleep in your house tonight. We are not going to sleep in the forest.'

Sudheer strode into the lighted room, but backed out almost immediately, holding his fingers to his nose.

'What dead animal are you keeping here?' he cried.

'They are sheepskins, for curing,' said the old man. 'What is wrong?'

'Nothing, nothing,' said Sudheer, not wishing to hurt our host's feelings so soon; but later he whispered to me, 'There is such a stink, I doubt if we will wake up in the morning.'

We stumbled into the room, and I dumped my bundle on the ground. The room was bare except for dilapidated sheep and deer skins hanging on the walls. There was a small fire in a corner of the room. Sudheer and I got as close to it as we could, stamping our feet and chafing our hands. The old man sat down on his haunches and glared suspiciously at us. Sudheer looked at him, and then at me, and shrugged eloquently.

'May we know your name?' I asked.

'It is Ram Singh,' said the old man grudgingly.

'Well, Ram Singh, my host,' said Sudheer solicitously, 'have you had your meal as yet?'

'I take it in the morning,' said Ram Singh.

'And in the evening?' Sudheer's voice held a note of hope.

'It is not necessary to eat more than once a day.'

'For a rusty old fellow like you, perhaps,' said Sudheer, 'but we have got blood in our veins. Is there nothing here to eat? Surely you have some bread, some vegetables?'

'I have nothing,' said the old man.

'Well, we will have to wait till morning,' said Sudheer. 'Rusty, take out the blanket and the bottle of rum.'

I took the blanket which Hathi had given me out from my bag, and a flask of rum slipped out from the folds. Ram Singh showed unmistakable signs of coming to life.

'Is that medicine you have?' asked the old man. 'I have been suffering from headaches for the last month.'

'Well, this will give you a worse headache,' said Sudheer, gulping down a mouthful of rum and licking his lips. 'Besides, for people who eat only once a day it is dangerous stuff.'

'We could get something to eat,' said the old man eagerly.

'You said you had nothing,' I said teasingly, taking the bottle from Sudheer and putting it to my lips.

'There are some pumpkins on the roof,' said the old man. 'And I have a few potatoes and some spices. Shall I make a curry?'

And an hour later, warmed by rum and curry, we sat round the fire in a most convivial fashion. Sudheer and I had gathered our only blanket about our shoulders, and Ram Singh had covered himself in sheepskins. He had been asking us questions about life in the cities—a life that was utterly foreign to him.

'You are men of the world,' he said. 'You have been in most of the cities of India, you have known all kinds of men and women. I have never travelled beyond Lansdowne, nor have I seen the trains and ships which I hear so much about. I am seventy and I have not seen these things, though I have sons who have been away many years, and one who has even been out of India with his regiment. I would like to ask your advice. It is lonely living alone, and though I have had three wives, they are all dead.'

'If you have had three wives,' said Sudheer, 'you are a man of the world!'

He had his back to the wall, his feet stuck out towards the fire. I was half-asleep, my head resting on Sudheer's shoulder.

'My daughters are all married,' continued Ram Singh. 'I would like to get married again, but tell me, how should I go about it?'

Sudheer laughed out loud. I thought to myself that the old man in his youth must have been as crafty a devil as the Lafunga himself.

'Well, you would have to pay for her, of course,' said Sudheer.

'Tell me of a suitable woman. She should be young, of course. Her nose—what kind of nose should she have?'

'A flat nose,' said Sudheer, without the ghost of a smile. 'The nostrils should not be turned up.'

'Ah! And the shape of her body?'

'Not too manly. She should not be crooked. Do not expect too much, old man!'

'Her head?' asked the old man eagerly. 'What should her head be like?'

Sudheer gave this a moment's consideration. 'The head should not be bald,' he said.

Ram Singh nodded his approval; it looked as if his opinion of Sudheer was going up by leaps and bounds.

'And her colour, should it be white?'

'No, not very white.'

'Black?'

'Not too black. But she would have to be evil-smelling, otherwise she would not stay with you.'

A bear kept us awake during the early part of the night. It clambered up on the roof and made a meal of the old man's store of pumpkins.

'Can it get in?' I asked.

'It comes every night,' said Ram Singh. 'But it is a vegetarian and eats only the pumpkins.'

There was a thud as a pumpkin rolled off the roof and landed on the ground. Then the bear climbed down from the roof and shambled off into the forest.

The fire was glowing feebly, but Sudheer and I were warm beneath our blanket and, being very tired, were soon asleep, despite the efforts of an army of bugs to keep us awake. But at about midnight we were woken by a loud cry and starting up, found the lantern lit, and the old man throwing a fit.

Ram Singh was leaping about the room, waving his arms, going into contortions, and bringing up gurgling sounds from the back of his throat.

'What is the matter?' I shouted. 'Have you gone mad?'

For reply, the old man gurgled and shrieked, and continued his frenzied dance.

'A demon!' he shouted. 'A demon has entered me!'

Sudheer and I exchanged glances, trying hard to not laugh.

'It's the medicine you gave me!' cried Ram Singh. 'The medicine was evil, it is all your doing!' And he continued dancing about the room.

'Should I throw the medicine away?' asked Sudheer.

'No, don't do that!' shouted Ram Singh, appearing normal for a moment. 'Throw yourself on the ground!'

Sudheer obliged and threw himself on the ground.

'On your back!' gasped the old man.

Sudheer turned over on to his back. I simply watched, fascinated.

'Raise your left foot,' ordered the old man. 'Take it in your mouth. That will charm the demon away.'

'I will not put my foot in my mouth,' said Sudheer getting to his feet, having lost faith in the genuineness of the old man's fit. 'I don't think there is any demon in you. It is probably your curry. Have something more to drink, and you will be all right.'

He produced the all but empty flask of rum, made the old man open his mouth, and poured the rest of the spirit down his throat.

Ram Singh choked, shook his head violently, and grinned at Sudheer. 'The demon has gone now,' he said.

'I am glad to know it,' said Sudheer. 'But you have emptied the bottle. Now let us try to sleep again.'

But the cold had come in through the blanket by then, and I found sleep difficult. Instead, I began to think of the purpose of my journey, and wondered if it would not have been wiser to stay in Dehra. Outside, the air was still; the wind had stopped whistling through the pines. Only a jackal howled in the distance. The old man was tossing and turning on his sheepskins.

'Ram Singh,' I whispered. 'Are you awake?'

Ram Singh groaned softly.

'Tell me,' I said, 'have you heard of a woman living alone in these parts?'

'There are many old women here.'

'No, I mean a well-to-do woman. She must be about fifty. At one time she was married to a white sahib.'

'Ah, I have heard of such a woman . . . She was beautiful when she was young, they tell me.'

I kept quiet. I was afraid to ask any further questions, afraid to know too much, afraid of finding out too soon that there was nothing from my father for me and nowhere to go.

'Ram Singh,' I whispered after some time. 'Where does this woman live?'

'She had her house on the road to Rishikesh . . .'

'And the woman, where is she? Is she dead?'

'I do not know, I have not heard of her recently,' said Ram Singh. 'Why do you ask of her? Are you related to the sahib?'

'No,' I lied. 'I have heard of her, that's all.'

Silence. The old man grumbled to himself, muttering quietly, and then began to snore. The jackal was silent, the wind was up again, the moon was lost in the clouds. I felt Sudheer's hand slip into my own and press my fingers. I was surprised to find him awake.

'Forget it,' whispered Sudheer. 'Forget the dead, forget the past. Trouble your heart no longer. I have enough for both of us, so let us live on it till it finishes, and let us be happy, Rusty, my friend, let us be happy . . .'

I did not reply, but held the Lafunga's hand and returned the pressure of his fingers to let him know that I was listening.

'This is only the beginning,' said Sudheer. 'The world is waiting for us.'

I woke first. Looking up at the skylight, I saw the first glimmer of dawn. Without waking Sudheer or the old man, I unlatched the door and stepped outside.

Before me lay a world of white.

It had snowed in the early hours of the morning while we had been sleeping. The snow lay thick on the ground, carpeting the hillside. There was not a breath of wind; the pine trees stood blanched and still, and a deep silence hung over the forest and the hills.

I did not feel like waking the others immediately. I wanted this all to myself—the snow and the silence and the coming of the sun . . .

Towards the horizon, the sky was red. And then the sun rose over the hills and struck the snow, and I ran to the top of the hill and stood in the dazzling sunlight, shading my eyes from the glare, taking in the range of mountains and the valley and the stream that cut its way through the snow like a dark trickle of oil. I ran down the hill and into the house.

'Wake up!' I shouted, shaking Sudheer. 'Get up and come outside!'

'Why—have you found your treasure?' complained Sudheer sleepily. 'Or has the old man had another fit?'

'More than that—it has snowed!'

'Then I shall definitely not come outside,' he said. And turning over, he went to sleep again.

LADY WITH A HOOKAH

I glimpsed the house as we came through the trees, and I knew at once that it was the place we had been looking for. It had obviously been built by an Englishman, with its wide veranda and sloping corrugated roof, like the house in Dehra where I had lived with my guardian. It stood in the knoll of a hill, surrounded by an orchard of apple and plum trees.

'This must be the place,' said Sudheer. 'Shall we just walk in?'

'Well, the gate is open,' I said.

We had barely entered the gate when a huge black Tibetan mastiff appeared on the front veranda. It did not bark, but a low growl rumbled in its throat. And that was a more dangerous portent. The dog bounded down the steps and made for the gate, and Sudheer and I scrambled back up the hillside forgetting our weariness. The dog remained at the gate, growling as before.

A servant boy appeared on the veranda and called out, 'Who is it? What do you want?'

'We wish to see the lady who lives here,' replied Sudheer.

'She is resting,' said the boy. 'She cannot see anyone now.'

'We have come all the way from Dehra,' said Sudheer. 'My friend is a relative of hers. Tell her that, and she will see him.'

'She isn't going to believe that,' I whispered fiercely.

The boy, with a doubtful glance at both of us, went indoors and was gone for some five minutes. When he reappeared on the veranda, he called the dog inside and chained it to the railing. Then he beckoned to us to follow him. We went in cautiously through the gate.

The boy stared appraisingly at us for a few moments before saying, 'She is at the back. Come with me.'

We went round the house along a paved path, and on to another veranda which looked out on the mountains. I stared at

the view, and took my eyes off it only when Sudheer tugged at
my sleeve; then I looked into the veranda, but I could see
nothing at first because of a difference in light. Only when I
stepped into the shade was I able to make out someone—a
woman reclining, barefoot and wearing a white sari, on a string
cot. An elaborate hookah was set before her, and its long,
pliable stem rose well above the level of the bed, so that she
could manoeuvre it with comfort.

She looked surprisingly young. I had expected to find an older
woman. My aunt, I suppose I could call her that, did not look
over forty-five. Having met an aged friend of my father's in Mr
Pettigrew, I had expected my aunt to be an elderly woman. She
obviously came from a village in the higher ranges and this
accounted for her good colour, her long black hair—and her
hookah. She looked physically strong, and her face, though
lacking femininity, was strikingly handsome.

'Please sit down,' she said; and Sudheer and I, finding that
chairs had materialized from behind while we had stood staring
at her, sank into them. The boy pattered away into the interior
of the house.

'You have come a long way to see me,' she said. 'It must be
important.' And she looked from Sudheer to me, probably
curious to know which of us concerned her. Her eyes rested on
me, on my eyes, and she said, 'You are angrez, aren't you?'

'Yes,' I said. 'I came to see you, because—because you knew
my father—and I was told—I was told you would see me . . .' I
did not quite know what to say, or how to say it.

'Your father?' she said encouragingly, and I noticed a flicker
of interest in her eyes. 'Who is your father?'

'He died when I was much younger,' I said. And when I told
her Father's name, she thrust the hookah aside and leaned
forward to look closely at me. 'You are his son, then . . .'

I nodded.

'Yes, you are his son. You have his eyes and nose and forehead.

I would have known it without your telling me if it had not been so dark in here.' With an agility that was quite surprising, she sprang off the cot and pulled aside the curtains that covered one side of the veranda. Sunlight streamed in, bringing out the richness of her colouring.

'So you are only a boy,' she said, smiling at me indulgently. 'You must be seventeen—eighteen—I remember you only as a child . . . fourteen, fifteen years ago . . .' She put her hands to her cheeks, as though she felt the lines of advancing age; but her cheeks, I observed, were still smooth, her youth was still with her. It came of living in the hills, of having just enough of everything and not too much.

'I came to you because you knew my father well.'

We were sitting again, and Sudheer's long legs stretched across the width of the veranda. I sat beside my aunt's cot.

'I wish there was something of your father's that I could give you,' she said. 'He did not leave much money. I would have offered to look after you, but I was told you had a guardian to take care of you. You must have been in good hands. Later, after my husband's death, I tried to get news of you; but I lived far from any town and was out of touch with what was happening elsewhere. I am alone now. But I don't mind. Your uncle left me this house and the land around it. I have my dog.' She stroked the huge mastiff who sat devotedly beside her. 'And I have the boy. He is a good boy and looks after me well. You are welcome to stay with us, Rusty.'

'No, I did not come for that,' I said. 'You are very generous, but I do not want to be a burden on anyone.'

'You will be no burden. And if you are, it doesn't matter.' She shook her head sadly. 'Your father would have wished to give you a wonderful future, but he could not . . . But let us not depress ourselves. Come, tell me about your tall friend, and what you propose to do, and where you are going from here. It is late, and you must take your meal with us and stay the night.

You will need an entire day if you are going to Rishikesh. I have enough rooms and beds here.'

We sat together in the twilight, and I told my aunt about my quarrel with my guardian, of my friendship with Kishen and Devinder and Sudheer the Lafunga. When it was dark, she drew a shawl around her shoulders and took us indoors; and Baiju, the boy, brought us food on brass thalis, from which we ate seated on the ground. Afterwards, we talked for about an hour, and the Lafunga expressed his admiration for a woman who could live alone in the hills without giving way to loneliness or despair. I tried smoking the hookah, but it gave me a splitting headache, and when eventually I went to bed I could not sleep. Sudheer set up a rhythmic snoring, each snore gaining in tone and vibrancy, reminding me of the brain-fever bird I often heard in Dehra.

I left my bed and walked out on the veranda. The moon showed through the trees, and I walked down the garden path where fallen apples lay rotting in the moonlight. When I turned at the gate to walk back towards the house, I saw someone standing in the veranda. Could it be a ghost? No, it was my aunt in her white sari, watching me.

'What is wrong, Rusty?' she asked, as I approached. 'Why are you wandering about at this time? I thought you were a ghost— I was frightened, because I haven't seen one in years.'

'I've never seen one at all,' I said. 'What are ghosts really like?'

'Oh, they are usually the spirits of immoral women, and they have their feet facing backwards. They are called churels. There are other kinds, too. But why are you out here?'

'I have a headache. I couldn't sleep.'

'All right. Come and talk to me.' And taking me by the hand, she led me into her large moonlit room and made me lie down. Then she took my head in her hands, and with her strong cool fingers pressed my forehead and massaged my temples; and she began telling me a story, but her fingers were more persuasive than her tongue, and I fell asleep before the tale could be finished.

Next morning while Sudheer slept late, she took me around the house and grounds.

'I have some of your books,' she said, when we came indoors. 'You are probably too old for some of them now, but your father asked me to keep them for you. Especially Alice in Wonderland. He was particular about that one, I don't know why.'

She brought the books out, and the sight of their covers brought back to me the whole world of my childhood—lazy afternoons in the shade of a jackfruit tree, a book in my hand, while squirrels and magpies chattered in the branches above; the book-shelf in my grandfather's study. These same books—Alice had been there, and *Treasure Island*, and *Mister Midshipman Easy*—they had been my grandfather's, then my father's and finally my own. I had read them all by the time I was eight; after that the books had been with Father, and I did not see them again after going to live in my guardian's house.

Now after all these years they had turned up once more, in the possession of my strange aunt who lived alone in the mountains.

I decided to take the books because they had once been part of my life. They were the only link that remained now between my father and myself—they were my only legacy.

'Must you go back to Dehra?' asked my aunt.

'I promised my friends I would return. Later, I will decide what I should do and where I should go. During these last few months I have been a vagrant. And I used to dream of becoming a writer!'

'You can write here,' she said. 'And you can be a farmer, too.'

'Oh no, I will just be a nuisance. And anyway, I must stand on my own feet. I'm too old to be looked after by others.'

'You are old enough to look after me,' she said, putting her hand on mine. 'Let us be burdens on each other. I am lonely sometimes. I know you have friends, but they cannot care for you if you are sick or in trouble. You have no parents. I have no children. It is as simple as that.'

She looked up as a shadow fell across the doorway. Sudheer was standing there in his pyjamas, grinning sheepishly at us.

'I'm hungry,' he said. 'Aunty, will you feed us before we reluctantly leave your house?'

THE ROAD TO RISHIKESH

Sudheer and I set out on foot for Rishikesh, that small town straddling the banks of the Ganges where the great river emerges from the hills to stretch itself across the wide plains of northern India. It was in this town of saints and mendicants and pilgrims that Sudheer proposed to set up headquarters. Dehra was no longer safe, he said, with the police and the seth still looking for him. He had already spent a considerable sum from the money he had appropriated, and he hoped that in Rishikesh, where all manner of men congregated, there would be scope for lucrative projects. And from Rishikesh, I could take a bus to Dehra whenever I felt like returning. There was no immediate plan in my mind, but I was content to be on the road again with the Lafunga, as I had been with Kishen. I knew that I would soon tire of this aimless wandering, and wondered if I should return to my aunt after all. But for the time being I was content to wander; and with the Lafunga beside me, I felt carefree and reckless, ready for almost anything.

At noon, we arrived at a small village on the Rishikesh road. From here a bus went twice daily to Rishikesh, and we were just in time to catch the last one.

Though there was no snow, there had been rain.

The road was full of slush and heaps of rubble that had fallen from the hillside. The bus carried very few passengers. Sacks of flour and potatoes took up most of the space.

The driver—unshaven, smoking a bidi—did not inspire

confidence. Throughout the journey he kept up a heated political discussion with a passenger seated directly behind him. With one hand on the steering-wheel, he used the other hand to make his point, gesticulating and shouting in order to be heard above the rattle of the bus.

Nevertheless, Sudheer and I enjoyed the ride. Sudheer's head hit the roof quite often, and this made me burst out in laughter and Sudheer sought comfort from the other passengers' discomfiture.

A stalwart, good-looking young farmer sitting opposite Sudheer said, 'I would feel safer if this was a government bus. Then, if we were killed, there would at least be some compensation for our families—or for us, if we were not dead!'

'Yes, let us be cheerful about these things,' said Sudheer. 'Take our driver, for instance. Do you think he is troubled at the thought of being an irresponsible fellow who could very well be the cause of our deaths? Not he!'

'Very true, he seems to be far removed from such worries!' said the farmer.

We gazed out of the window, down a sheer 200-foot cliff that fell to a boulder-strewn stream. The road was so narrow that we could not see the edge. Trees stood out perpendicularly from the cliff-face. A waterfall came gushing down from the hillside and sprayed the top of the bus, splashing in at the windows. The wheels of the bus turned up stones and sent them rolling downhill; they mounted the rubble of a landslip and went churning through a stretch of muddy water.

The driver was so immersed in his discussion that when he saw a boulder right in the middle of the road he did not have time to apply the brakes. It must be said to his credit that he did not take the bus over the cliff. Instead, he rammed it into the hillside, and there it stuck. Being quite used to accidents of this nature, the driver sighed, re-lit his bidi, and returned to his argument.

As there were only eight miles left for Rishikesh, the passengers decided to walk.

Sudheer once again got into conversation with the farmer, whose name we now knew to be Ganpat. Most of the produce in the bus was Ganpat's; no doubt the bus would take an extra day to arrive in Rishikesh, and that would give him an excuse for prolonging his stay in town and enjoying himself out of sight of his family.

'Is there any place in Rishikesh where we can spend the night?' asked Sudheer.

'There are many dharamsalas for pilgrims,' said Ganpat.

Finding some purpose to our enforced trek, we now set out with even longer and more vigorous strides. Ganpat had a fine sun-darkened body, a strong neck set on broad shoulders, and a heavy, almost military, moustache. He wore his dhoti well; his strong ankles and broad feet were burnished by the sun, hardened by years of walking barefoot through the fields.

Soon he and the Lafunga had discovered something in common—they were both connoisseurs of beautiful women.

'I like them tall and straight,' said Ganpat, twirling his moustache. 'They must not be too fussy, and not too talkative. How does one please them?'

'Have you heard of the great sage Vatsayana? He had three wives. One he pleased with secret confidences, the other with secret respect, and the third with secret flattery.'

'You are a strange fellow,' said Ganpat.

END OF A JOURNEY

It was the festival of the Full Moon. The temples at Rishikesh lay bathed in a soft clear light. The broad, slow-moving Ganges caught the moonlight and held it, to become a river of liquid silver. Along the shore, devotees floated little lights downstream. The wicks were placed in earthen vessels, where they burned for a few minutes, a red-gold glow. I lay on the sand and watched them float by, one by one, until they went out or were caught amongst rocks and shingle.

Sudheer and Ganpat had gone into the town to seek amusement, but I had preferred to stay by the river, at a little distance from the embankment where hundreds of pilgrims had gathered.

I could have slept on the sand if it had been summer, but it was cold, and my blanket was no protection against the icy wind that blew down from the mountains. I went into a lighted dharamsala and settled down in a corner of the crowded room. Rolling myself into my blanket, I closed my eyes, listening to the desultory talk of pilgrims sheltering in the building.

But sleep evaded me. Suddenly, I remembered that little black notebook which belonged to Sudheer. It was still in my pocket. I took it out and opened it only to realize that it was a diary— Sudheer's diary. I flipped through the notebook, which was crammed with all sorts of details, until I came to the last entry. For a second I held myself back thinking about how impolite it was to read someone else's diary. But curiosity urged me on, and soon I was engrossed in it.

It read:

Today, I woke Hastini in the middle of her afternoon siesta by tickling her under the chin with a feather.

'And who were you with last night, little brother?' she asked, running her fingers through my thick brown hair. 'You are smelling of some horrible perfume.'

'You know I do not spend my nights with anyone,' I said. 'The perfume is from yesterday.'

'Someone new?'

'No, my butterfly. I have known her for a week.'

'Too long a time,' said Hastini petulantly. 'A dangerously long time. How much have you spent on her?'

'Nothing so far. But that is not why I came to see you. Have you got twenty rupees?'

'Villain!' she cried. 'Why do you always borrow from me when you want to entertain some stupid young thing? Are you so heartless?'

'My little lotus flower!' I protested, pinching her rosy cheeks. 'I am not borrowing for any such reason. A friend of mine has to leave Dehra urgently, and I must get the money for his train fare. I owe it to him.'

'Since when do you have a friend?'

'Never mind that. I have one. And I come to you for help because I love you more than anyone else. Would you prefer that I borrow the money from Mrinalini?'

'You dare not,' said Hastini. 'I will kill you if you do.'

This healthy rivalry for my affections between these two girls is something I can always count on if I need a favour from them. Perhaps it is the great difference in their proportions that animates the rivalry. Mrinalini envies the luxuriousness of Hastini's soft body, while Hastini envies Mrinalini's delicacy, poise, slenderness of foot and graceful walk. Mrinalini is the colour of milk and honey, she has the daintiness of a deer, while Hastini possesses the elegance of an elephant. Hastini can twang the sitar, dance (though with a heavy tread) and has various other accomplishments. Mrinalini is also dear to me—she is sweet, but dominated by her mother who also keeps most of the money Mrinalini makes.

'So where is the money?' I asked.

'You are so impatient! Sit down, sit down. I have it here beneath the mattress.'

I put my hand beneath the mattress and probed about in search of the money.

'Ah, here it is! You have a fortune stacked away here. Yes, ten rupees, fifteen, twenty—and one for luck . . . Now give me a kiss!'

About an hour later I was in the street again. I turned off at a little alley, throwing my half-eaten apple at a stray dog. Then I climbed a flight of stairs—wooden stairs that were loose and rickety, liable to collapse at any moment . . .

Mrinalini's half-deaf mother was squatting on the kitchen floor, making a fire in an earthen brazier. I poked my face round the door and shouted: 'Good morning, Mother, hope you are making me some tea. You look fine today!' And then, in a lower tone, so that she could not hear: 'You look like a dried-up mango.'

'So it's you again,' grumbled the old woman. 'What do you want now?'

'Your most respectable daughter is what I want,' I said.

'What's that?' She cupped her hand to her ear and leaned forward.

'Where's Mrinalini?' I shouted.

'Don't shout like that! She is not here.'

'That's all I wanted to know.' I walked through the kitchen, through the living-room, and on to the veranda balcony, where I found Mrinalini sitting in the sun, combing out her long silken hair.

'Let me do it for you,' I said, and I took the comb from her hand and ran it through the silky black hair. 'For one so little, so much hair. You could conceal yourself in it and not be seen, except for your dainty little feet.'

'What are you after, Sudheer? You are so full of compliments today. And watch out for Mother—if she sees you combing my hair, she will have a fit!'

'And I hope it kills her.'

'Sudheer!'

'Don't be so sentimental about your mother. You are her little gold mine, and she treats you as such—soon I will be having to fill in application forms before I can see you! It is time you kept your earnings for yourself.'

'So that it will be easier for you to help yourself?'

'Well, it would be more convenient. By the way, I have come to you for twenty rupees.'

Mrinalini laughed delightedly and took the comb from me. 'What were you saying about my little feet?' she asked slyly.

'I said they were the feet of a princess, and I would be very happy to kiss them.'

'Kiss them, then.'

She held one delicate golden foot in the air, and I took it in my hands (which were as large as her feet) and kissed her ankle.

'That will be twenty rupees,' I said.

She pushed me away with her foot. 'But Sudheer, I gave you fifteen rupees only three days ago. What have you done with it?'

'I haven't the slightest idea. I only know that I must have more. It is most urgent, you can be sure of that. But if you cannot help me, I must try elsewhere.'

'Do that, Sudheer. And may I ask, whom do you propose to try?'

'Well, I was thinking of Hastini.'

'Who?'

'You know, Hastini, the girl with the wonderful figure . . .'

'I should think I do! Sudheer, if you dare to take so much as a rupee from her, I'll never speak to you again!'

'Well then, what shall I do?'

Mrinalini beat the arms of the chair with her little fists and cursed me under her breath. Then she got up and went into the kitchen. A great deal of shouting went on in there before Mrinalini came back with flushed cheeks and fifteen rupees.

'You don't know the trouble I had getting it,' she said. 'Now don't come asking for more until at least a week has passed.'

'After a week, I will be able to supply you with funds. I am engaged tonight on a mission of some importance. In a few days I will place golden bangles on your golden feet.'

'What mission?' asked Mrinalini, looking at me with an anxious frown. 'If it is anything to do with the seth, please leave it alone. You know what happened to Satish Dayal. He was smuggling opium for the seth, and now he is sitting in jail, while the seth continues as always.'

'Don't worry about me. I can deal with the seth.'

'Then be off! I have to entertain a foreign delegation this evening. You can come tomorrow morning if you are free.'

'I may come. Meanwhile, goodbye!'

I felt a little embarrassed at having pried into Sudheer's personal life in this manner without even his knowledge. Anyway, I had now found out how Sudheer had got funds to give Devinder that day. But his encounters with Hastini and Mrinalini, though interesting, had managed to make me feel drowsy. Soon I was fast asleep.

Rishikesh comes to life at an early hour. The priests, sanyasis and their disciples rise at three, as soon as there is a little light in the sky, and begin their ablutions and meditation. From about five o'clock, pilgrims start coming down to the river to bathe. Saffron-robed sadhus and wandering mendicants walk along the steps of the river, whilst the older and senior men sit on small edifices beneath shady trees, where they receive money and gifts from pilgrims, and dispense blessings in return.

I had bathed early, leaving Sudheer and Ganpat asleep in the dharamsala. These two revellers had come in at two o'clock in the morning, disturbing others in the shelter. They did not get up until the sun had risen. Then Ganpat crossed the river in a ferry boat in order to visit the temples on the other side, to propitiate the gods with offerings of his own. Sudheer made his way outside to try and acquire a suitable disguise, as he had to visit Dehra for a few days. Dressed as he was, he would soon be spotted by the seth's informers. Later, he met me at the bus-stand.

'I will be back tomorrow,' said Sudheer. 'I can't take you with me because in Dehra my company would be dangerous for you.'

'Why must you be going to Dehra, then?' I asked.

'Well, there are one or two people who owe me money,' he said. 'And though, as you know, we have plenty to go on with, these people are not loved by me, so why should they keep my money? And another thing. I must return the money I borrowed from Hastini and Mrinalini.'

After the bus moved off I strolled through the bazaar, going from one sweet shop to another, assessing the quality of their different wares. Eventually I bought eight annas worth of hot, fresh, golden jalebis, and carrying them in a large plate made of banana leaves, went down to the river.

At the river-side grew a banyan tree, and I sat in its shade and ate my sweets. The tree was full of birds—parrots and bulbuls and rosy pastors—feeding on the ripe red figs of the banyan. It was nice and peaceful to just lean back against the trunk of the tree, listen to the chatter of the birds and study their plumage.

When the sweets were finished, I wandered along the banks of the river. On a stretch of sand two boys were wrestling. They were on their knees, arms interlocked, pressing forward like mad bulls, each striving to throw the other. The taller boy had the advantage at first; the smaller boy, who was dark and pockmarked, appeared to be yielding. But then there was a sudden flurry of arms and legs, and the small boy sat victorious across his opponent's chest.

When they saw me watching them, the boys asked me if I too would like to wrestle. But I declined the invitation. I had eaten too many jalebis and felt sick.

I walked until the sickness had passed. Soon I was hungry again and returning to the bazaar, I feasted on puris and a well-spiced vegetable curry.

Well stuffed with puris, I returned to the banyan tree and slept right through the afternoon and the night.

It was a wonderful morning in Rishikesh. There was a hint of spring in the air. Birds flashed across the water, and monkeys chased each other over the rooftops. I lay on a stretch of sand, drinking in the crisp morning air, letting the sun sink into my body.

I had risen early and had gone down to the river to bathe. The touch of the water brought memories of my own secret pool that lay in the forest behind the church. Perhaps Devinder would be there now; and Goonga would be sitting on a buffalo.

I sat on the sand, nostalgically thinking of my friends. Though there was another pull now from the house in the hills, I felt fairly certain that I ought to go back to Dehra. I decided to leave Rishikesh as soon as the Lafunga returned. After all, Sudheer was experienced in the ways of the world, and was never lacking in friends. Devinder and Kishen were of my age. They probably needed companionship, and I wasn't too happy being on my own either.

I lay on the white sand until the voices of distant bathers reached me, and the sun came hurrying over the hills. Slipping on my shirt and trousers, I went to the bazaar, where I found a little tea shop. And there I drank a glass of hot, sweet milky tea and ate six eggs, much to the amazement of the shopkeeper.

After that, I went down to the bus-stand to see if Sudheer had returned. The second bus from Dehra had arrived, but Sudheer was not to be seen anywhere. I was about to go back when, turning, I found myself looking into the eyes of a distinguished-looking young sadhu, who had three vermilion stripes across his forehead, an orange robe wound about his thighs and shoulders, and an extremely unsaintly grin on his face. The disguise might have deceived me, but not the grin.

'So now you have become a sadhu,' I said. 'And for whose benefit is this?'

'It was for business in Dehra,' said Sudheer. 'I did not wish to be seen by the seth or his servants. Let us find a quiet place where we can talk. And let us get some fruit, I am hungry.'

I bought six apples from a stall and took Sudheer to the banyan tree. We sat on the ground, talking and munching apples.

'Did you see your friends?' I asked.

'Yes, I went to them first. The bus ride had made me tired and angry, and there is no one like Hastini for soothing and refreshing one. Then at midnight, I paid a clandestine visit to Mrinalini. Knowing that I would have to stay away for some time, I wished to see her just once again, in order to make her a gift and a promise of my fidelity.

'It took me a few seconds to climb the treacherous flight of stairs that leads to Mrinalini's rooms. Every time I climb those stairs, they sway and plunge about more heavily.

'Mrinalini was preparing herself for a visitor, I think; she was sitting in front of that cracked, discoloured mirror which distorts her fine features into hideous dimensions. She had once told me that whenever she looked into the distorting mirror and saw the bloated face, the crooked eyes, the smear of paint, she always felt that one day she would look like that. By contrast she had said that my reflection whenever it appeared beside hers in the mirror, reminded her of a horse—a horse with a rather long and silly face. And seeing it yesterday there, she laughed.

'"What are you laughing at?" I asked.

'"At you, of course! You look so stupid in the mirror!"

'"I did not know that," I said, my vanity a little hurt. "Hastini does not think so."

'"Hastini is a fool. She likes you because she thinks you are handsome. I like you because you have a face like a horse."

'"Well, your horse is going to be away from Dehra for some time. I hope you will not miss him."

'"You are always coming and going, but never staying," she said a little sulkily.

'"That's life."

'"Doesn't it make you lonely?" she asked, moving away from the mirror, and going to the bed. She made herself comfortable against a pillow . . . she looked so beautiful that I felt miserable at the thought of staying away from her.

'"When I am lonely, I do something," I said, trying to keep a hold over my emotions. "I go out and do something foolish or dangerous. When I am not doing things, I am lonely. But I was not made for loneliness."

'"I am lonely sometimes."

'"You! With your mother? She never leaves you alone. And you have visitors nearly every day, and many new faces."

'"Yes. The more people I see, the lonelier I get. You must have some companion, someone to talk to and quarrel with, if you are not to be lonely. You can find such a companion, Sudheer. But who can I find? My mother is old and deaf and heartless," she said, sounding really unhappy.

'"One day I will come and take you away from here. I have some money now, Mrinalini. As soon as I have started a business in another town, I will call you there. Meanwhile, why not stay with Hastini?"

'"I hate her."

'"You do not know her yet. When you know her, you will love her!"

'"You love her."

'"I love her because she is so comfortable to be with. I love you because you are so sweet. Can I help it if I love you both?" I spoke truthfully, Rusty, for a change. I seldom got to speak so openly with Mrinalini, and last night I just didn't want her to harbour any false illusions about me.

'"You are strange," said Mrinalini with one of her rare smiles. "Go now. Someone will be coming."

'"Then keep this for me," I said.

'I took the thin gold ring which was on my finger, and slipped it on to the third finger of her right hand.

'"Keep it for me till I return," I said. "And if I do not return, then keep it for ever. Sell it only if you are in need. All right?"

'She stared at the ring for some time, turning it about on her finger so that the light fell on it in different places. Then she slipped it off her finger and hid it in her blouse.

'"If I keep it on my hand, my mother will be sure to take it."

'I was exasperated by the never-ending control her old mother had over this girl. Quietly I said, "If only you would allow me, I'd finish off your mother for you."

'"Don't talk like that! She has not long to live . . . "

'"She is doing her best to outlive all of us . . . But don't worry, I will not even touch her, I promise you. I will simply frighten her to death. I could pounce on her from a dark alley, let off a firecracker . . . "

'"Sudheer!" cried Mrinalini. "How can you be so cruel?"

'"It would be a kindness," I said laughingly.

'"Go now! Stay away from Dehra as long as you can."

'So you see, Rusty, Mrinalini is still waiting for her mother to die. In life, people do nothing but wait for other people to die. Do I look all right?' he asked suddenly.

'You look as handsome as ever.'

'I know that. But do I look like a sadhu?' Obviously Sudheer had some new plans up his sleeve.

'Yes, a very handsome sadhu.'

'All the better. Come, let us go.'

'Where do we go?' I asked.

'To look for disciples, of course. A sadhu such as I must have disciples and they should be rich disciples. There must be many fat, rich men in the world who are unhappy about their consciences. Come, we will be their consciences! We will be respectable, Rusty. There is more money to be made that way. Yes, we will be respectable—what an adventure that will be!'

We began walking towards the bazaar.

'Wait!' I said. 'I cannot come with you, Sudheer!'

Sudheer came to an abrupt halt. He turned and faced me, a puzzled and disturbed expression on his face.

'What do you mean, you cannot come with me?'

'Sudheer, I must return to Dehra. I may come this way again, if I want to live with my aunt.'

'But why? You have just left her. You came to the hills for money, didn't you? And she didn't have any money.'

'I wanted to see her, too. I wanted to know what she was like. It wasn't just a matter of money.'

'Well, you saw her. And there is no future for you with her, or in Dehra. What's the use of returning?'

'I don't know, Sudheer. What's the use of anything for that matter? What would be the use of staying with you? I want to give some direction to my life. I want to work, I want to be free, I want to be able to write. I can't wander about the hills and plains with you for ever.'

'Why not? There is nothing to stop you, if you like to wander. India has always been the home of wanderers.'

'I might join you again if I fail at everything else.'

Sudheer looked sullen and downcast.

'You do not realize . . .' he began, but stopped, groping for the right words; he had seldom been at a loss for words. 'I have got used to you, that is all,' he said.

'And I have got used to you, Sudheer. I don't think anyone else has ever done that.'

'That's why I don't want to lose you. But I cannot stop you from going.'

'I shall come to see you, I will, really . . .'

Sudheer brightened up a little. 'Do you promise? Or do you say that just to please me?'

'Both.'

Then Sudheer was his old self again, smiling and digging his fingers into my arms. 'I'll be waiting for you,' he said. 'Whenever you want to look for treasure, come to me! Whenever you are looking for fun, come to me!'

Then he was silent again, and a shadow passed across his face. Was he afraid of being lonely? 'Let us part now,' he said. 'Let us not prolong it. You go down the street to the bus-stand, and I'll go the other way.'

He held out his hand to me. And then saying, 'Your hand is not enough,' he put his arms around me, and embraced me.

People stopped to stare; not because two youths were demonstrating their affection for each other—that was common enough—but because a sadhu in a saffron robe was behaving out of character.

When Sudheer realized this, he grinned at the passers-by; and they, embarrassed by his grin, and made nervous by his height, hurried on down the street.

Sudheer turned and walked away.

I watched him for some time. He stood out distinctly from the crowd of people in the bazaar, tall and handsome in his flowing robe.

FIRST AND LAST IMPRESSIONS

Because I had told no one of my return, there was no one to meet me at Dehra station when I stepped down from a third-class compartment. But on my way through the bazaar I met one of the tea-shop boys who told me that Devinder might be found near the Clock Tower. And so I went to the Clock Tower, but I could not find my friend. Another familiar, a shoeshine boy, said he had last seen Devinder near the Court, where business was brisk that day.

I was feeling tired and dirty after my journey, so I decided to look for Devinder later, and made my way to the church compound and left my bag there. Then I went through the jungle to the pool.

Goonga was already there, bathing in the shallows, gesticulating and shouting incomprehensibles at a band of langurs who were watching him from the sal trees. When Goonga saw me, he chortled with delight and rushed out of the water to give me a hug.

'And how are you?' I asked.

'Goo,' said Goonga.

He was evidently very well. Devinder had been feeding him, and he no longer needed to prowl around tea shops and receive kicks and insults in exchange for a glass of tea or a stale bun.

I took off my clothes and leapt into the cold, sweet, delicious water of the pool. I floated languidly on the water, gazing up through the branches of an overhanging sal, through a pattern of broad leaves, into a blind-blue sky. Goonga sat on a rock and grinned at the monkeys, making encouraging sounds. Looking from Goonga to the monkeys and back to the hairy, long-armed youth, I wondered how anyone could doubt Darwin's theories.

And quite obviously, I belong to the same species, I thought to myself, joining Goonga on the rock and making noises of my own. 'Oh, to be a langur, without a care in the world. Acorns and green leaves to feed on, lots of friends and no romantic complications. But no books either. I suppose being human has its advantages. Not that books would make any difference to Goonga.'

I was soon dry. I lay on my tummy, flat against the warm, smooth rock surface. I wanted to sink deep into that beautiful rock.

'Goo,' said Goonga, as though he approved.

Then the sun was in the pool and the pool was in the sky and the rock had swallowed me up, and when I woke I thought Goonga was still beside me. But when I raised my head and looked, I saw Devinder sitting there—Devinder looking cool and clean in a white shirt and pyjamas, his tray lying on the ground a little way off.

'How long have you been here?' I asked.

'I just came. It is good to see you. I was afraid you had left for good.'

'I'm hungry,' I said.

'I'm glad you haven't lost your appetite. I have brought you something to eat.' He produced a paper bag filled with bazaar food and a couple of oranges.

While I ate, I told Devinder of my journey. He was disappointed.

'So there was nothing for you, except a few books. I know

money isn't everything, but it's time you had some of it, Rusty. How long can you carry on like this? You can't sell combs and buttons like me—you wouldn't know how to. You're a dreamer, a kind of poet, but you can't live on dreams. You don't have rich friends and relatives, like Kishen, to provide intervals of luxury. You're not like Sudheer, able to live on your wits. There's only this aunt of yours in the hills—and you can't spend the rest of your life lost in the mountains like a hermit. It will take you years to become a successful writer. Look at Goldsmith— borrowing money all the time! And you haven't even started yet.'

'I know, Devinder. You don't have to tell me. Tomorrow I'll go and see Mr Pettigrew. Perhaps he can help me in some way— perhaps he can find me a job.'

We fell silent, gazing disconsolately into the pool.

'Have you seen Kishen?' I asked.

'Once, in the bazaar. He was with that girl, his cousin, I think. They were on bicycles. I think they were going to the cinema. Kishen seemed happy enough. He stopped and spoke to me and asked me when you would be back. They will soon be sending him back to school. That's good, isn't it? He'll never be able to manage without a proper education. Degrees and things.'

'Well, Sudheer has managed well enough without one. You might call him self-educated. And Kishen is worldly enough. And sufficiently shrewd as well. No one is likely to get the better of him. All the same, you're right. A couple of degrees behind your name could make all the difference, even if you can't put them down in the right order!'

Already the dream was fading. Life is like that. You can't run away from it and survive. You can't be a vagrant for ever. You're getting nowhere, so you've got to stop somewhere. Kishen had stopped. He'd thrown in his lot with the settled incomes—he had to. Even Mowgli left the wolf-pack to return to his own people. And India was changing. This great formless mass was taking some sort of shape at last. I, too, had to stop at that point, and find a place for myself, or go forward to disaster.

'I'll see him tomorrow,' I said to Devinder, stirring from my thoughts. 'I'll see Kishen and say goodbye.'

I decided to leave my books with Mr Pettigrew instead of in the church vestry, a transient abode. So I put them in my bag, and after tea with Devinder near the Clock Tower, set out for the tea gardens.

I crossed the dry river-bed and yellow mustard fields which stretched away to the foothills, and found Mr Pettigrew sitting on his veranda as though he had not moved from his cane chair since I had last visited him. He gazed out across the flat tea bushes and seemed to look through me. So I thought I had not been recognized. Perhaps the old man had forgotten me!

'Good morning,' I greeted him. 'I'm back.'

'The poinsettia leaves have turned red,' said Pettigrew. 'Another winter is passing.'

'Yes.'

'Full sixty hot summers have besieged my brow. I'm growing old so slowly. I wish there could be some action to make the process more interesting. Not that I feel very active, but I'd like to have something happening around me. A jolly old riot would be just the thing. You know what I mean, of course?'

'I think so,' I replied.

It was loneliness again. In a week I had found two lonely people—my aunt and this elderly gentleman, moving slowly through the autumn of their lives. It was beginning to affect me. I looked at Mr Pettigrew and wondered if I would be like that one day—alone, not very strong, living in the past, with a bottle of whisky to sustain me through the still, lonely evenings. I had friends—but so did Pettigrew, in his youth. I had books to read, and books to write—but Pettigrew had books, too. Did they make much difference? Weren't there any permanent flesh and blood companions to be found outside the conventions of marriage and business?

Pettigrew seemed suddenly to realize that I was still standing beside him. A spark of interest showed in his eyes. It flickered and grew into comprehension.

'Drinking in the mornings, that's my trouble. You returned very soon. Sit down, my boy, sit down. Tell me—did you find the lady? Did she know you? Was it any good?'

I sat down on a step, for there was no chair on the veranda apart from Mr Pettigrew's.

'Yes, she knew me. She was very kind and wanted to help me. But she had nothing of mine, except some old books which my father had left with her.'

'Books! Is that all? You've brought them with you, I see.'

'I thought perhaps you'd keep them for me until I'm properly settled somewhere.'

Mr Pettigrew took the books from me and thumbed through them.

'Stevenson, Ballantyne, Marryat, and some early P.G. Wodehouse. I expect you've read them. And here's *Alice in Wonderland*. "How doth the little crocodile . . . " Tenniel's drawings. It's a first edition, methinks! It couldn't be—or could it?'

Mr Pettigrew then became silent for a while. He studied the title page and the back of the title-leaf with growing interest and solicitude and then with something approaching reverence.

'It could be, at that,' said Pettigrew, almost to himself, and I was bewildered by the transformation on the old man's face. Ennui had given place to enthusiasm.

'Could be what, sir?'

'A first edition.'

'It was once my grandfather's book. His name is on the flyleaf.'

'It must be a first. No wonder your father treasured it.'

'Is being a first edition very important?'

'Yes, from the book-collector's point of view. In England, on the Continent and in America, there are people who collect rare works of literature—manuscripts, and the first editions of books that have since become famous. The value of a book depends on its literary worth, its scarcity and its condition.'

'Well, Alice is a famous book. And this is a good copy. Is a first edition of it rare?'

'It certainly is. There are only two or three known copies.'

'And do you think this is one?'

'Well, I'm not an expert, but I do know something about books. This is the first printing. And it's in good condition, except for a few stains on the fly-leaf.'

'Let's rub them off.'

'No, don't touch a thing—don't tamper with its condition. I'll write to a bookseller friend of mine in London for his advice. I think this should be worth a good sum of money to you—several hundred pounds.'

'Pounds!' I exclaimed disbelievingly.

'Five or six hundred, maybe more. Your father must have known the book was valuable and meant you to have it one day. Perhaps this was his legacy.'

I kept quiet, taking in the import of what Mr Pettigrew had told me. I had never had much money in my life. A few hundred pounds would take me anywhere I wanted to go. But it was also, I knew, quite easy to go through any sum of money, no matter how large the amount.

Pettigrew was glancing through the other books. 'None of these are firsts, except the Wodehouse novels, and you'll have to wait some time with those. But Alice is the real thing. My friend will arrange its sale.'

'It would be nice to keep it,' I said, thinking of how the book had passed through two generations of my family.

Mr Pettigrew looked up in surprise. 'In other circumstances, my boy, I'd say keep it. Become a book-collector yourself. But when you're down on your beam-ends, you can't afford to be sentimental. Now leave this business in my hands, and let me advance you some money. Furthermore, this calls for a celebration!'

He poured himself a stiff whisky and offered me a drink.

'I don't mind if I do,' I said, bestowing a smile on the old man.

Later, after lunching with Mr Pettigrew, I sat out on the veranda with the old man and discussed my future.

'I think you should go to England,' said Mr Pettigrew.

'I've thought of that before,' I said, 'but I've always felt that India is my home.'

'But can you make a living here? After all, even Indians go abroad at the first opportunity. And you want to be a writer. You can't become one overnight, certainly not in India. It will take years of hard work, and even then—even if you're good— you may not make the reputation that means all the difference between failure and success. In the meantime, you've got to make a living at something. And what can you do in India? Let's face it, my boy, you've only just finished school. There are graduates who can't get jobs. Only last week a young man with a degree in the Arts came to me and asked my help in getting him a job as a petty clerk in the tea-estate manager's office. A clerk! Is that why he went to college—to become a clerk?'

I did not argue the point. I knew that it was only people with certain skills who stood a chance. It was an age of specialization. And I did not have any skills, apart from some skill with words.

'You can always come back,' said Mr Pettigrew. 'If you are successful, you'll be free to go wherever you please. And if you aren't successful, well then, you can make a go of something else—if not in England, then in some other English-speaking country, America or Australia or Canada or the Cook Islands!'

'Why didn't you leave India, Mr Pettigrew?'

'For reasons similar to yours. Because I had lived many years here in India and had grown to love the country. But unlike you, I'm at the fag-end of my life. And it's easier to fade away in the hot sun than in the cold winds of Blighty.'

He looked out rather wistfully at his garden, at the tall marigolds and bright clumps of petunia and the splurge of bougainvillaea against the wall.

'My journeyings are over,' he mused. 'And yours have just begun.'

It was dark when I slipped over a wall and moved silently round the porch of Mrs Bhushan's house. There was a light showing in the front room, and I crept up to the window and looked in, pressing my face against the glass. I felt the music in the room even before I heard it. It came vibrating through the glass with a pulsating rhythm. Kishen and Aruna, both barefoot, were gyrating on the floor in a frenzy of hip-shivering movement. Their faces were blank. They did not sing. All expression was confined to their plunging torsos.

I felt that it was not a propitious moment for calling on my old friend. This was confirmed a few minutes later by the throaty blare of a horn and the glare of a car's headlights. Mrs Bhushan's Hillman was turning in at the gate. The music came to a sudden stop. I dodged behind a rose-bush, stung my hands on nettle, and remained hidden until Mrs Bhushan alighted from her car. I was moving cautiously through the shrubbery when one of the dogs started barking. Others took up the chorus.

I was soon clambering over the wall, with two or three cockers snapping at my feet and trousers. I ran down the road until I found the entrance to a dark lane, down which I disappeared.

I slowed to a walk as I approached the crowded bazaar area. I felt annoyed and a little depressed at not having been able to see Kishen, but I had to admit that Kishen appeared to be quite happy in Mrs Bhushan's house. Aruna had made all the difference; for Kishen was beginning to grow up.

Perhaps, I thought, I'd better not see him at all.

START OF A JOURNEY

Events moved swiftly—as they usually do, once a specific plan is set in motion—and within a few weeks I was in possession of a passport, a rail ticket to Bombay, my boat ticket, an income tax clearance certificate (this had been the most difficult to obtain, in spite of the fact that I had no income), a smallpox vaccination certificate, various other bits and pieces of paper, and about fifty rupees in cash advanced by Mr Pettigrew. The money for Alice would not be realized for several months, and could be drawn upon in London.

I was late for my train. The tonga I had hired turned out to be the most ancient of Dehra's dwindling fleet of pony-drawn carriages. The pony was old, slow and dyspeptic. It stopped every now and then to pass quantities of wind. The tonga driver turned out to be a bhang addict who had not woken up from his last excursion into dreamland. The carriage itself was a thing of shreds and patches. It lay at an angle, and rolled from side to side. This motion seemed designed to suit the condition of the driver who dozed off every now and then.

'If it hadn't been for your luggage,' said Devinder, 'we would have done better to walk.'

At our feet was a new suitcase and a spacious holdall given to me by Mr Pettigrew. Devinder, the tonga driver and I were the only occupants of the carriage.

I couldn't help thinking of a similar situation many years back when my grandmother and I were travelling by a pony cart to the Dehra railway station. We had to take the train to Lucknow, stay with Aunt Emily for a few days, and then go on to Bombay. From there we were to take the ship to London. Even though that carriage had been slow, we had managed to catch the train as it always left after its scheduled time. Despite this, we couldn't make it to England for Grandmother passed away suddenly in Lucknow, and I was sent back to Dehra.

This time, however, I wanted to make sure that nothing went wrong. I wanted to reach London at all cost, by all means.

'Please hurry,' I begged of the tonga driver. 'I'll miss the train.'

'Miss the train?' mumbled the tonga driver, coming out of his coma. 'No one ever misses the train—not when I take them to the station!'

'Why, does the train wait for you to arrive?' asked Devinder. 'Oh, no,' said the driver. 'But it waits.'

'Well, it should have left at seven,' I said. 'And it's five past seven now. Even if it leaves on time, which means ten minutes late, we won't catch it at this speed.'

'You will be there in ten minutes, sahib.' And the man called out an endearment to his pony.

Neither Devinder nor I could make out what the tonga driver said, but it did wonders to the pony. The beast came to life as though it had been injected with a new wonder hormone. Devinder and I were jerked upright in our seats. The pony kicked up its hind legs and plunged forward, and cyclists and pedestrians scattered for safety. We raced through the town, followed by oaths and abuses from a vegetable-seller whose merchandise had been spilled on the road. Only at the station entrance did the pony slow down and then, as suddenly and unaccountably as it had come to life, it returned to its former dispirited plod.

Paying off the man, we grabbed hold of the luggage and tumbled on to the railway platform. Here we banged into Kishen who, having heard of my departure (from the barber, who had got it from an egg vendor, who had got it from Devinder), had come to see me off.

'You didn't tell me anything,' said Kishen with an injured look. 'You seem to have forgotten me altogether.'

'I hadn't forgotten you, Kishen. I did come to see you—but I couldn't bring myself to say goodbye. It seems final, saying goodbye. I wanted to slip away quietly, that's all.'

'How selfish you are!' said Kishen.

A last-minute quarrel with Kishen was the last thing I wanted.

'We must hurry,' said Devinder urgently. 'The train is about to leave.'

The guard was blowing his whistle, and there was a final scramble among the passengers. If sardines could have taken a look at the situation in the third-class railway compartments of that train that day, they would not have anything to complain about. It was a perfect example of the individual being swallowed up by the mass, of a large number of identities merging into one corporate whole. Your leg, you discover, is not yours but your neighbour's; the growth of hair on your shoulder is someone's beard and the cold wind whistling down your neck is his asthmatic breath; a baby materializes in your lap and is reclaimed only after it has wet your trousers; and the corner of a seat which you had happily thought was your own green spot on this earth is suddenly usurped by a huge Sikh with a sword dangling at his side. I knew from experience in third-class compartments that if I did not get into one of them immediately, my way would be permanently barred.

'There's no room anywhere,' said Kishen cheerfully. 'You'd better go tomorrow.'

'The boat sails in three days,' I said.

'Then come on, let's squeeze you in somewhere.'

Managing the luggage ourselves, and ignoring the protests of the station coolies, we hurried down the length of the platform looking for a compartment less crowded than most. We discovered an open door and a space within, and my worldly goods were bundled into it.

'It's empty!' I said delightedly, after getting into the compartment. 'There's no one in it.'

'Of course not,' said Kishen. 'It's a first-class compartment.'

But the train was already in motion and there was no time to get out.

'You can shift into another compartment after Hardwar,' said Devinder. 'The train won't be so crowded then.'

I closed the door and stuck my head out of the window. Perhaps this mad, confusing departure was the best thing that could have happened. It was impossible to say goodbye in dignified solemnity. And I would have hated a solemn, tearful departure. Devinder and Kishen had time only to look relieved—relieved at having been able to get me into the train. They would not realize, till later, that I was going out of their lives forever.

I waved to them from the window, and they waved back, smiling and wishing me luck. They were not dismayed at my departure. Rather, they looked pleased that my life had taken a new direction; they were impressed by my good fortune, and they took it for granted that I would come back some day, with money and honours. Such is the optimism of youth.

I waved until my friends were lost in the milling throng on the platform, until the station lights were a distant glow. And then the train was thundering through the swift falling darkness of India. I looked in the glass of the window and saw my own face dimly reflected. And I wondered if I would ever come back.

There was someone else's reflection in the glass, and I realized that I was not alone in the compartment. Someone had just come out of the washroom and was staring at me in some surprise. A familiar face, a foreigner. The man I had met at the Raiwala waiting-room, when I had been travelling with Kishen to Dehra in different circumstances.

'We meet again,' said the American. 'Remember me?'

'Yes,' I said. 'We seem to share a fondness for trains.'

'Well, I have to make this journey every week.'

'How is your work?'

'Much the same. I'm trying, but with little success, to convince farmers that a steel plough will pay greater dividends than a wooden plough.'

'And they aren't convinced?'

'Oh, they're quite prepared to be convinced. Trouble is, they find it cheaper and easier to repair a wooden plough. You see how complicated everything is? It's a question of parts. For want of a bolt, the plough was lost, for want of a plough the crop was lost, for want of a crop . . . And where are you going, friend? I see you're alone this time.'

'Yes, I'm going away. I'm leaving India.'

'Where are you going? England?'

I nodded and looked out of the window in time to see a shooting star skid across the heavens and vanish. A bad omen; but I was defiant of omens.

'I'm going to England,' I said. 'I'm going to Europe and America and Japan and Timbuctoo. I'm going everywhere, and no one can stop me!'

A Far Cry from India

IT WAS WHILE I was living in Jersey, in the Channel Islands, that I really missed India.

Jersey was a very pretty island, with wide sandy bays and rocky inlets, but it was worlds away from the land in which I had grown up. You did not see an Indian or Eastern face anywhere. It was not really an English place either, except in parts of the capital, St Helier, where some of the business houses, hotels and law firms were British-owned. The majority of the population—farmers, fishermen, councillors—spoke a French patois which even a Frenchman would have disowned. The island, originally French, and then for a century British, had been briefly occupied by the Germans. Now it was British again, although it had its own legislative council and made its own laws. It exported tomatoes, shrimps and Jersey cows, and imported people looking for a tax haven.

During the summer months the island was flooded with English holidaymakers. During the long, cold winter, gale-force winds swept across the Channel and the island's waterfront had a forlorn look. I knew I did not belong there and I disliked the place intensely. Within days of my arrival I was longing for the languid, easy-going, mango-scented air of small-town India: the gulmohur trees in their fiery summer splendour; barefoot boys riding buffaloes and chewing on sticks of sugarcane; a hoopoe on the grass, bluejays performing aerial acrobatics; a girl's pink dupatta flying in the breeze; the scent of wet earth after the first rain; and most of all my Dehra friends.

So what on earth was I doing on an island, twelve by five miles in size, in the cold seas off Europe? Islands always sound as though they are romantic places, but take my advice, don't live on one—you'll feel deeply frustrated after a week.

I had come here to try my luck at getting my first novel published. There really wasn't much scope for struggling young English authors in India at my time. And I was certainly not going to pursue any other profession.

I had finished school, and then for a couple of years I had been loafing around in Dehra, convinced that my vagrancy in the company of a few friends would give me the right outlook, material and environment to write my first novel.

I'd always wanted to be a writer for nothing made me happier than being surrounded by books, reading them and then writing. Books had been my sole companions during the many lonely periods of my life. My parents had separated when I was just four and my mother had remarried. I had stayed mostly with Father (wherever his job took us) or with my paternal grandparents in Dehra sometimes. But when I was just eleven, I lost my father to malaria. I stayed for a while with Grandmother, but she too passed away. I was then shunted around for some time—first I stayed with my mother and stepfather, then I was put under the care of my father's cousin Mr John Harrison. I finished my schooling but was at a loose end when circumstances forced me to leave Mr Harrison's house. I became a tutor to Kishen (who was not much younger than me), and lived in a tiny room on the roof of the Kapoors' house, thus making my first serious attempt at defining my own identity.

But life, as usual, had other things in store for me. I was soon without a stable shelter over my head or any means to make a living. I learnt to live each day as it came and to take the tough in my stride. All this only helped to fuel my ambition of becoming a writer someday soon. One day, quite out of the blue, I happened to meet an old acquaintance of my father—Mr Pettigrew, and through him chanced upon a few books left to me by Father.

One of them was a first edition of Lewis Caroll's *Alice in Wonderland*. I followed Mr Pettigrew's advice to sell this rare find to a book collector in London. This fetched me a few hundred pounds with which I planned to buy myself a passage to England. Somehow Aunt Emily (my father's cousin) got to know of my future plans and wrote saying that her family (which had settled in Jersey) would be happy to accommodate me with them until I found a job in London. This settled the matter for me, and soon enough I found myself on Ballard Pier and there followed the long sea voyage on the P&O liner, *Strathnaver*. (Built in the 1920s, it had been used as a troopship during the War and was now a passenger liner again.) In the early 1950s, the big passenger ships were still the chief mode of international travel. A leisurely cruise through the Red Sea, with a call at Aden; then through Suez, stopping at Port Said (you had a choice between visiting the pyramids or having a sexual adventure in the port's back alleys); then across the Mediterranean, with a view of Vesuvius (or was it Stromboli?) erupting at night; a look-in at Marseilles, where you could try out your school French and buy naughty postcards; finally docking at Tilbury, on the Thames estuary, just a short train ride away from the heart of London.

At Bombay, waiting for the ship's departure, I had spent two nights in a very seedy hotel on Lamington Road, and probably picked up the hepatitis virus there, although I did not break out in jaundice until I was in Jersey. Bombay never did agree with me. (Now that it has been renamed Mumbai, maybe I'll be luckier.)

I liked Aden. It was unsophisticated. And although I am a lover of trees and forests, there is something about the desert (a natural desert, not a man-made one) that appeals to my solitary instincts. I am not sure that I could take up an abode permanently surrounded by sand, date-palms and camels, but it would be preferable to living in a concrete jungle—or in Jersey, for that matter!

And camels do have character.

Have I told you the story of the camel fair in Rajasthan? Well, there was a brisk sale in camels and the best ones fetched good prices. An elderly dealer was having some difficulty in selling a camel which, like its owner, had seen better days. It was lean, scraggy, half-blind and moved with such a heavy roll that people were thrown off before they had gone very far.

'Who'll buy your scruffy, lame old camel?' asked a rival dealer. 'Tell me just one advantage it has over other camels.'

The elderly camel owner drew himself up with great dignity and with true Rajput pride, replied: 'There is something to be said for character, isn't there?'

Did I have 'character' as a boy? Probably more than I have now. I was prepared to put up with discomfort, frugal meals and even the occasional nine-to-five job provided I could stay up at night in order to complete my book or write a new story. Almost fifty years on, I am still leading a simple life—a good, strong bed, a desk of reasonable proportions, a coat-hanger for my one suit and a comfortable chair by the window. The rest is superstition.

When that ship sailed out of Aden, my ambitions were tempered by the stirrings of hepatitis within my system. That common toilet in the Lamington Road hotel, with its ever-growing uncleared mountain of human excreta, probably had something to do with it. The day after arriving at my uncle's house in Jersey, I went down with jaundice and had to spend two or three weeks in bed. But rest and the right diet brought about a good recovery. And as soon as I was back on my feet, I began looking for a job.

I had only three or four pounds left from my travel money, and I did not like the idea of being totally dependent on my relatives. They were a little disapproving of my writing ambitions. Besides, they were sorry for me in the way one feels sorry for an unfortunate or poor relative—simply because he or she is a relative. They were doing their duty by me, and this was noble of them; but it made me uneasy.

St Helier, the capital town and port of Jersey, was full of solicitors' offices, and I am not sure what prompted me to do the rounds of all of them, asking for a job; I think I was under the impression that solicitors were always in need of clerical assistants. But I had no luck. At twenty, I was too young and inexperienced. One firm offered me the job of tea-boy, but as I never could brew a decent cup of tea, I felt obliged to decline the offer. Finally I ended up working for a pittance in a large grocery store, Le Riche's, where I found myself sitting on a high stool at a high desk (like Herbert Pocket in Great Expectations), alongside a row of similarly positioned clerks, making up bills for despatch to the firm's regular clients.

By then it was mid-winter, and I found myself walking to work in the dark (7.30 a.m.) and walking home when it was darker still (6 p.m.)—they gave you long working hours in those days! So I did not get to see much of St Helier except on weekends.

Saturdays were half-holidays. Strolling home via a circuitous route through the old part of the town, I discovered a little cinema which ran reruns of old British comedies. And here, for a couple of bob, I made the acquaintance of performers who had come of age in the era of the music halls, and who brought to their work a broad, farcical humour that appealed to me. At school in Simla, some of them had been familiar through the pages of a favourite comic, Film Fun—George Formby, Sidney Howard, Max Miller ('The Cheeky Chappie', known for his double entendres), Tommy Trinder, Old Mother Riley (really a man dressed up as a woman), Laurel and Hardy and many others.

I disliked Le Riche's store. My fellow junior clerk was an egregious fellow who never stopped picking his nose. The senior clerk was interested only in the racing results from England. There were a couple of girls who drooled over the latest pop stars. I don't remember much about this period except that when King George VI died, we observed a minute's silence. Then back to our ledgers.

George VI was a popular monarch, a quiet self-effacing man, and much respected because he had stayed in London through the Blitz when, every night for months, bombs had rained on the city. I thought he deserved more than a minute's silence. In India we observed whole holidays when almost any sort of dignitary or potentate passed away. But here it was 'The King is dead. Long live the Queen!' And then, 'Stop dreaming, Bond. Get on with bills.'

The sea itself was always comforting and on holidays or summer evenings I would walk along the seafront, watching familiar rocks being submerged or exposed, depending on whether the tide was coming in or going out. On Sundays I would occasionally go down to the beach (St Helier's was probably the least attractive of Jersey's beaches, but it was only a short walk from my aunt's house) and sometimes I'd walk out with the tide until I came to a group of prominent rocks, and there I'd sunbathe in solitary and naked splendour. Not since the year of my father's death had I been such a loner.

I could swim a little but I was no Johnny Weissmuller and I took care to wade back to dry land once the tide started turning. Once a couple had been trapped on those rocks; their bodies had been washed ashore the next day. At high tide I loved to watch the sea rushing against the sea wall, sending sprays of salt water into my face. Winter gales were frequent and I liked walking into the wind, just leaning against it. Sometimes it was strong enough to support me and I fell into its arms. It wasn't as much fun with the wind behind you, for then it propelled you along the road in a most undignified fashion, so that you looked like Charlie Chaplin in full flight.

Back in the little attic room which I had to myself, I kept working on my novel, based on the diaries I had kept during my last years in Dehra. It remained a journal but I began to fill in details, trying to capture the sights, sounds and smells of that little corner of India which I had known so well. And I tried to recreate the nature and character of some of my friends—Somi, Ranbir, Kishen—and the essence of that calf-love I'd felt for Kishen's mother. I could have left it as a journal, but in that case it would not have found a publisher. In the 1950s, no publisher would have been interested in the sentimental diaries of an unknown twenty-two year old. So it had to be turned into a novel.

Days of Wine and Roses

LOOKING BACK ON the two years I spent in London, I realize that it must have been the most restless period of my life, judging from the number of lodging houses and residential districts I lived in—Belsize Park, Haverstock Hill, Swiss Cottage, Tooting and a couple of other places whose names I have forgotten. I don't quite know why but I was never long in any one boarding house. And unlike a Graham Greene character, I wasn't trying to escape from sinister pursuers. Unless you could call Nirmala a sinister pursuer.

This good-hearted girl, the sister of an Indian friend, took it into her head that I needed a sister, and fussed over me so much, and followed me about so relentlessly that I was forced to flee my Glenmore Road lodgings and move to south London (Tooting) for a month. I preferred north London because it was more cosmopolitan, with a growing population of Indian, African and continental students. I had, initially, tried living in a students' hostel for a time but the food was awful and there was absolutely no privacy. So I moved into a bedsitter and took my meals at various snack bars and small cafés. There was a nice place near Swiss Cottage where I could have a glass or two of sherry with a light supper, and after this I would walk back to my room and write a few pages of my novel.

My meals were not very substantial and I must have been suffering from some form of malnutrition because my right eye started clouding over and my sight was partially affected. I had to go into hospital for some time. The condition was diagnosed as Eale's Disease, a rare tubercular condition of the eye, and I felt quite thrilled that I could count myself among the 'greats' who had also suffered from this disease in some form or another— Keats, the Bröntes, Stevenson, Katherine Mansfield, Ernest Dowson—and I thought, If only I could write like them, I'd be happy to live with a consumptive eye!

But the disease proved curable (for a time, anyway), and I went back to my job at Photax on Charlotte Street, totting up figures in heavy ledgers. Adding machines were just coming in but my employers were quite happy with their old ledgers—and so was I. I became quite good at adding pounds, shillings and pence, for hours, days, weeks, months on end. And quite contented too, provided I wasn't asked to enter the higher realms of mathematical endeavour. Maths was never my forte, although I kept reminding myself that Lewis Carroll, one of my all-time favourites, also wrote books on mathematics.

This mundane clerical job did not prevent me from pursuing the literary life, although for most of the time it was a solitary pursuit—wandering the streets of London and the East End in search of haunts associated with Dr Johnson, Dickens and his characters, W.W. Jacobs, Jerome K. Jerome, George and Weedon Grossmith; Barrie's Kensington Gardens; Dickens's dockland; Gissing's mean streets; Fleet Street; old music halls; Soho and its Greek and Italian restaurants.

In these latter I could picture the melancholic 1890s poets, especially Ernest Dowson writing love poems to the vivacious waitress who was probably unaware of his presence. For a time I went through my Dowson period—wistful, dreamy, wallowing in a sense of loss and failure. I had even memorized some of his verses, such as these lovely lines:

They are not long, the days of wine and roses:
Out of a misty dream
Our path emerges for a while, then closes
Within a dream.

Poor Dowson, destined to die young and unfulfilled. A minor poet, dismissed as inconsequential by the critics, and yet with us still, a singer of sad but exquisite songs.

A little down the road from my office was the Scala Theatre, and as soon as I had saved enough for a theatre ticket (theatre-going wasn't expensive in those days), I went to see the annual Christmas production of Peter Pan, which I'd read as a play when I was going through the works of Barrie in my school library. This production had Margaret Lockwood as Peter. She had been Britain's most popular film star in the forties and she was still pretty and vivacious. I think Captain Hook was played by Donald Wolfit, better known for his portrayal of Svengali.

My colleagues in Photax, though not in the least literary, were a friendly lot. There was my fellow clerk, Ken, who shared his marmite sandwiches with me. There was Maisie of the auburn hair, who was constantly being rung up by her boyfriends. And there was Clarence, who was slightly effeminate and known to frequent the gay bars in Soho. (Except that the term 'gay' hadn't been invented yet.) And there was our head clerk, Mr Smedly, who'd been in the Navy during the War, and was a musical-theatre buff. We would often discuss the latest musicals—*Guys and Dolls*, *South Pacific*, *Paint Your Wagon*, *Pal Joey*—big musicals which used to run for months, even years.

The window opposite my desk looked out on a huge hoarding, and it was always an event when a new poster went up on it. Weeks before the film was released, there was a poster of Judy Garland in her comeback film, *A Star Is Born*, and I can still remember the publicity headline: 'Judy, the World Is Waiting for Your Sunshine!' And, of course, there was Marilyn Monroe in *Niagara*, with Marilyn looking much bigger than the waterfall, and that fine actor, Joseph Cotten, nowhere in sight.

My heart, though, was not in the Photax office. I had no ambitions to become head clerk or even to learn the intricacies of the business. It was a nine-to-five job, giving me just enough money to live on (six pounds a week, in fact), while I scribbled away all my evenings, working on the second (or was it the third?) draft of my novel.

How I worked at that book! I was always being asked to put things in or take things out. At first the publishers suggested that it needed 'filling out'. When I filled it out, I was told that it was now a little too descriptive and would I prune it a bit? And what started out as a journal and then became a first-person narrative finally ended up in the third person. But the editors only made suggestions; they did not tamper with my language or style. And the 'feel' of the story—my love for India and my friends in particular—was ever present, running through it like a vein of gold.

Much of the publishers' uncertain and contradictory suggestions stemmed from the fact they relied heavily on their readers' recommendations. A 'reader' was a well-known writer or critic who was asked (and paid) to give his opinion on a book. My manuscript was sent to the celebrated literary critic, William Atkins, who said I was a 'born writer' and likened me to Sterne, but also said I should wait a little longer before attempting a novel. Another reader, Leslie Lamb, said he had enjoyed the story but that it would be a gamble to publish it.

Fortunately, Antony Dahl was the sort of publisher who was ready to take a risk with a new, young author, so instead of rejecting the book, he bought an option on it, which meant that he could sit on it for a couple of years until he had made up his mind!

My mentor at this time was Donna Stephen, Dahl's editor and junior partner. She was at least ten years older than me but we became good friends. She invited me to her flat for meals and sometimes accompanied me to the pictures or the theatre. She was tall, auburn-haired and attractive in a sort of angular English way. Donna was fond of me. She could see I was suffering from malnutrition and as she was a good cook (in addition to being a good editor), she shared her very pleasant and wholesome meals with me. There is nothing better than good English food, no matter what the French or Italians or Chinese may say. A lamb chop, a fish nicely fried, cold meat with salad, or shepherd's pie, or even an Irish stew, are infinitely more satisfying than most of the stuff served in continental or Far Eastern restaurants. I suppose it's really a matter of childhood preferences. For, deep down in my heart, I still fancy a kofta curry because koftas were what I enjoyed most in Granny's house. And oh, for one of Miss Kellner's meringues—but no one seems to make them any more.

I really neglected myself during the first year I spent in London. Never much of a cook, I was hard put to fry myself an egg every morning before rushing off to catch the tube for Tottenham Court Road, a journey of about twenty-five minutes. In the lunch break I would stroll across to a snack bar and have the inevitable baked beans-on-toast. There wasn't time for a more substantial meal, even if I could afford it. In the evenings I could indulge myself a little, with a decent meal in a quiet café; but most of the time I existed on snacks. No wonder I ended up with a debilitating disease!

Perhaps the first relaxing period of my London life was the month I spent in the Hampstead General Hospital, which turned out to be a friendly sort of place.

I was sent there for my Eale's disease, and the treatment consisted of occasional cortisone injections to my right eye. But I was allowed—even recommended—a full diet, supplemented by a bottle of Guinness with my lunch. They felt that I needed a little extra nourishment—wise doctors, those!

The bottle of Guinness made me the envy of the ward, but I made myself popular by sharing the drink with neighbouring patients when the nurses weren't looking. One nurse was a ravishing South American beauty, and half the ward was in love with her.

It was a general ward and one ailing patient named George—a West Indian from Trinidad—felt that he was being singled out for experimentation by the doctors. He set up a commotion whenever he had to be given a rather painful lumbar puncture. I would sit on his bed and try to calm him down, and he became rather dependent on my moral support, insisting on my presence whenever he was being examined or treated.

While I was in hospital, I got in a lot of reading (with one eye), wrote a short story, and received visitors in style. They ranged from my colleagues at Photax, to Donna Stephen, my would-be publisher, to some of my Indian friends in Hampstead, to my latest landlady, a motherly sort who'd lost some of her children in Hitler's persecution of the Jews.

When I left the hospital I was richer by a few pounds, having saved my salary and been treated free on account of the National Health Scheme. The spots had cleared from my eyes and I'd put on some weight, thanks to the lamb chops and Guinness that had constituted my lunch.

Before I left, George, the West Indian, asked me for my home address, but for some strange reason I did not expect to see him again.

Return to Dehra

AFTER THE INSULARITY of Jersey, London had been liberating. Theatres, cinemas, bookshops, museums, libraries helped further my self-education. Not once did I give serious thought to joining a college and picking up a degree. In any case, I did not have the funds, and there was no one to sponsor me. Instead, I had to join the vast legion of the world's workers. But Kensington Gardens, Regent's Park, Hampstead Heath and Primrose Hill gave me the green and open spaces that I needed in order to survive. In many respects London was a green city. My forays into the East End were really in search of literary landmarks.

And yet something was missing from my life. Vu-Phuong had come and gone like the breath of wind after which she had been named. And there was no one to take her place.

The affection, the camaraderie, the easy-going pleasures of my Dehra friendships; the colour and atmosphere of India; the feeling of belonging—these things I missed . . .

Even though I had grown up with a love for the English language and its literature, even though my forefathers were British, Britain was not really my place. I did not belong to the bright lights of Piccadilly and Leicester Square; or, for that matter, to the apple orchards of Kent or the strawberry fields of Berkshire. I belonged, very firmly, to peepal trees and mango groves; to sleepy little towns all over India; to hot sunshine, muddy canals, the pungent scent of marigolds; the hills of home;

spicy odours, wet earth after summer rain, neem pods bursting; laughing brown faces; and the intimacy of human contact.

Human contact! That was what I missed most. It was not to be found in the office where I worked, or in my landlady's house, or in any of the learned societies which I had joined, or even in the pubs into which I sometimes wandered ... The freedom to touch someone without being misunderstood. To take someone by the hand as a mark of affection rather than desire. Or even to know desire. And fulfilment. To be among strangers without feeling like an outsider. For in India there are no strangers ...

I had been away for over four years but the bonds were as strong as ever, the longing to return had never left me.

How I expected to make a living in India when I returned was something of a mystery to me. You did not just walk into the nearest employment exchange to find a job waiting for you. I had no qualifications. All I could do was write and I was still a novice at that. If I set myself up as a freelance writer and bombarded every magazine in the country, I could probably eke out a livelihood. At that time there were only some half-a-dozen English language magazines in India and almost no book publishers (except for a handful of educational presses left over from British days). The possibilities were definitely limited; but this did not deter me. I had confidence in myself (too much, perhaps) and plenty of guts (my motto being, 'Never despair. But if you do, work on in despair'). And, of course, all the optimism of youth.

As Donna Stephen and Antony Dahl kept telling me they would publish my novel one day (I had finally put my foot, or rather, my pen, down and refused to do any more work on it), I wheedled a fifty-pound advance out from them, this being the standard advance against royalties at the time. Out of this princely sum I bought a ticket for Bombay on the *S.S. Batory*, a Polish passenger liner which had seen better days. There was a fee for a story I'd sold to the BBC and some money saved from my Photax salary; and with these amounts I bought a decent-looking suitcase and a few presents to take home.

I did not say goodbye to many people—just my office colleagues who confessed that they would miss my imitations of Sir Harry Lauder; and my landlady, to whom I gave my Eartha Kitt records—and walked up the gangway of the *Batory* on a chilly day early in October.

Soon we were in the warmer waters of the Mediterranean and a few days later in the even warmer Red Sea. It grew gloriously hot. But the *Batory* was a strange ship, said to be jinxed. A few months earlier, most of its Polish crew had sought political asylum in Britain. And now, as we passed through the Suez Canal, a crew member jumped overboard and was never seen again. Hopefully he'd swum ashore.

Then, when we were in the Arabian Sea, we had to get out of our bunks in the middle of the night for the ship's alarm bells were ringing and we thought the *Batory* was sinking. As there had been no lifeboat drill and no one had any idea of how a lifebelt should be worn, there was a certain amount of panic. Cries of 'Abandon ship!' mingled with shouts of 'Man overboard!' and 'Women and children first!'—although there were no signs of women and children being given that privilege. Finally it transpired that a passenger, tipsy on too much Polish vodka, had indeed fallen overboard. A lifeboat was lowered and the ship drifted around for some time; but whether or not the passenger was rescued, we were not told. Nor did I discover his (or her) identity. Whatever tragedy had occurred had been swallowed up in the immensity of the darkness and the sea.

The saga of the *Batory* was far from over.

No sooner had the ship docked at Bombay's Ballard Pier than a fire broke out in the hold. Most of the passengers lost their heavy luggage. Fortunately, my suitcase and typewriter were both with me and these I clung to all the way to the Victoria

Terminus and all the way to Dehra Dun. I knew it would be some time before I could afford more clothes or another typewriter.

When the train drew into Dehra I found Devinder waiting to greet me. (Somi and Ranbir were now both in Calcutta.)

Devinder had come on his cycle.

I got up on the crossbar of Devinder's bike and he took me to his place (he was staying in the outhouse of a tea-planter) in style, through the familiar streets of the town that had so shaped my life.

The Odeon was showing an old Bogart film; the small roadside cafés were open; the bougainvillaea were a mass of colour; the mango blossoms smelt sweet; Devinder chattered away; and the girls looked prettier than ever.

And I was twenty-four that year.

Summertime in Old New Delhi

THE NEXT YEAR I left Dehra for Delhi, and lived in the capital for a few years—freelancing, and for a time working with an international relief agency. I wasn't too happy to be in Delhi, but I'd felt the need to move, for Dehra had limited scope for young Indian authors writing in English. I could not fall in love with Delhi, my heart was always in the hills and small towns of north India.

But there were things I came to like about Delhi, even in summer. The smell of a hot Indian summer is one smell that can never be forgotten. It is not just the thirsty earth with its distinctive odour, but all other ingredients of a hot weather in the plains that go to make this season almost intolerable on the one hand and sweetly memorable on the other. For who can forget that summer brings the jasmine, whose sweet scent drifts past us on the evening breeze along with the stronger odours and scents of mango blossom, raat-ki-rani and cowdung smoke.

Although I have spent most of my life in the hills, I had stayed in some fairly hot places—humid Kathiawar ports, dusty old New Delhi, and the steamy Java—and I was no stranger to prickly heat, mosquito bites, intermittent fever and dysentery and other hot-weather afflictions. Today's residents of the capital complain of pollution and overcrowding, and I wouldn't exchange my mountain perch for the pleasure of being fried crisp, but at least half of them have air-conditioning, coolers, refrigerators and other means to keep the heat at bay. In 1940s'

Delhi you were lucky to have a small table-fan, and that was effective only if the bhisti, or water-carrier, came around with his goat-skin bag, splashing water on to the khus-khus matting draped from your door or window; otherwise the fan simply blew hot air at you. I was in Delhi in the early '40s, living with my father, and I shall never forget the fragrant, refreshing smell of the wet khus reed which cooled the rooms and verandas of New Delhi bungalows (the only high-rise building in those days was the Qutab Minar).

Father and I lived in a small RAF hutment on the fringe of the scrub jungle near Humayun's tomb. This was then furthest Delhi, where one could expect to find peacocks in the garden and a snake in the bathroom. The bhisti and the khus-khus helped us to survive that summer. As did the box-like wind-up gramophone on which I played endless records which had to be stored flat in order to prevent them from warping and assuming weird shapes in the heat. My father liked opera, and on his day off he would play his Caruso records. It was strange to lie beside him on a perspiration-soaked bed, listening to Caruso sing *Che Gelida Manina*:

> *Your tiny hand is frozen,*
> *Let me warm it into life!*

I was ten, a child of warm climates, and I had no idea what it was like to have one's hand frozen. Dipping my hands in ice-cream was the nearest I'd come to it.

In 1959 I was living on the outskirts of a greater, further New Delhi. The influx of refugees from the Punjab after Partition had led to many new colonies springing up on the outskirts of the capital, and at the time the furthest of these was Rajouri Garden. Needless to say, there were no gardens there. The treeless colony was buffeted by hot, dusty winds from Haryana and Rajasthan. The houses were built on one side of Najafgarh Road. On the other side, as yet uncolonized, were extensive fields of wheat and other crops still belonging to the original inhabitants. In an attempt to escape the city life that constantly oppressed me, I would walk across the main road and into the fields, finding old wells, irrigation channels, camels and buffaloes, and sighting birds and small creatures that no longer dwelt in the city. In an odd way, it was my reaction to city life that led to my taking a greater interest in the natural world. Up to that time, I had taken it all for granted.

The notebook I kept at the time is before me now, and my first entry describes the bluejays or rollers that were so much a feature of those remaining open spaces. At rest, the bird is fairly nondescript, but when it takes flight it reveals the glorious bright blue wings and the tail, banded with a lighter blue. It sits motionless . . . But the large dark eyes are constantly watching the ground in every direction. A grasshopper or cricket has only to make a brief appearance, and the bluejay will launch itself straight at its prey. In the spring and early summer the 'roller' lives up to its other name. It indulges in love flights in which it rises and falls in the air with harsh grating screams—a real rock-'n'-roller!

Some way down the Najafgarh Road was a large village pond and beside it a magnificent banyan tree. We have no place for banyan trees today, they need so much space in which to spread their limbs and live comfortably. Cut away its aerial roots and the great tree topples over—usually to make way for a spacious apartment building. This one had about a hundred pillars supporting the boughs, and above them there was this great leafy crown like a pillared hall. It has been said that whole armies could shelter in the shade of an old banyan. And probably at one time they did. I saw another sort of army visit the banyan by the village pond when it was in fruit. Parakeets, mynas, rosy pastors, crested bulbuls without crests, barbets and many other birds crowded the tree in order to feast noisily on big, scarlet figs. Season's eatings!

Even further down the Najafgarh Road was a large jheel, famous for its fishing. I wonder if any part of the jheel still exists, or if it got filled in and became a part of greater Delhi. One could rest in the shade of a small babul or keekar tree and watch the kingfisher skim over the water, making just a slight splash as it dived and came up with small glistening fish. Our common Indian kingfisher is a beautiful little bird with a brilliant blue back, a white throat and orange underparts. I would spot one perched on an overhanging bush or rock, and wait to see it plunge like an arrow into the water and return to its perch to devour the catch. It came over the water in a flash of gleaming blue, shrilling its loud 'tit-tit-tit'.

The kingfisher is the subject of a number of legends, and the one I remember best, recounted by Romain Rolland, tells us that it was originally a plain grey bird that acquired its resplendent colours by flying straight towards the sun when Noah let it out of the Ark. Its upper plumage took the colour of the sky above, while the lower was scorched a deep russet by the rays of the setting sun.

Summer and winter, I scorned the dust and the traffic, and walked all over Delhi—from Rajouri Garden to Connaught Place, which must have been five or six miles, and on other occasions, from Daryaganj to Chandni Chowk, and from Ajmeri Gate to India Gate! That is the best way to get to know a city. I had walked all over London. Now I did the same thing in Delhi, investigating old tombs and monuments, historic streets and buildings, or simply sitting on the grass near India Gate and eating jamuns. I liked the sour tang of the jamun fruit which was best eaten with a little salt. And I liked the deep purple colour of the fruit. Jamuns were one of the nicer things about Delhi.

From Small Beginnings

ON THE FIRST clear September day, towards the end of the rains, I visited the pine-knoll, my place of peace and power.

Mussoorie . . . never ever thought that this would be the place where I'd finally settle down.

After my mother passed away (soon after her operation), I returned to Dehra, and life went back to its routine ways. Not for very long though, for, one day I received a legal notice informing me about a house in Mussoorie that I had inherited. I had inherited it from Uncle Ken (of all people). I was shocked, to say the least. I had had no idea that Uncle Ken had come back to India from England, and worse still, hadn't known about his whereabouts or his death until now. I was restless with curiosity. Had Uncle Ken cared for me so much as to leave behind a house—his house—for me? Why hadn't he contacted me all these years? Mussoorie wasn't far from Dehra, after all.

Plagued by these questions I set out to take a look at this inheritance of mine. It did not disappoint—it was a charming little cottage on the slope of a hill, and had a splendid view.

I pondered on my next course of action. It would probably be easy for me to sell off the cottage to someone and forget about it. But would that be Uncle Ken's wish? Perhaps he had been fond of his house and had wanted it to be occupied by someone who was family. And I was the only living member of our family in India. I didn't want to leave Dehra; many of the best years of my life had been spent in Dehra. However, this house in Mussoorie gave me the perfect opportunity and reason to finally settle down, put my roots down, for I'd always been lured by the hills ever since my schooldays in Simla. Yes, I'd make that cottage in Mussoorie my permanent residence. So, here I was—in Mussoorie.

I tramped through late monsoon foliage—tall ferns, bushes festooned with flowering convolvulus—and crossed the stream by way of its little bridge of stones before climbing the steep hill to the pine slope.

This is where I would write my stories. I could see everything from here—my cottage across the valley; behind and above me, the town and the bazaar, straddling the ridge; to the left, the high mountains and the twisting road to the source of the great river; below me, the little stream and the path to the village; the fields beyond; the wide valley below, and another range of hills and then the distant plains.

Today, as I look around, I can even see Prem Singh in the garden, putting the mattresses out in the sun. From here he is just a speck on the far hill, but I know it is Prem by the way he stands. A man may have a hundred disguises, but in the end it is his posture that gives him away. Like my grandfather, who was a master of disguise and successfully roamed the bazaars as fruit-vendor or basketmaker. But we could always recognize him because of his pronounced slouch.

Prem Singh doesn't slouch, but he has this habit of looking up at the sky (regardless of whether it's cloudy or clear), and at the moment he's looking at the sky.

Eight years with Prem. He was just a sixteen-year-old boy when I first saw him, and now he has a wife and child.

I had been in the cottage for just over a year . . . He stood on the landing outside the kitchen door. A tall boy, dark, with good teeth and brown, deep-set eyes, dressed smartly in white drill— his only change of clothes. Looking for a job. I liked the look of him, but . . .

'I already have someone working for me,' I said.

'Yes, sir. He is my uncle.'

In the hills, everyone is a brother or an uncle.

'You don't want me to dismiss your uncle?'

'No, sir. But he says you can find a job for me.'

'I'll try. I'll make enquiries. Have you just come from your village?'

'Yes. Yesterday I walked ten miles to Pauri. There I got a bus.'

'Sit down. Your uncle will make some tea.'

He sat down on the steps, removed his white keds, wriggled his toes. His feet were both long and broad, large feet but not ugly. He was unusually clean for a hill boy. And taller than most.

'Do you smoke?' I asked.

'No, sir.'

'It is true,' said his uncle. 'He does not smoke. All my nephews smoke but this one. He is a little peculiar, he does not smoke— neither bidi nor hookah.'

'Do you drink?'

'It makes me vomit.'

'Do you take bhang?'

'No, sahib.'

'You have no vices. It's unnatural.'

'He is unnatural, sahib,' said his uncle.

'Does he chase girls?'

'They chase him, sahib.'

'So he left the village and came looking for a job.' I looked at him. He grinned, then looked away and began rubbing his feet.

'Your name is . . .?'

'Prem Singh.'

'All right, Prem, I will try to do something for you.'

I did not see him for a couple of weeks. I forgot about finding him a job. But when I met him again, on the road to the bazaar, he told me that he had got a temporary job in the Survey, looking after the surveyor's tents.

'Next week we will be going to Rajasthan,' he said.

'It will be very hot. Have you been in the desert before?'

'No, sir.'

'It is not like the hills. And it is far from home.'

'I know. But I have no choice in the matter. I have to collect some money in order to get married.'

In his region there was a bride price, usually of two thousand rupees.

'Do you have to get married so soon?'

'I have only one brother and he is still very young. My mother is not well. She needs a daughter-in-law to help her in the fields and the house, and with the cows. We are a small family, so the work is greater.'

Every family has its few terraced fields, narrow and stony, usually perched on a hillside above a stream or river. They grow rice, barley, maize, potatoes—just enough to live on. Even if their produce is sufficient for marketing, the absence of roads makes it difficult to get the produce to the market towns. There is no money to be earned in the villages, and money is needed for clothes, soap, medicines, and for recovering the family jewellery from the moneylenders. So the young men leave their villages to find work, and to find work they must go to the plains. The lucky ones get into the army. Others enter domestic service or take jobs in garages, hotels, wayside tea shops, schools . . .

In Mussoorie the main attraction is the large number of schools which employ cooks and bearers. But the schools were full when Prem arrived. He'd been to the recruiting centre at Roorkee, hoping to get into the army; but they found a deformity in his right foot, the result of a bone broken when a landslip carried him away one dark monsoon night. He was lucky, he said, that it was only his foot and not his head that had been broken.

He came to the house to inform his uncle about the job and to say goodbye. I thought, another nice person I probably won't see again; another ship passing in the night, the friendly twinkle of its lights soon vanishing in the darkness. I said 'Come again', held his smile with mine so that I could remember him better, and returned to my study and my typewriter. The typewriter is the repository of a writer's loneliness. It stares unsympathetically back at him every day, doing its best to be discouraging. Maybe I'll go back to the old-fashioned quill pen and marble ink-stand; then I can feel like a real writer—Balzac or Dickens—scratching away into the endless reaches of the night . . . Of course, the days and nights are seemingly shorter than they need to be! They must be, otherwise why do we hurry so much and achieve so little, by the standards of the past . . .

Prem went, disappeared into the vast faceless cities of the plains, and a year slipped by, or rather I did, and then there he was again, thinner and darker and still smiling and still looking for a job. I should have known that hill men don't disappear altogether. The spirit-haunted rocks don't let their people wander too far, lest they lose them forever.

I was able to get him a job in the school. The Headmaster's wife needed a cook. I wasn't sure if Prem could cook very well but I sent him along and they said they'd give him a trial. Three days later the Headmaster's wife met me on the road and started gushing all over me. She was the type who gushed.

'We're so grateful to you! Thank you for sending me that lovely boy. He's so polite. And he cooks very well. A little too hot for my husband, but otherwise delicious—just delicious! He's a real treasure—a lovely boy.' And she gave me an arch look—the famous look which she used to captivate all the good-looking young prefects who became prefects, it was said, only if she approved of them.

I wasn't sure that she didn't want something more than a cook, and I only hoped that Prem would give every satisfaction.

He looked cheerful enough when he came to see me on his off-day.

'How are you getting on?' I asked.

'Lovely,' he said, using his mistress's favourite expression.

'What do you mean—lovely? Do they like your work?'

'The memsahib likes it. She strokes me on the cheek whenever she enters the kitchen. The sahib says nothing. He takes medicine after every meal.'

'Did he always take medicine—or only now that you're doing the cooking?'

'I am not sure. I think he has always been sick.'

He was sleeping in the Headmaster's veranda and getting sixty rupees a month. A cook in Delhi got a hundred and sixty. And a cook in Paris or New York got ten times as much. I did not say as much to Prem. He might ask me to get him a job in New York. And that would be the last I saw of him! He, as a cook, might well get a job making curries off-Broadway; I, as a writer, wouldn't get to first base. And only my Uncle Ken knew the secret of how to make a living without actually doing any work. But then, of course, he had three sisters. And each of them was married to a fairly prosperous husband. So Uncle Ken divided his year among them. Three months with Aunt Mabel in Nainital. Three months with Aunt Beryl in Kashmir. Three months with Aunt Emily in Lucknow. And three months with Grandmother who was his aunt, and who was always very fond of him. In this way he never overstayed his welcome. Uncle Ken had it worked out to perfection.

But I had no sisters and I couldn't live forever on the royalties of a single successful novel. So I had to write others. So I came to the hills.

The hill men go to the plains to make a living. I had to come to the hills to try and make mine.

'Prem,' I said, 'why don't you work for me?'

'And what about my uncle?'

'He seems ready to desert me any day. His grandfather is ill, he says, and he wants to go home.'

'His grandfather died last year.'

'That's what I mean—he's getting restless. And I don't mind if he goes. These days he seems to be suffering from a form of sleeping sickness. I have to get up first and make his tea . . .'

Sitting here under the cherry tree, whose leaves are just beginning to turn yellow, I rest my chin on my knees and gaze across the valley to where Prem moves about in the garden. Looking back over the eight years he has been with me, I recall some of the nicest things about him. They come to me in no particular order—just pieces of cinema—coloured slides slipping across the screen of memory . . .

Prem rocking his infant son to sleep—crooning to him, passing his large hand gently over the child's curly head; Prem following me down to the police station when I was arrested, (on a warrant from Bombay, charging me with writing an allegedly obscene short story!) and waiting outside until I reappeared; his smile, his large, irrepressible laughter, most in evidence when he was seeing an old Laurel and Hardy movie.

Of course there were times when he could be infuriating, stubborn, deliberately pig-headed, sending me little notes of resignation—but I never found it difficult to overlook these little acts of self-indulgence. He had brought much love and laughter into my life, and what more could a lonely man ask for?

It was his stubborn streak that limited the length of his stay in the Headmaster's household. Mr Good was tolerant enough. But Mrs Good was one of those women who, when they are pleased with you, go out of their way to help, pamper and flatter, but when displeased, become vindictive, going out of their way to harm or destroy. Mrs Good sought power—over her husband, her dog, her favourite pupils, her servant . . . She had absolute power over the husband and the dog, partial power over her slightly bewildered pupils, and none at all over Prem, who missed the subtleties of her designs upon his soul. He did not respond to her mothering, or to the way in which she tweaked him on the cheeks, brushed against him in the kitchen and made admiring remarks about his looks and physique. Memsahibs, he knew, were not for him. So he kept a stony face and went diligently about his duties. And she felt slighted, put in her place. Her liking turned to dislike. Instead of admiring remarks, she began making disparaging remarks about his looks, his clothes, his manners. She found fault with his cooking. No longer was it 'lovely'. She even accused him of taking away the dog's meat and giving it to a poor family living on the hillside— no more heinous crime could be imagined! Mr Good threatened him with dismissal. So Prem became stubborn. The following day he withheld the dog's food altogether, threw it down the khud where it was seized upon by innumerable strays, and he went off to the pictures.

That was the end of his job. 'I'll have to go home now,' he told me. 'I won't get another job in this area. The Mem will see to that.'

'Stay a few days,' I said.

'I have only enough money with which to get home.'

'Keep it for going home. You can stay with me for a few days, while you look around. Your uncle won't mind sharing his food with you.'

His uncle did mind. He did not like the idea of working for his nephew as well; it seemed to him no part of his duties. And he was apprehensive that Prem might get his job.

So Prem stayed no longer than a week.

Here on the knoll the grass is just beginning to turn yellow. The first clouds approaching winter cover the sky. The trees are very still. The birds are silent. Only a cricket keeps singing on the oak tree. Perhaps there will be a storm before evening. A storm like the one in which Prem arrived at the cottage with his wife and child—but that's jumping too far ahead . . .

After he had returned to his village, it was several months before I saw him again. His uncle told me he had taken up a job in Lucknow. There was an address. It did not seem complete, but I resolved that when I was next in Lucknow I would try to see him.

The opportunity came in May, as the hot winds of summer blew across the plains. It was the time of year when people who can afford it, try to get away to the hills. I dislike Lucknow at the best of times, and I hate it in summer. People compete with each other in being bad-tempered and mean. But I had to go down— I don't remember why, but it must have seemed very necessary at the time—and I took the opportunity to try and see Prem.

Nothing went right for me. Of course the address was all wrong, and I wandered about in a remote, dusty, treeless colony called Vasant Bagh (Spring Garden) for over two hours, asking all the domestic servants I came across if they could put me in touch with Prem Singh of Village Koli, Pauri Garhwal. There were innumerable Prem Singhs, but apparently none who belonged to Village Koli. I returned to my hotel and took two days to recover from heatstroke before returning to Mussoorie, thanking God for mountains!

And then the uncle gave notice. He'd found a better-paid job in Dehra Dun and was anxious to be off. I didn't try to stop him.

For the next six months I lived in the cottage without any help. I did not find this difficult. I was used to living alone. It wasn't service that I needed but companionship. In the cottage it was very quiet. The ghosts of long-dead residents were sympathetic but unobtrusive. The song of the whistling thrush was beautiful, but I knew he was not singing for me. Up the valley came the sound of a lute, but I never saw the flute player. My affinity was with the little red fox who roamed the hillside below the cottage. I met him one night and wrote these lines:

As I walked home last night
I saw a lone fox dancing
In the cold moonlight.
I stood and watched—then

Took the low road, knowing
The night was his by right.
Sometimes, when words ring true,
I'm like a lone fox dancing
In the morning dew.

During the rains, watching the dripping trees and the mist climbing the valley, I wrote a great deal of poetry. Loneliness is of value to poets. But poetry didn't bring me much money, and funds were low. And then, just as I was wondering if I would have to give up my freedom and take a job again, a publisher bought the paperback rights of one of my children's stories, and I was free to live and write as I pleased—for another three months!

That was in November. To celebrate, I took a long walk through the Landour Bazaar and up the Tehri road. It was a good day for walking; and it was dark by the time I returned to the outskirts of the town. Someone stood waiting for me on the road above the cottage. I hurried past him.

If I am not for myself,
Who will be for me?
And if I am not for others,
What am I?
And if not now, when?

I startled myself with the memory of these words of Hillel, the ancient Hebrew sage. I walked back to the shadows where the youth stood, and saw that it was Prem.

'Prem!' I said. 'Why are you sitting out here, in the cold? Why did you not go to the house?'

'I went, sir, but there was a lock on the door. I thought you had gone away.'

'And you were going to remain here, on the road?'

'Only for tonight. I would have gone down to Dehra in the morning.'

'Come, let's go home. I have been waiting for you. I looked for you in Lucknow, but could not find the place where you were working.'

'I have left them now.'

'And your uncle has left me. So will you work for me now?'

'For as long as you wish.'

'For as long as the gods wish.'

We did not go straight home, but returned to the bazaar and took our meal in the Sindhi Sweet Shop—hot puris and strong sweet tea.

We walked home together in the bright moonlight. I felt sorry for the little fox dancing alone.

When You Can't Climb
Trees Any More

A YEAR LATER I found myself sitting in a taxi that was headed for Dehra. Though I was happily ensconced in Mussoorie, I'd miss Dehra once in a while and be reflecting back on the many years that I had spent there. I decided to visit the town every now and then to put my restless thoughts and memories to rest.

When I finally got there, I felt a bit lost. Now what? What exactly did I want to do in Dehra? None of my old friends had stayed back in Dehra. Neither did I have any relatives here. Maybe I should look up old Miss Pettibone . . . I'd promised to keep in touch with her, but had sent her just a letter or two in the beginning—when I had moved. After that, I had not been in touch with her, neither had she written at all. But then, I didn't expect her to write—she was so very old and not very well either. Never mind, I told myself, I will surprise her and apologize for being such a cad all these years. But first I would get her something.

I went to the mall and bought her a jar of orange marmalade and some bacon, and made my way to her cottage. I entered through the gate and walked up the small path. The garden which she was so fond of hardly remained . . . it was just a jungle of weeds and all kinds of wild plants. As for the cottage, it wore a deserted look. The smile died on my lips and I started feeling a bit apprehensive. Just as I was turning away from the front door, I saw the postman come up near the gate. It was the same old postman Dehra had had all these years . . . he just looked more wizened and lean.

'Ah, Bond sahib. Good to see you after all these years. But what are you doing here?'

'I've come to visit Miss Pettibone. Can you tell me where she'll be now? I had no idea she had moved.'

'So you haven't heard . . . Miss Pettibone, she passed away three years after you left. As you know, she was very old and weak. She lay crippled by a paralytic stroke for a long time, and had one of her distant relatives looking after her. But she didn't recover from that stroke . . . she seemed to have given up on life suddenly, and wanted nature to take its own course.'

'But what about this cottage?'

'This house is now disputed property. You see, she didn't leave any will and now all her relatives—I'm sure she never even knew how some of them were related to her—have turned up to claim this property as theirs and quite predictably, this house has been closed up till a legal verdict is taken on it.'

I felt ashamed of my negligence towards this gentle old lady who had been so kind and friendly towards me. Now there was nothing I could do for her. Disappointed and upset, I walked down the hill slowly. I began to wonder if it had been such a good idea to come back to Dehra after all. It might have been better not to know of these sad things at all.

Brooding, I let my feet take me wherever they wanted to go, and after some time saw that I was now facing Astley Hall. I was suddenly afraid to go into the building. What if more disappointments lurked around the corner? Moti Bibi came out of her shop. But she didn't seem to recognize me.

'Moti Bibi, don't you know me? Bond?'

She looked up at me and smiled and said, 'Of course I recognized you, but wasn't sure if you'd remember me. You've come to meet your friend, isn't it? Good. Well, don't keep standing there, go right upstairs.'

Which friend, I asked myself. I stood back and took stock of the building. It looked older and more decrepit than before, but it was the first-floor balcony which caught my attention. On it were a row of potted plants—ferns, a palm, a few bright marigolds, zinnias and nasturtiums—they made the balcony stand out from others. It was impossible to miss it.

I was quite sure they were my plants—the plants that my friend Sitaram had stolen for me, and which I had left behind in Moti Bibi's care when I was leaving Dehra. They still looked healthy, but who was taking care of them now? Could it be . . .?

With my heart racing, I bounded up the stairs—all twenty-two of them—and knocked at the door of the flat.

Chance gives and takes away and gives again. The door was opened by none other than Sitaram himself. For a second he looked as surprised as I was and, grinning in that typical Sitaram manner, welcomed me in.

'Truly filmi style,' he said, still grinning.

'What do you mean?' I asked.

'Well, your reappearance at our doorstep.'

'"Our"? Who else is staying with you? Oh, your parents. I'd forgotten about them.'

'Not them, not them. My wife, Mr Rusty, lives with me now.'

Wife! Before I could ask him anything else, a young woman entered the room and I got up in confusion. I knew her . . . had seen her; but couldn't remember who she was. She looked at me directly and seeing my lost expression, gave a little laugh. Sitaram too burst into laughter. Radha! The name leapt into my mind. The maid who had worked in the flat next to mine in the very same building. I regained my composure and said, 'Nice to see you again, Radha. Nicer to know you have married this rogue. How long has it been?'

'I know what's on your mind,' said Sitaram. 'You are asking yourself how Radha and I happen to be married to each other. Well, as you know, I was in Simla for a few years, roughing it out as an underpaid, but overworked waiter. A few months after you left I came back to Dehra. Let's say I was forced to come back. I was accused of stealing cutlery and soap bars in the hotel. Can you imagine that? I admit I had been reckless and mischievous in the past, but this allegation was completely baseless. I couldn't prove my innocence, so I left and came back here. But when I got here, my parents told me you'd gone away. Moti Bibi gave me all your plants and I continued staying with my parents. But even then I was bored and lonely and used to come over to Astley Hall.

'I'd go up to the terrace and sit there, watching the kites in the sky. Sometimes I met Radha there—she'd come upstairs to hang out the washing and we'd get talking. Soon, I realized that I liked her a lot. What I liked most about her was her smile. It dropped over her face slowly, like sunshine moving over brown hills. She seemed to give out some of that glow that was in her face. I felt it pour over me. And this golden feeling did not pass when she left the terrace. That was how I knew she was going to mean something special to me.

'Radha's folks were poor, but in time I was to realize that I was even poorer. When I discovered that plans were afoot to marry her to a widower of sixty, I plucked up enough courage to declare that I would marry her myself. But my youth was no consideration. The widower had a generous gift of money for Radha's parents. Not only was this offer attractive, it was customary. What had I to offer? Nothing—I did not even possess a job that would take care of our basic needs if we got married. Nor did I have rich parents or relatives to speak and act on my behalf.

'I thought of running away with Radha. When I mentioned it to her, her eyes lit up. She thought it would be great fun. Women in love can be just as reckless as men! She did not even seem to worry about where we would go and how we would live. There would be no home to crawl back to for either of us. But we had loved passionately and fiercely and felt compelled to elope, regardless of the consequences. We longed for something more permanent than the few stolen moments we shared together—on the stairs, on the terrace, in the deserted junkyard behind the shops.

'And so we ran away to Simla where I had some friends. I didn't have your address with me, or I would have brought her straight to your place. Anyway, God has been kind to me ever since. We got jobs in the canteen of a missionary school in Simla, and then after a year, I got a job in Dehra. Now, she looks after the house while I work in a jam factory close by. Tell me, Rusty, aren't you happy for us?'

Of course I was. I was glad that Sitaram had not only found true love, but also managed to do something which I never could—have the courage and belief to sustain that love. My trip to Dehra was justified. And now, there was one more place I had to go to.

I headed towards my grandmother's house.

When the trees saw me, they made as if to turn in my direction. A puff of wind came across the valley from the distant snows. A long-tailed blue magpie took alarm and flew noisily out of an oak tree. The cicadas were suddenly silent. But the trees remembered me. They bowed gently in the breeze and beckoned me nearer, welcoming me home. Three pines, a straggling oak and a wild cherry. I went among them and acknowledged their welcome with a touch of my hand against their trunks—the cherry's smooth and polished; the pine's patterned and whorled; the oak's rough, gnarled, full of experience. He'd been there longest, and the wind had bent and twisted a few of his upper branches, so that he looked shaggy and undistinguished. But like the philosopher who is careless about his dress and appearance, the oak has secrets, a hidden wisdom. He has learnt the art of survival!

While the oak and the pines were older than me and my

father, and had been here many, many years, the cherry tree was exactly thirty-nine years old. I knew, because I had planted it.

On one of my vacations from boarding school, I'd come to Dehra to spend a few weeks with Grandmother. Uncle Ken had given me this cherry seed, and on an impulse I thrust it into the soft earth, and then went away and forgot all about it. A few months later I found a tiny cherry tree in the long grass. I did not expect it to survive. But the following year it was two feet tall. And then some goats ate its leaves and a grass-cutter's scythe injured the stem, and I was sure it would wither away. But it renewed itself, sprang up even faster, and within three years it was a healthy, growing tree, about five feet tall.

After Grandmother's house was sold, I left Dehra for a while for some years—forced by circumstances—but I did not forget the cherry tree. I thought about it fairly often, sent telepathic messages of encouragement in its direction. And when, several years ago, I returned in the autumn, my heart did a somersault when I found my tree sprinkled with pale pink blossoms. (The Himalayan cherry flowers in November.) And later, when the fruit was ripe, the tree was visited by finches, tits, bulbuls and other small birds, all come to feast on the sour, red cherries.

That summer when the house was standing empty (I think it was between owners) I spent a night on the pine-knoll, sleeping on the grass beneath the cherry tree. I lay awake for hours, listening to the chatter of the stream and the occasional tonk-tonk of the nightjar, and watching through the branches overhead, the stars turning in the sky. And I felt the power of the sky and the earth, and the power of a small cherry seed . . .

Now I stood on the grass verge by the side of the road and looked over the garden wall at the old house. It hadn't changed much. There's little anyone can do to alter a house built with solid blocks of granite brought from the riverbed. But there was a new outhouse and there were fewer trees. I was pleased to see that the jackfruit tree still stood at the side of the building, casting its shade on the wall. I remembered my grandmother saying: 'A blessing rests on the house where falls the shadow of a tree.' And so the present owners must also be the recipients of the tree's blessings.

At the spot where I stood there had once been a turnstile, and as a boy I would swing on it, going round and round until I was quite dizzy. Now the turnstile had gone and the opening walled up. Tall hollyhocks grew on the other side of the wall.

'What are you looking at?'

It was a disembodied voice at first. Moments later a boy stood framed between dark red hollyhocks, staring at me.

It was difficult to guess his age. He might have been twelve or he might have been sixteen.

'I'm looking at the house,' I said.

'Why? Do you want to buy it?'

'Is it your house?'

'It's my father's.'

'And what does your father do?'

'He's only a Colonel.'

'Only a Colonel?'

'Well, he should have been a Brigadier by now.'

I burst out laughing.

'It's not funny,' he said. 'Even mummy says he should have been a Brigadier.'

It was on the tip of my tongue to make a witty remark ('Perhaps that's why he's still a Colonel'), but I did not want to give offence. We stood on either side of the wall, appraising each other.

'Well,' he said finally. 'If you don't want to buy the house, what are you looking at?'

'I used to live here once.'

'Oh.'

'Many years ago. When I was a boy—younger than you . . . until my grandmother died and then we sold the house and went away.'

He was silent for a while, taking in this information. Then he said, 'And you'd like to buy it back now, but you don't have the money?'

'No, I wasn't thinking of buying it back. I wanted to see it again, that's all. How long have you lived here?'

'Only three years,' he smiled. He'd been eating a melon and there was still juice at the corners of his mouth. 'Would you like to come in—and look—once more?'

'Wouldn't your parents mind?'

'They've gone to the Club. They won't mind. I'm allowed to bring my friends home.'

'Even adult friends?'

'How old are you?'

'Oh, a little old, but feeling young today.' And to prove it I decided I'd climb over the wall instead of going in by the gate. I got up on the wall all right, but had to rest there, breathing heavily. 'Middle-aged man on the flying trapeze,' I muttered to myself.

'Let me help you,' said the boy and gave me his hand.

I slithered down into a flower-bed, shattering the stem of a hollyhock.

As we walked across the grass I noticed a stone bench under a mango tree. It was the bench on which my grandmother used to sit when she tired of pruning rose bushes and bougainvillaea.

'Let's sit here,' I said. 'I don't want to go inside.'

He sat beside me on the bench. It was March and the mango tree was in bloom. A sweet, heavy fragrance drenched the garden.

We were silent for some time. I closed my eyes and remembered other times—the music of a piano, the chiming of a grandfather clock, the constant twitter of budgerigars on the veranda, my grandfather cranking up the old car . . .

'I used to climb the jackfruit tree,' I said, opening my eyes. 'I didn't like the jackfruit, though. Do you?'

'It's all right in pickles.'

'I suppose so . . . The tree was easy to climb. I spent a lot of time in it.'

'Do you want to climb it again? My parents won't mind.'

'No, I don't think so. Not after climbing the wall! Let's just sit here for a few minutes and talk. I mention the jackfruit tree because it was my favourite place. Do you see that thick branch stretching out over the roof? Half-way along it there's a small hollow in which I used to keep some of my treasures.'

'What kind of treasures?'

'Oh, nothing very valuable. Marbles I'd won. A book I wasn't supposed to read. A few old coins I'd collected. Things came and went. There was my grandfather's medal, well not his exactly, because he was British and the Iron Cross was a German decoration, awarded for bravery during the War—that's the First World War—when Grandfather fought in France. He got it from a German soldier.'

'Dead or alive?'

'Pardon? Oh, you mean the German. I never asked. Dead I suppose. Or perhaps he was a prisoner. I never asked Grandfather. Isn't that strange?'

'And the Iron Cross? Do you still have it?'

'No,' I said, looking him in the eye. 'I left it in the jackfruit tree.'

'You left it in the tree!'

'Yes, I was so busy at the time—packing, and saying goodbye to friends, and thinking about the ship I was going to sail on—that I just forgot all about it.'

He was silent, considering, his finger on his lips, his gaze fixed on the jackfruit tree.

Then, quietly, he said, 'It may still be there. In the hollow of the branch.'

'Yes,' I said. 'After forty years, it may still be there. Unless someone else found it.'

'Would you like to take a look?'

'I can't climb trees any more.'

'I can! I'll go and see. You just sit here and wait for me.'

He sprang up and ran across the grass, swift and sweet of limb. Soon he was in the jackfruit tree, crawling along the projecting branch. A warm wind brought little eddies of dust along the road. Summer was in the air. Ah, if only I could climb trees again!

'I've found something!' he cried.

And now, barefoot, he ran breathlessly towards me, in his outstretched hand a rusty old medal.

I took it from him and turned it over on my palm.

'Is it the Iron Cross?' he asked eagerly.

'Yes, this is it.'

'Now I know why you came. You wanted to see if it was still in the tree.'

'I don't know. I'm not really sure why I came. But you can keep the Cross. You found it, after all.'

'No, you keep it. It's yours.'

'But it might have remained in the tree for a hundred years if you hadn't gone to look for it.'

'Only because you came back—'

'On the right day, at the right time, and with the right person.' Getting up, I squeezed the hard rusty medal into my little friend's left palm. 'No, it wasn't the Cross I came for. It was my lost youth.'

Somehow, he understood this, even though his own youth still lay ahead of him; he understood it, not as an adult, but with the wisdom of the child that was still part of him. He walked with me to the gate and stood there gazing after me as I walked away. Where the road turned, I glanced back and waved to him. Then I quickened my step and moved briskly towards the bus stop. There was a spring in my step and happiness in my heart. I felt at peace with the world and now wanted to go back to my own home in Mussoorie.

As Time Goes By

PREM'S BOYS ARE growing tall and healthy, on the verge of manhood. How can I think of growing old, when faced with the full vigour and confidence of youth? They remind me of Somi and Ranbir, who were the same age when I knew them in Dehra during my teenage years. But remembering Somi and Ranbir reminds me of death—for Ranbir had died a young man—and I look at Prem's boys again, haunted by the thought of suddenly leaving this world, and pray that I can be with them a little longer.

Somi and Ranbir . . . I remember: it was going to rain. I could see the rain moving across the hills, and I could smell it on the breeze. But instead of turning back, I walked on through the leaves and brambles that grew over the disused path, and wandered into the forest. I had heard the sound of rushing water at the bottom of the hill, and there was no question of returning until I had found the water.

I had to slide down some smooth rocks into a small ravine, and there I found the stream running across a bed of shingle. I removed my shoes and socks and started walking up the stream. Water trickled down from the hillside, from amongst ferns and grass and wild flowers, and the hills, rising steeply on either side, kept the ravine in shadow. The rocks were smooth, almost soft, and some of them were grey and some yellow. The pool was fed by a small waterfall, and it was deep beneath the waterfall. I did not stay long, because now the rain was swishing over the sal trees, and I was impatient to tell the others about the pool.

Somi usually chose the adventures we were to have, and I would just grumble and get involved in them; but this pool was my own discovery, and both Somi and Ranbir gave me credit for it. We decided to call it 'Rusty's Pool'.

I think it was the pool that brought us together more than anything else. We made it a secret, private pool, and invited no others except for Kishen—the boy I tutored to earn my living when I was forced to leave my guardian, Mr Harrison's house. Ranbir was the best swimmer. He dived off rocks and went gliding about under the water, like a long, golden fish. Somi threshed about with much vigour but little skill. I could dive off a rock too, but I usually landed on my belly.

There were slim silverfish in the waters of the stream. At first we tried catching them with a line, but they usually took the bait and left the hook. Then we brought a bedsheet and stretched it across one end of the stream, but the fish wouldn't come near it. Eventually Ranbir, without telling us, brought along a stick of dynamite, and Somi, Kishen and I were startled out of a siesta by a flash across the water and a deafening explosion. Half the hillside had tumbled into the pool, and Ranbir along with it; but we got him out, as well as a good supply of stunned fish which were too small for eating.

The effects of the explosion gave Somi another idea, and that was to enlarge our pool by building a dam across one end. This we accomplished with our joint labour. But one afternoon, when it rained heavily, a torrent of water came rushing down the stream, bursting the dam and flooding the ravine. Our clothes were all carried away by the current, and we had to wait for night to fall before creeping home through the darkest alleyways, for we used to bathe quite naked; it would have been unmanly to do otherwise.

Our activities at the pool included wrestling and buffalo-riding. We wrestled on a strip of sand that ran beside the stream, and rode on a couple of buffaloes that sometimes came to drink and wallow in the more muddy parts of the stream. We would sit astride the buffaloes, and kick and yell and urge them forward, but on no occasion did we ever get them to move. At the most, they would roll over on their backs, taking us with them into a pool of slush.

But the buffaloes were always comfortable to watch. Solid, earthbound creatures, they liked warm days and cool, soft mud. There is nothing so satisfying to watch as buffaloes wallowing in mud, or ruminating over a mouthful of grass, absolutely oblivious to everything else. They watched us with sleepy, indifferent eyes, and tolerated the pecking of crows. Did they think all that time, or did they just enjoy the sensuousness of soft, wet mud, while we perspired under a summer sun . . .? No, thinking would have been too strenuous for those supine creatures; to get neck-deep in water was their only aim in life.

It didn't matter how muddy we got ourselves, because we had only to dive into the pool to get rid of the muck. In fact, mud-fighting was one of our favourite pastimes. It was like playing with snowballs, only, we used mud balls.

If it was possible for Somi, Ranbir and Kishen and me to get out of our houses undetected at night, we would come to the pool and bathe by moonlight, and at these times we would bathe silently and seriously, because there was something subduing about the stillness of the jungle at night.

I don't exactly remember how we broke up, but we hardly noticed it at the time. That was because we never really believed we were finally parting, or that we would not be seeing the pool again. After about three years, Somi finished his schooling, and he and his family left for Calcutta. The last time I heard from him, many years ago, he was working in a pharmacy in Calcutta; he remembered the pool in a sentimental way, but not as I remembered it.

Before Somi Ranbir had left town, and I did not see him again, until after I returned from England. Then he was in Air Force uniform, tall, slim, very handsome, completely unrecognizable as the chubby boy who had played with me in the pool. Three weeks after this meeting I heard that he had been killed in an air crash. Sweet Ranbir . . . I feel you are close to me now . . .

And what of the pool?

I looked for it, after an interval of more than thirty years, but couldn't find it. I found the ravine, and the bed of shingle, but there was no water. The stream had changed its course, just as we had changed ours.

I turned away in disappointment, and with a dull ache in my heart. It was cruel of the pool to disappear; it was the cruelty of time. But I hadn't gone far when I heard the sound of rushing water, and the shouting of children; and pushing my way through the jungle, I found another stream and another pool and about half-a-dozen children splashing about in the water.

They did not see me, and I kept in the shadow of the trees and watched them play. But I didn't really see them. I was seeing Somi and Ranbir and the lazy old buffaloes, and I stood there for almost an hour, a disembodied spirit, romping again in the shallows of our secret pool. Nothing had really changed. Time is like that.